UNSEEN

HEATHER CRITCHLOW

canelo
CRIME

First published in the United Kingdom in 2026 by

Canelo Crime, an imprint of
Canelo Digital Publishing Limited,
20 Vauxhall Bridge Road,
London SW1V 2SA
United Kingdom

A Penguin Random House Company
The authorised representative in the EEA is Dorling Kindersley Verlag GmbH.
Arnulfstr. 124, 80636 Munich, Germany

A CIP catalogue record for this book is available from the British Library.

ISBN 978 1 83598 102 3

Cover design by Andrew Smith

Printed and bound in Great Britain by Clays Ltd, Elcograf S.p.A.

Look for more great books at
www.canelo.co | www.dk.com

1

MIX
Paper
FSC™ C018179

Unseen

Heather Critchlow grew up in rural Aberdeenshire and trained as a business journalist after studying history and social science at the University of Cambridge. Her short stories have appeared in crime fiction anthologies *Afraid of the Light*, *Afraid of the Christmas Lights* and *Afraid of the Shadows*. She lives in St Albans.

Also by An Author

The Cal Lovett Files

Unknown
Unseen

In memory of Isobel Fettes

PROLOGUE

BELLA

The fear response is instant, physical. Bella's bladder voids and there is a sheet of ice down her back, sweat breaking out as she shakes with terror. Her arm jerks, striking the teapot off the side, and it smashes on the floor, dregs of tea and shards of crockery mixing with the pungent ammonia, sullying everything.

She had been cooking dinner, pottering around the kitchen wiping the surfaces and marvelling at the fact that her husband and teenage sons were unable to see crumbs and stains. *Maybe it's biological*, she had been thinking archly, like dogs not being able to see certain colours. *Maybe they can't help it*. As always, she had carefully pressed down on the feeling that she should have sisters to commiserate with on this point.

Just an ordinary Tuesday night. Noah hollering up the stairs to Ben to bring his washing down, the casserole bubbling on the stove, billows of steam plunging into the atmosphere with the promise of rich ragu. The cat under her feet again, seeking its dinner, and the news coming onto the television in the background, marking the crossover to six. Soon they would all be around the table, messy and chaotic and loud.

This cacophony of sound, life and normality patches over the past, though it can never undo it. Her dad would be arriving shortly for his dinner, like every Tuesday, and she'd be surrounded by men she cherishes, places set only in her mind for the women who should have been there too. It's as safe as she ever feels, enveloped by these known men, though that is an illusion. There hasn't been safety since she was five years old. But the illusion is all she has – built and crafted painstakingly over the horrors of the past.

When the news comes on the radio, Bella has a handful of crumbs scooped and nestled in her dishcloth. She doesn't listen to the news. She *can't*. There are things that tip her off the tightrope of normality. If Noah or either of the boys had been in the room, they would have turned it off without being asked. They may not be able to see crumbs, but they all know enough to know this is non-negotiable.

Maybe the years have made her complacent. Instead of crossing the room to the radio, she shakes and rinses the cloth first.

It takes only a few seconds.

Those few seconds change everything.

If it wasn't for them, she wouldn't be listening to his voice. Old footage, though she doesn't know that yet. A man speaking outside court after his acquittal for murder.

Bella is now forty-four years old, so that means it has been thirty-nine years since she heard her mother's laugh, or the chatter and babble of her sisters. It's also thirty-nine years since she heard *this* voice. The voice of the man who took all of that away from her.

It had always been a blessing that she couldn't remember. That's what everyone said. That's what Dad said. A relief to him that his remaining child didn't fall asleep visualising the slaughter of her mother and sisters.

But she remembers something now. Suddenly and viscerally. His voice. She cannot even spin to look at his face before her body reacts violently to the sound of him. The past bursting back through the protective covers in her mind.

After a trial held at great expense and with unprecedented media attention, a man was convicted and sentenced to life in prison. A violent drug addict with a string of offences to his name. There was evidence, there was a confession. It was supposed to be over.

-

When her husband rushes into the room, alerted by the shattering crockery, he finds Bella has fallen from her tightrope. She is crumpled on the floor in a puddle of her own urine, the casserole is bubbling up too high, the cat is yowling, the teapot is shattered and the tap is running.

'Bella… Bella! Can you hear me?'

His hands on her shoulders, shaking her, gently at first, then harder.

Her gaze, fixed to his, unable to speak, though inside she is screaming. Her skin is pale and clammy and he searches her for injuries, frantic, calling her back to him.

Bella cowers now like she did in the field that day. The familiar kitchen looks different to her. The world has been altered. All of the certainties she had about herself and her life have vanished. It seems aeons must have passed, universes whirled and collided, but it has been seconds, for the man is still on the screen and when she can she raises a hand and points a finger so Noah can follow.

'It's *Him*,' she whispers to her terrified husband. 'He killed them.'

CHAPTER ONE

CAL

The sky above the imposing Lawnmarket building is mottled grey and the stiff Edinburgh wind bites at his face. Inside, Cal is burning. The need to see justice in its full flaming glory threatens to consume him, but wishing is never enough. What if the accused gets only a year? Or let out on suspension? How will Cal cope? Clearing his throat, he straightens his tie, unaccustomed to the throttling feeling of wearing one.

In all other aspects of his life, he is mild and relaxed, but when it comes to Jason Barr, reason leaves Cal hanging. He lies awake at night, imagining the man torn limb from limb, bloodied and cracked apart, made to suffer a slow and painful death in retribution for the one Barr meted out to his older sister Margot all those years ago.

It's frightening to have this anger nesting inside him – a dark secret he keeps even from those closest to him. He looks at them now: Shona and Chrissie, the two people left in this world he would do anything for. It means everything to have his partner and daughter by his side today, even if they are unlikely to see the kind of Old Testament justice he craves inside Edinburgh's High Court of Justiciary.

'Shall we go in?' Shona smiles and stretches out a hand.

Her easy smile helps stifle the heat of his nerves. Once the sentencing is done, he needs to move on, let go. As a true crime podcaster, there is always a new case, a better focus than raking over the past. This hatred is like bile and it's going to dissolve him from inside if he doesn't put a stop to it. He knows that, but it is easier said than done. Time and time again he tries and fails.

'You okay, Dad?'

Chrissie looks strange to him in conventional florals instead of her student uniform of frayed jeans, clumpy boots and dark eyeliner. It's a relief to see her red curls defying efforts to tame them, slipping from the bun she keeps touching, self-consciously.

'Fine,' he says, forcing a smile. 'Just hoping he gets a good long stretch.'

He holds tight to Shona's hand, squeezing it for reassurance as they step inside. Jason Barr has already been found guilty of taking Cal hostage at knifepoint last year. He's been locked away ever since and today is the final underline, that's all. No big deal. It's just that, having watched Barr brought to trial and acquitted for Margot's murder, he takes nothing for granted.

-

Taking their seats in the public gallery, they flip down the bases of the air force blue-upholstered chairs and wait. The wooden-toned walls give the court an orange glow and Cal finds it surprisingly claustrophobic. Maybe it's the Perspex shield between them and the rest of the room that makes it feel that way.

The sentencing of Jason Barr is the first item on the agenda and he recognises one or two reporters taking their seats, notepads in hand. An overweight man in an ill-fitting shirt fastened over a substantial gut nods at him. Cal grimaces – the man is the crime reporter for one of the Scottish tabloids that has indulged in horrifically misogynistic coverage on Margot's case through the years. Since Barr attacked Cal, the tabloid has pivoted, changing position without embarrassment or apology. Clearly it's different when a man is the victim, he thinks, that red heat rising inside him again.

There is some sort of delay. Those waiting in the gallery grow restless, shifting in their seats. A couple of people surreptitiously pull phones from pockets and check messages, but Cal has turned his off and won't risk being asked to leave. Instead, he watches the clerk of the court and presses down on the dread. The man seems, if not flustered, then put out, conducting whispered conversation with advocates for the prosecution and defence. Barr has not yet been brought in and there is no sign of the judge.

Eventually, thirty minutes behind schedule, the judge takes her seat on the bench. Cal notes the stern irritation on the woman's face as she addresses Barr's advocate – a thin man with a wiry moustache. The judge is in her late sixties with a no-nonsense reputation and fierce elegance to her that Cal admires. He hopes she isn't going to let them down today.

Now, she clears her throat in obvious frustration and her clipped *Prime of Miss Jean Brodie* tones cut through the courtroom restlessness.

'My Lord. Your client does not appear to be here.'

The advocate bows his head.

'Apologies, Madam. He has declined to be present, and we ask that sentencing takes place in his absence,' he stutters.

The judge purses her lips and peers at the unlucky man from her elevated position on the bench.

'Am I to understand that he is actually here, inside the building?'

'Well, Judge… almost. He has been brought from the prison, but he is refusing to leave the secure transportation.'

Cal feels the bubbles of anger rising from their persistent simmer. *Of course.* Nothing is ever simple with Jason Barr. So, he's about to be denied the satisfaction of seeing his attacker sentenced even for this lesser charge. An involuntary growl leaves his lips. Shona places her hand over his, her fingers soft and cool, bringing him back to himself. He glances at Chrissie, whose eyes are wide. She saw Barr attack him last year – she needs to see the man punished. His daughter looks up at him, uncertain, and Cal forces himself to roll his eyes and smile when he actually wants to punch the transparent screen in front of them.

But the judge isn't ready to capitulate.

'I require that he is brought in here without delay.'

The advocate opens his mouth to argue, then seems to think better of it and nods before excusing himself, eyebrows drawn together in a deep frown. Cal leans forward in his seat and presses his hands together, hoping.

It seems an age before the advocate is back again.

'Madam, my apologies. He has said he will come in but he has asked for a closed court.'

The advocate's eyes dart towards the gallery and Cal feels his stomach drop. Chrissie clasps his arm.

The impatience on the judge's face swells to a furious storm cloud, and when she speaks her voice is ice.

'My Lord. The accused is not in a position to dictate. He will be brought before me to hear his sentence or I will hold him in contempt and add that to the imprisonment I intend to bestow. I will not have the administration of justice interfered with. Have him brought into court. Now.'

Cal wants to stand up and cheer. The advocate stutters and hustles from the room.

The only sound is that of a reporter scribbling to his right and the judge shuffling papers in front of her. While they wait on tenterhooks, Cal finds his mind straying to Margot – the older sister he lost when he was nine years old. A lump forms in his throat and he tries to swallow it. He doesn't want to get upset today. Doesn't want to remember her tucking him into bed or holding his hand as they crossed the road to the ice cream van. Neither does he want to remember that she was abducted walking home from a night out after an argument with her boyfriend. Or that she lay hidden in a scrapyard for more than thirty years. He closes his eyes, wishing for this all to be over.

And there he is: ex-nightclub bouncer Jason Barr, flanked by two prison officers. He's changed since Cal last saw him. Always bulky and strong, Barr looks diminished, perhaps unable to maintain his extreme weightlifting regime in HMP Edinburgh, where he has been remanded since his arrest. His chin is stubbled and he looks dirty, unkempt even. When he sits, Barr stares at his handcuffed wrists, not looking up.

'Nice of you to join us, Mr Barr,' the judge says, and Cal feels the chill from his seat.

Every muscle in his body is tight. This is it.

The judge starts to speak, reading from papers in front of her. The words wash over Cal, failing to properly penetrate his skull because he can't stop staring at Barr. He's trying to listen, grasping for the words, but there's a buzzing in his head and a fidgeting in his fingers. Last year, he had the chance to let this man die. It was a split-second decision and he made the wrong choice. He knows that now. No matter what happens today, he realises he will not have peace while Barr lives. He is serving his own life sentence.

Tuning back in, Cal hears the judge refer to him.

'I have read the impact this crime had on the victim, the victim's daughter and the police officers who were there that day in their statements. This is not your first violent crime and so I am minded to impose a significant custodial sentence. In addition, there are aggravating factors, given the use of a knife in the abduction, the danger to the victim and the attending officers.'

Still, Barr refuses to look at the judge.

'I want to commend Cal Lovett's presence of mind in making the decision to guide you away from a populated holiday area. Your actions were both intentional and reckless that day and the attack was prolonged. I have seen no evidence of remorse and although you did enter a guilty plea, it was not until after the start of the trial and jury selection. Having taken all of these factors into account…'

Cal feels hope rise further. There is no slick media and defence team pulling the wool over the court's eyes, this time. This is a judge who seems to see straight through Barr to the monster who lies behind. His heartrate quickens and he struggles to listen as the charges are read and the sentences allocated. He tries adding them together, unsure how it works out. Shona grips his hand and he looks at her shining eyes in confusion.

'With this in mind I sentence you to ten years' imprisonment backdated to your initial remand into custody. You will serve at least five years before you can be considered for parole. It will be for the parole board to decide when you are ultimately released.'

Cal can't help it. He's on his feet, tears in his eyes and the word 'yes' escaping his lips before he can stop himself.

The judge jerks her attention to him, but before she can reprimand him, he holds a hand up in apology and sinks back into his chair, contrite. He doesn't think he imagines the brief softening of the hawk-like gaze, and he tries to transmit his gratitude through the stuffy atmosphere.

However, his movement has also attracted Barr's attention. The predator unable to resist the prey. For the first time since he was brought into court, the ex-bouncer's head swivels and his gaze rakes the gallery until their eyes lock. There *is* someone who knows about the red-hot hatred burning inside, Cal realises. He can see it in the way Barr looks at him, too.

–

They don't speak as they leave the court building, all too stunned to know what to say. There is a fine drizzle making the pavements gleam and the cars are swishing through puddles. Cal smiles at Shona and Chrissie, suddenly exhausted.

'Ten years,' Chrissie says, faintly.

'It's something,' Shona says, watching Cal carefully, her words half question.

He stretches his arms out and pulls them both into a tight hug.

'It is,' he says. 'Better than nothing.' And then he releases them and finds himself lost, unprepared for the moments that come after this one. There is only ever imperfect justice for Cal when it comes to Barr. It took so long to bring him to trial for the murder of Margot. He will never get over hearing that *not guilty* verdict, realising that what seemed so obvious to him could not be proven beyond reasonable doubt. What now?

Seeming to sense his discombobulation, Shona scans the street, then turns to Chrissie.

'Do you have time for lunch?'

She nods, little drops of rain gleaming on her curls.

'I've got a study group at two but I'm fine until then. Let me just check my emails to be sure.'

She pulls out her phone and Cal is reminded of his own handset in his pocket.

'I should call Sarah,' he says, kissing Shona on the cheek.

The producer of his *Finding Justice* podcast has been as invested in this case as in any of his series. He can't wait to tell her the result. But when he turns on his phone, he sees he has several missed calls. All from the same number.

'Oh,' his heart drops. 'No.'

Shona frowns, peering over his arm at the phone.

'What's up?'

'It's Mum's care home. They've called a few times.'

'Maybe she just wants to know the result of the sentencing?'

Chrissie's voice wobbles a little. She is clutching at straws. They all know his mother is beyond caring about Jason Barr.

He presses the phone to his ear and waits for the care home reception to answer, picturing the neat building miles away in the Midlands near where he grew up. It seems to take an age, listening to gentle hold music that sounds discordant. The rain is getting heavier. When they finally pick up, he has to wait for Spencer, the care home manager, to come to the line.

'Cal,' he says, breathless, as if he has been running. 'I'm sorry for all the missed calls.'

'It's fine. What's wrong?'

Everything slows.

'I'm afraid your mother has worsened,' Spencer says, kind and careful as he is trained to be. 'I think you need to come now.'

CHAPTER TWO

CAL

Dusk is encroaching when he finally reaches the care home, car crunching over the gravel. Cal's eyes are gritty and he massages his neck as he swings his legs out of the car into the cold air and hurries to the reception. What if he's too late? A small and terrible part of him wishes it so.

Spencer greets him at the door.

'How is she?'

'The doctor has been in. We think your mother has a severe urine infection and she's now been given strong antibiotics. She's sleeping. I'm sorry to drag you here from Edinburgh.'

'No,' Cal tells him, following the man through the labyrinth of corridors. 'I'm glad you did.'

'I think we're at a tipping point. Sometimes people rally, your mum is a strong woman, but I didn't want to risk waiting.'

It's strange, hearing an outside view of her. He thinks of his mother as cold, difficult, shut off. But in other lights she is different. When you weren't the grieving child depending on her.

'I appreciate it,' he murmurs.

They reach the door and Spencer pauses, hand on the brass lever.

'Would you like me to come in?'

Cal shakes his head. 'I won't wake her,' he says. 'I'll just sit.'

The television is on low in the background, a lamp casting a soft orange glow over the room and a thick warmth from a pumping radiator makes his cheeks flush. Stepping forward tentatively, he studies her, sleeping in front of him. His mother's face is different, changed in only a few weeks since he was last here, her flesh sinking and vanishing, the shape of her skull almost visible beneath the papery skin. Slowly her chest rises and falls, seeming to take so much longer than it once did. He finds himself waiting, holding his own breath and checking that her chest rises again.

Cal sits in a chair by the bed. On the flickering screen, he watches the news ticker announcing the sentencing of Jason Barr in Edinburgh's High Court. Satisfaction and sadness commingle. Yes, the ex-bouncer has been given ten years, and in the past he did time for assaulting women he watched and followed from the nightclub where he worked, but it isn't enough.

He hates the fact that this need sits inside him. It burns and flays him every day. Jason Barr killed his sister. He buried her in a tarpaulin beneath a scrapyard and she rotted there alone. And he has evaded justice for that crime. Any other sentence is partial justice.

Cal slips into a watchful meditation, afraid to touch his mother, or breathe too loudly. A couple of times, Spencer appears in the doorway, whispering to Cal to press the call button if he needs anything, bringing him a cup of tea and some chocolate digestives. He has not eaten; he is in another world. He drifts in and out of sleep, jerking awake to check she is still with him.

In the early hours, his mother shifts beside him, moaning and trying to open her eyes. He sees fear there, confusion. Where is she? He reaches for her hand, taking the fragile limb in his. She is cold and he pulls up one of the many blankets covering her.

'It's me, Mum. Cal.'

'Chris?'

She peers at him, confused, using his old name, the name he changed when he left home, wanting to leave the notoriety of being the boy with the missing sister behind him – that and the saturated unhappiness of their family life. He had needed to slough it off like a reptile casting and finding new skin and life beneath.

He smiles, though his face hurts.

'Yes, it's me. I'm here.'

She closes her eyes. 'Tell your father he's left the door open.'

She sinks into sleep, her breathing easier. He lays her hand gently on the bed, tucking it in to keep her warm. They have not touched in years, he realises.

-

Cal dozes in the chair, slipping into a deep sleep when dawn breaks and the birds start their morning chorus. It feels safer in the light. When he wakes, a care assistant is turning his mother gently, the curtains open and golden light streaming in. His mouth feels dry, his tongue thick and breath rancid. Cal rubs his face to wake himself properly, the rasp of his stubble loud in the hushed room.

The woman hears and smiles.

'How is she?'

'I think she's stabilised.'

He sits up.

'Really?'

'She's had a good night and those antibiotics must finally be kicking in. Not sure she's ready to leave us yet, are you Vivian? Maybe it's your son being here.' She smiles at Cal and he chooses not to deny that his presence will be making a difference. Theirs was not a happy family even before Margot was taken from them. When she disappeared, his parents closed off completely, sunk by guilt and loss.

'Spencer's gone off shift. He didn't want to wake you. You can go for a rest and a shower if you like. We'll call you if things change.'

Cal feels the exhaustion of the sentencing, the journey and the thought that his mother is dying slam into him. His heart aches. He knows that even if she rallies today, she doesn't have long now and there is so much that is unsaid. It's too late to fix their relationship, all that's left is to be there beside her as she goes and hope it's enough. Should he be saying important things to her, though, unburdening himself? That feels like a cruelty, a selfish act.

It frightens him, the responsibility. Soon, Cal will be the only one of his nuclear family left. There will be no one who knows what he was like as a child, no one to recount histories, no one to remember. No one left to avenge Margot but him.

CHAPTER THREE

BELLA

They leave her in bed. A doctor visits. She is vaguely aware, but her mind is elsewhere.

It was a clear blue day. Their father was away working, as he often was, but it didn't matter because their house was always full of fun and mess, and Mummy would be right there with them in the thick of it. Even now, Bella has a memory of finger painting on a sun-drenched kitchen table in the Strathmore Valley house. She never went back there after it happened. Her father couldn't bear it.

That day they needed to walk Jet and Mummy said if they were good and came round the fields first they could bring their swimming things and then they'd all go in the river. She was Izzy then, not Bella. Izzy liked it when Jet plunged into the water with them – the collie would shake and shake when she got out of the river, covering them with droplets that rainbow-shimmered in the sunshine.

She misses that dog like a pang. After it all happened, Jet didn't leave her side. They were inseparable, bonded by loss. When Jet died of old age, Bella was thirteen and her heart broke. She cried more then than she did when her mother and sisters were murdered. Sometimes, even now, she'll see a collie and her heart will clench so hard she can't breathe.

Izzy was the middle one. Daddy called her Medium. Not as big and responsible as Gail, who'd started having sleepovers with her friends, giggling and shutting the door so Izzy couldn't hear. But not as little as Philly – who they still all called the baby even though she was more than two. Philly would insist on wearing red wellington boots on that walk even though it was boiling.

The oilseed rape was tall and pungent, so tall she couldn't see over the top of it. Jet liked to pelt through the bright yellow flowers, no sign of her but a swish and rustle, before she'd explode out of it in front of them. Mummy said they mustn't let the farmer see her doing it. Izzy had her swimming costume on under her T-shirt and shorts, her towel rolled with a pair of knickers inside it. Gail was carrying a beach bag with hers and Philly's towels and the water and snacks. Mummy was carrying Philly, the dog's lead in her hand. They were the girls, all of them, a big female clan of love and warmth and noise. How was she to know it wouldn't last forever?

-

One memory slides away and another slots into place. There was a night before that day, when Daddy was away for work. It must have been winter because it was dark outside, the bulbs all on, and the air in the house could cut you with cold. Despite it, Izzy liked the feeling of their house in the sea of dark fields, like an island of light. Back then, she didn't know to be afraid of the dark. The sound of the knocker being rapped hard when they were all just getting out of the bath, still swaddled in towels. The baby was wearing a yellow towel with a hood, pink and clean and cuddled on Mummy's knee on the bathroom floor, giggling as Mummy dried between her toes. Gail was already in her nightie and Izzy was sitting with a huge towel around her, making a tent in the warm steam.

Mummy eased herself up from her kneeling position and dried her hands on a towel, asking Gail and Izzy to watch their sister. Her face was flushed and warm with wisps of fair hair rising in the steam like a halo, her dress was spattered with water and there were pools on the floor.

Izzy was holding Philly's clean plump hands, singing a song to keep her from wriggling, when she heard Mummy's voice get louder than usual, like she was telling someone off. Not quite a shout but a crossness, then the door closing loudly. Izzy looked at Gail and she seemed surprised too. There was a long silence as they waited, then Izzy snuck to the top of the stairs and looked down. Mummy holding a bunch of pretty flowers, her head bent. She dropped them on the floor and turned to come back up and so Izzy scuttled back to the bathroom.

After that, she remembers her mother shutting the curtains, pulling them together more quickly and carefully than she usually did, scanning the frosted driveway below before she pressed the edges closely together so there was no gap.

'When will Daddy be back?'

'Tomorrow. He'll be back tomorrow. Do you miss him?'

'Yes,' she and Gail had chorused.

But it wasn't really true. Of course, Izzy loved Daddy. She loved the way his stubbly skin prickled her face and how he could lift her and toss her in the air so it seemed like she was flying, but she didn't miss him that much when he was gone. She had her mother and her sisters and Jet and all the colour and love and fun they offered. Mummy was everything to her and her sisters: their whole world.

CHAPTER FOUR

CAL

There's a woman outside the house. Cal, alerted by the car crunching onto the gravel, watches her from the window. It's unusual to have unexpected guests out here on the edge of Aberdeen's green belt, surrounded by farms and fields.

He's been in the living room all morning, going through the boxes of things he brought back from his mother's, rolling ornaments into newspaper so he can take them to the charity shop. It feels wrong, discarding once-treasured possessions, but they need to sell the house and release money to top up her care. After days of sitting by her bedside, he has had to travel home. She could be in this state for months, eating just enough to stay alive.

Cal watches the dark-haired woman. She must be in her forties, neat in a black skirt, green jumper and ankle boots, her curly hair skimming her shoulders. She doesn't look like a salesperson. Instead of moving towards their covered porch, she's twisting one hand around a thin wrist, staring at the converted barn like it's the gallows. His curiosity swells.

Setting down the paper parcel he's holding, Cal crosses the room and walks down the hallway to the front door, stepping blinking onto the sunny path. It is bright but cold, not even May yet. The woman is retreating, reaching for her car door handle.

'Excuse me,' he calls. 'Can I help you?'

Her face is a quiver of nerves and apologies. She opens her mouth and the words seem to stutter out, almost against her will.

'Cal Lovett?'

Barefoot, he moves onto the gravel, afraid if he stops to slip on shoes the woman will vanish. The stones are sharp and cold seeps through his skin.

'Yes, that's me.'

'The podcaster?'

He gets that feeling he has sometimes in his line of work, of meeting a kindred spirit. There is loss in her eyes, deep and old, perhaps, but there all the same.

'That's right.'

'I'm sorry to come here like this. I shouldn't be imposing.'

It's intrusive, a stranger showing up on the doorstep, and it should unsettle him, but Cal can't be afraid of this slight woman. She moves a little closer still, then stops a few metres away, wringing her hands. He gestures to the door.

'Do you want to come in for a chat?'

Wordlessly, she follows him into the house.

'It's a bit of a mess,' he explains, leading her through the box-lined hallway into the kitchen at the rear, with its view of fields and the swell of Bennachie in the far distance.

'I'm sorting some of my mother's things. She isn't well. I don't think we've got much longer.'

'I'm so sorry,' she says, genuine emotion in her words.

'Thank you.' He doesn't say that his mother is difficult and impenetrable and that their relationship is a constant source of pain and confusion to him.

The woman twists her fingers together again. 'I am so sorry for intruding.'

'Please,' he says, before she can turn and flee. 'Stay for a drink. You'd be doing me a favour. It's not much fun sorting all these things and I could do with some human company for a moment.'

She looks around. 'I didn't see our home being packed up after my mother died. I never went back there. I wonder, sometimes, what happened to everything.'

Cal reads the grief etched into the words. There is a heaviness in him at the thought of what she is soon bound to ask for – his help. So often, he hears stories of such pain and sadness that he desperately wants to help, but with limited time and resources he can only take on a few cases. But he can listen. Listening counts.

'You haven't told me your name,' he says, gently, as he pours the hot water onto teabags and opens the fridge for the milk.

'I'm not usually like this, I'm so sorry. I've just not been… well recently. Something happened that brought everything crashing back and no one will believe me, and I don't know what to do.' Her mouth twists in a rueful half-smile. 'That's why I'm standing on your doorstep like a mad woman.'

'Take a deep breath,' he says.

Cal feels a strong connection to this woman and he doesn't know why.

'My name is Bella Davies,' she says. 'That's my married name but I had already changed it when I was a child. My father changed it because he couldn't bear to remember. I was christened Isabella. I used to be known as Izzy.'

Foreboding thrums in Cal. A common enough name, and yet with it comes a glimmer of recognition, something he cannot yet decipher, a train speeding towards him down the tracks. He is powerless to stop it.

She takes a deep breath and ploughs on, desperation and fear in her voice like she has to get this out now or she'll lose the courage. 'Once upon a time I used to be Isabella Carlo. I had two sisters. My mother was Allegra Carlo.'

Cal drops the teaspoon he is holding and it clatters across the floor.

He stares into her eyes.

Allegra Carlo is a name he knows.

-

Cal has to resist the urge to shudder, or cover his eyes, or turn away. He is filled both with foreboding and a sense of inevitability as he invites Bella to sit down. If he looks up, he'll see the shimmer of his sister, red lipped and waving to him, blowing a kiss as she leaves for a night out. It's these memories that make his efforts to move on without justice for her impossible. For now, he redoubles his focus on the woman sitting opposite him. She is fraying at the edges: her skin is glacial beneath her makeup, her pale pink nail polish chipped and cuticles ragged. There are one or two strands of grey in her hair.

'You might not know about them,' she says, dread on her face as she grips her mug with both hands and looks at him through the steam.

'I do,' he says, wanting to save her from reliving it. He keeps his voice gentle but there is no way to soften the memory.

He doesn't know whether to tell her that he knows a great deal more than that, that he looked into the case, thinking it might be something he could investigate. In the initial confusion after the attack, it was reported that Izzy Carlo had died. That toddler Philippa had survived. Dominic Carlo's efforts to keep their subsequent lives private means some papers still confuse the facts to this day. Cal takes a breath.

'I know what happened to your mother and sisters. To you. Jet.'

At the dog's name, the woman's eyes become liquid. She fishes for a tissue in her handbag.

'I don't know what's wrong with me. It's been thirty-nine years. I barely remember them. I'm fine. I grew up, I have a family.'

'Sometimes it just hits you,' Cal says, feeling Margot in the air around him, in the very fibres of his being. 'It never really goes away.'

She holds his gaze for a moment, as if deciding what to say.

'Is that how you feel about your sister?'

Cal swallows.

'Yes,' he says. 'I think about her all the time. I probably wouldn't think about her half as much if she'd lived. We might not have got on, might have seen each other once a year at Christmas, might have fallen out, who knows? We never got the chance. She's in my mind every day.'

Bella leans forward. 'That's it. It's not just what was taken from me and Dad then, it's what has been taken from us every day since. I have these fantasies about having my sisters and us being close and going shopping together, finishing each other's sentences. I think about how their children would be cousins to mine and we'd all rent a big house in the country together every Christmas… They're such detailed dreams. It's crazy.'

'It's not crazy,' Cal says, shaking his head. 'Not at all.'

They smile at each other, joined in mutual understanding.

'I don't watch the news,' Bella says. 'I can't. For years, Dad wouldn't let me, wouldn't have papers in the house or the news on TV, but when I was a teenager I thought I knew better so I went looking online for the coverage.' Her voice drops to a whisper. 'I shouldn't have. I found things out that…'

She presses her fingers to her lips, holding in the pain. 'I've tried to blank it out.'

'So you don't remember what happened that day?'

Bella shakes her head. 'No. When I woke up in hospital I didn't know. My gran had to tell me they were gone. Dad wouldn't talk about it.' Her eyes are round with the horror of it. 'I know now it was a blessing because it's starting to come back to me and I can't bear it. I don't know if the memories are real or things that I read.'

Having dived into the details of the Carlo murders, which were committed in such a brazen and depraved way, Cal can't imagine how she must feel to have the event lurking in her mind. It could send you mad.

'I know it doesn't bring them back,' he says, grasping for anything he can to reassure her. 'But Lachlan Merrick is locked away and he'll be an old man when he is released, if ever. You're safe from him.'

'That's just it,' she says. Her hands twist together, her body twitches in agitation.

'What is?' Cal asks gently, afraid for this woman who is so fragile she might shatter.

'I don't think it was him at all.'

There it is again: that cold sense of inevitability. He swallows.

'Why not?'

Bella looks tentative, treading carefully so as not to hurt him. They're like two birds with broken wings, flapping hopelessly.

'I heard a voice on television just a few days ago, and it all came flooding back to me. I had a visceral reaction to it. I collapsed. I was terrified. I knew it was *him*.'

'You don't think it was Lachlan Merrick who killed your family?'

She shakes her head. 'No, I don't.'

Cal's thoughts collide in his mind and he tries to grasp what she's saying to him.

'But, he worked on the nearby farm, he was a drug addict and many people testified that he was obsessed with your mother. He confessed.'

'I know. I remember that. He was. He did.'

'You think he's innocent?'

'I know he is,' she says. 'The man I heard on TV was the man who attacked us. I would swear on their memories. On Mum and Gail and Philly.' She hugs herself, hands gripping her arms tight, holding everything together.

'Who did you hear?' Cal asks, the buzzing in his ears making him dizzy.

'It was Jason Barr.'

CHAPTER FIVE

CAL

Cal stares at Bella. Outside, the farmer is bringing feed for the sheep and the sound of them calling to each other as they flock drifts into his ears. For them, it's a normal day and the world is still turning.

'I'm sorry,' Bella says in front of him, her face coming into focus again, concerned at how obviously floored he is by her declaration. 'I didn't mean to blindside you with this. I should have emailed, I just couldn't find the words. A friend told me you live here and it's so close to Aberdeen and it just seemed… fate.'

Cal clears his throat.

'No, no, it's fine. Look, I'm so sorry, Bella, but confession time, I have actually looked into your case already.'

'You have?' She frowns. 'Why?'

'Someone already suggested to me that Jason Barr could have been the one who killed your mother and sisters, and attacked you. After he got off, I couldn't cope with the thought that we would never have justice for Margot. I kept thinking if I could just put him in the frame for another case then we could nail him and it would all be okay.'

He takes a breath, remembering how obsessed he was with Barr and the gross injustice of the trial he'd waited so long for. At the time he couldn't see how unhealthy it was and the horrible impact his disintegration had on those around him. Everyone keeps telling him he has to move forward and accept the things he cannot alter. And they're right. He doesn't want to go back to chasing shadows and hopelessness.

Bella's face clouds but Cal presses on, determined to get this out before he can't.

'I looked into Lachlan Merrick, read all the clippings, the trial transcripts, everything in the public domain I could lay my hands on. Honestly, there's nothing more I'd like than being able to pin your family's murders on Jason Barr. I don't hate anyone, Bella, I'm not that sort of man, but I hate him. I wish he was dead for what he did to my sister.'

She nods fiercely.

'And it breaks me up that I feel that way because that's another thing he's done to me. Peace of mind he's stolen. I truly wish he would die and end the agony. But it wasn't him. Lachlan was seen in the area that morning, he'd been bothering your mother for a while, he was out of his face on drugs, and his fingerprint was found on the Tupperware in your mother's bag, her shirt in his wardrobe. When they brought him in, he made a confession.'

A tear traces its way down Bella's cheek.

'I know,' she says. 'I know all this. My husband has been trying to talk me out of coming to see you. He doesn't know I'm here. He thinks I need help, therapy or counselling, not to dig it all up again.'

'Therapy might help with the memories bubbling up,' Cal suggests. 'Though I generally want to scream when people suggest it to me.'

'The worst thing is that I haven't been able to talk to my dad about it,' Bella says. 'I can't do that to him. He's in his eighties and it would torture him. But I can't look him in the face, while I know what I know.'

There's a barrier between them now. She toys with her chipped nail polish, flakes of it falling onto the table. Cal feels suddenly exhausted and overwhelmed. He wishes he could lie down and sleep, wake up and find it's all been a dream and he's back in the before. He doesn't want to hear the memories of a terrorised five-year-old who watched her mother and sisters die.

'I know it sounds crazy,' Bella says softly. 'But it's the truth.'

Cal thinks his heart might break as she stands.

'I could have another look,' he tries as she walks to the hallway. 'Maybe just so you could see what I found. I'd be happy to share my notes and talk you through it.'

Bella shakes her head, sadly.

'Thank you, but no. I don't need someone to tell me what the official line is, who Merrick was or why it had to be him. I need someone who believes me.'

'I'm sorry.'

She seems so certain. If Cal hadn't already exhausted this avenue, he would believe every word she said. He certainly believes she believes it.

He follows her along the hallway, feeling inadequate and out of place. He's too tired, drained by his mother's illness and the burden of clearing the house, the sentencing and the emptiness that has followed. Not handling this as well as he should.

He's trying to grasp at something, some measure of hope or condolence, when she turns to look at him.

They're close, a foot apart in the constrained space of the hallway.

'Can I ask one thing?'

'Of course.'

'Who told you they thought Jason Barr might have killed my family?'

Her eyes glitter with desperation. Cal's mouth is dry. He has to wet his lips to speak. This won't be good for her; this is going to burst everything open. But it's not fair that he knows and she's in the dark.

'It was Naomi Barr.'

Bella stares at him. Her mouth opens and closes, then opens again.

'Naomi Barr? *Naomi Barr?* What… you mean, his…'

Cal meets her shocked expression, knowing as he does that he is opening the floodgates.

'Yes. His wife.'

CHAPTER SIX

BELLA

One day, Izzy, Mummy and Philly were taking Jet for a walk. It was late spring or early summer, the crops still knee-high, the days not yet long. Gail wasn't there, maybe she was at school or at one of her giggly friends' houses. Philly was in the pushchair, kicking her feet, so sooner or later she'd send one of the little red wellies flying and Izzy would have to retrieve it. Her sister was supposed to be asleep and Mummy said she'd probably drop off if they didn't look at her, so she raised the hood and lowered the back of the seat so Philly was lying down.

Jet had run ahead while they sorted the pushchair, then dropped low to the ground, alert and waiting for them.

'Jet says hurry up,' Izzy said.

'Is she herding us? Let's catch her!'

Mummy laughed, pushing Phil's buggy harder so it rattled and Izzy had to run to keep up with her, her chest sticking out and arms pumping. It was fun until her legs began to hurt too much and the distance between them started to open up and Izzy felt the panic of being left behind. Then her laughs turned to chest hitches and almost sobs, turning from happiness like a spinning coin.

'Wait! Mummy, wait!'

And Mummy spun round and held out her arms and Izzy tumbled into their warmth and safety and then it was all okay again. Kisses planted on her neck. *My sweet girl.*

After that summer, she was never again anyone's sweet girl. She was her father's only girl, the life buoy he clung to like a man overboard, tossed on the waves, swallowing water, ready to sink and never come up. They held each other above the surface and waited to be able to live again.

Because of the buggy, they couldn't go through the fields, so they'd walked all the way down the road to a little stretch of trees near the big farm, when Jet let out a loud volley of barks and a man stepped out from behind a tree. Izzy didn't see him at first because she was hopscotching on the middle of the deserted lane, focusing on the way her little pink trainers looked when she hit the tarmac. She only knew because Mummy came to a halt.

There, in the road ahead, was a tall man, wearing what looked like a blue sleep suit. He was thin and strange looking, chewing a piece of grass, staring at them with wide, red-rimmed eyes. There was room to go round him but it felt like he was blocking the way.

'Afternoon.' His voice was slow and stuttering, it sounded like he was asking them for something and she didn't know what.

'Come, Izzy,' Mummy said, her voice sharp like the knives in the kitchen she wasn't allowed to touch. 'This way.'

Mummy spun the buggy round so fast it tilted and Philly lurched inside it, waking from the nap she had finally slipped into. Philly started to grizzle but Mummy didn't comfort or soothe her like she normally would. She held out her hand to Izzy, impatient like she never was, and Izzy took it, frightened by how hard Mummy gripped her, tugging her close to her side. She felt like she was in trouble, that she'd done something wrong.

'Jet!'

Mummy whistled but Jet didn't come immediately. She backed away from the man, her hackles raised, barking all the while. The man didn't move or try and speak to Jet, didn't hold his hand out to her the way people usually did. Izzy twisted to see him as they hurried along and he was still there, staring at them.

Mummy kept walking, so fast Izzy had to trot to keep up. When Jet finally peeled away and raced after them, Mummy didn't tell her off for barking at the man.

'Good girl, Jet,' she said, instead. 'Good girl.'

CHAPTER SEVEN

CAL

Cal stares out at the field, not seeing the world outside, sinking instead into marshy despair and guilt. He keeps remembering Bella's expression as she said goodbye at the gate – the disappointment on her face, the sense that he was her final hope and he'd taken that hope and dashed it on the rocks. Her number is saved in his phone and he knows how easy it would be to spiral down that path.

It feels like things are writhing inside him, that he can never be clear of the evil that Jason Barr brought into his life all those years ago when he snatched the most precious thing from it. This, here, is the worst feeling of all – he isn't galvanised or angry, he's swamped by darkness he hoped had gone forever. He knows some of this introspection must be down to his mother's condition and having to clear the family home. It's not good for him.

It gets dark outside and finally he rouses himself and goes through to the kitchen, flicking on the lights as he does, trying to banish the shadows. But there, on the kitchen island, are their mugs from earlier – a silent admonishment that he can feel even when he's washed them up and put them away.

It's like being haunted by Jason Barr. He wishes he could take his own advice and move on now the man is in jail but he doesn't feel like he expected to. There is no sense of peace or the satisfaction of justice for his sister. He's seen that happen for other people and he knows that it helps. Instead, anger just bubbles and subsides in an internal volcano.

Sighing, Cal's gaze falls on his bag, sitting innocuously beside the door. Before he knows what he's doing, he has his laptop out and plugged in, the wire trailing to the kitchen table as he fires it up. His fingers fly across the keyboard and in only a few strokes he is back in the horror of the Allegra Carlo case. It's different now he's met Bella – Izzy as she used to be known. It seems more real and awful.

A crime of the 1980s, the Carlo case has largely faded from view, though mention of it still provokes shudders of recognition in many; it has leaked into the national consciousness. Cal was a child when it happened, only months before his own sister was taken, so didn't know about Scotland's most heinous set of murders back then. Until he did his research on the back of Naomi Barr's comments, he'd mistakenly believed a baby had survived the crime. In fact, Izzy was five years old, something that only serves to make it all the more horrifying. She was old enough to remember her mother and her sisters, to really be conscious of their absence.

Going through the old clippings, which are initially confused and hysterical, he can decipher that little Izzy Carlo was found by a passing motorist who was alerted by the family's collie running into the road, barking wildly. The driver saw the dog's bloody fur and thought it was injured, then followed when Jet darted back and forth barking at him, clearly trying to lead him somewhere. Part of him must have wished he'd never stopped.

The man came across a scene of carnage that one paper said he was never able to get over. He is dead now, but according to reports, the pet led him to a shallow ditch where he found Allegra's middle child curled, mute and bloodstained, her eyes wide. The man carried Izzy back to the road and drove her to the nearest house, which was a neighbour's. Her father could not be found for several hours, leaving his traumatised and blood-stained middle daughter with nurses in the local hospital.

He reads and reads, staring at the screen, absorbing the facts and the terror. He's always been a sponge for these kinds of details. They stay in his mind and return to him repeatedly, haunting his dreams.

When he has finished torturing himself with the bare facts of the case, Cal turns to Lachlan Merrick, searching and re-reading everything he can about the drug-addled and violent labourer who was arrested one month after the murders, who confessed, who rots in jail. He reads transcripts, media coverage, salacious and unpleasant details. He devours everything he can on Lachlan Merrick, but the truth is that there isn't that much to devour. Merrick admitted his crime, sparing the family the horror of a full trial and the history books of a full record.

His eyes grow bleary staring at the screen but he can't stop, obsessively raking for the details, looking for clues that the wrong man was convicted.

The problem is, Lachlan Merrick not only admitted it then, he maintains to this day that he killed Allegra and her girls. He hasn't tried to get the case overturned, sought appeals or protested his innocence. Initial attention was naturally on Dominic Carlo, but the bloody fingerprint didn't match. It was later found that Merrick's print was on the girls' lunchbox, Allegra's blood-soaked shirt was in his flat. It's cut and dried, brutal and unsophisticated. It was him. End of.

By the time he has exhausted all the information the internet can disgorge on the case, Cal has worked through the afternoon. Darkness is falling outside and the sheep are only light ghost blotches in the indigo, Bennachie a darker ink-blot on the sky. Shona will be back in a couple of hours. In the cloakroom downstairs, he splashes his face with cold water and stares into his bloodshot eyes in the mirror. His hair stands on end, streaks of grey mingling with the reddish brown, skin puffy and pale.

Get a grip, he tells himself silently. *It wasn't him*.

But there's a nagging feeling in the back of his mind. There are too many coincidences, too many times Barr's name has come up linked to this case. Can he really keep pushing those thoughts away?

He gives in and calls Sarah. His producer is used to his foibles and she takes no prisoners. She'll talk him out of his doubts and reassure him so then he can get on with his life, leaving Bella and her convictions behind him.

'You never call at this time.'

She's right to be suspicious. Already he feels better for the fact that she isn't treating him with kid gloves.

'I'm not really on my normal schedule,' he admits.

Her voice softens. 'How are you doing? I'm sorry to hear about your mum being unwell.'

'Thanks. She's responding to the antibiotics but she's pretty frail... Anyway... are you okay? You sound different.'

She exhales.

'It can wait.'

'Don't give me the kid glove treatment, Sarah, not today.'

A bark of laughter. 'Fine. I hadn't wanted to trouble you with this, but the new owners are looking at the podcast's viability.'

'What? I thought the danger had passed and they were going to keep things running.' Cal thinks back to the previous year's threat of redundancy, how gutted Sarah had been at the idea of losing her job.

'They're "streamlining". We've got one more quarter to prove our worth.'

Cal feels stunned by the revelation. When the new owners called to speak to him they'd given no indication of this intention.

'Anyway,' Sarah says, 'problem for another day. Why are you calling?'

He can tell she doesn't want to get bogged down in worrying so he accepts her desire for a change of subject, though the streamlining prospect leaves him uneasy.

'This morning a woman called Bella Davies came to see me.'

'Uh huh.'

He hears what sounds like a blender in the background. Cal's never seen Sarah's flat but he imagines an immaculate Scandi-style sanctuary with lots of pointy corners.

'She used to be called Izzy. Izzy Carlo.'

He waits.

'Sorry, not ringing any bells...'

'There was a brutal triple murder of a mother and two daughters in the Strathmore Valley area, not very far from Dundee. It happened before you were born. Izzy, the third child, survived the attack.' He can hear the tap of long fingernails on computer keys as she googles for the details. 'She thinks the wrong man is in jail for the murders. She thinks Lachlan Merrick is innocent.'

‘What? It says here the case was a slam dunk. That he pled guilty.’

‘He did. Bella’s still adamant they have the wrong man. She heard the voice of the person she says killed her mother and sisters on television a few days ago. She had a traumatic response to it and collapsed. There’s no doubt in her mind.’

‘And who does she say it was?’

Cal takes a breath.

‘Jason Barr.’

There’s a bark of laughter. Then a long silence. He waits for the inevitable onslaught of opinion. Sarah always has an opinion and she’s never reluctant to give it. It doesn’t come.

‘Sarah? Are you still there?’

‘Yeah, yeah, I’m here. Cal, this is…’

‘I know,’ he says. ‘It’s crazy. Impossible.’

‘Well. I was going to say huge.’

Cal frowns. ‘She *must* be mistaken, though.’

Even as he says the words they turn to sawdust in his mouth.

‘Yeah, she must be.’

But Sarah doesn’t sound as sure as he expected.

‘I mean, why would someone confess to such a horrible thing if he didn’t do it?’ he says.

Cal is desperate for her to help him shut this down in his mind. To railroad him as she always does. He’s not used to pushing and getting no resistance. This is disconcerting.

‘People do give false confessions, we know that,’ Sarah says, pensive.

‘Even all these years later, though? To have stuck to the story?’

‘I agree, it’s unlikely.’

He exhales.

'Right. Exactly.'

'Though, if she was right… what a story. This could be just what we need, Cal.'

'You're supposed to tell me it's a lot of rubbish and a bad idea to spend time on it.'

He stares at the stock image of Jason Barr on his laptop screen. It's open on the table where he and Bella had their coffee, the place where everything he thought he knew was tossed into the air.

'Maybe you're right,' she says, relenting. 'It's probably nothing; she was a little kid, it's crazy. Most likely a traumatic reaction to a similar sound.'

She pauses and he can almost hear the thoughts turning in her mind. When she speaks again, the words reverberate inside him.

'But what if it's not? What if this is the chance to put Jason Barr away forever?'

CHAPTER EIGHT

CAL

When there is a blast of cold air and Shona steps into the hallway of their converted barn, Cal slips back into his own skin with an exhale of relief. The moment she's over the threshold, Rocket noses open the door to the kitchen and lumbers along the hallway in excitement, tail and whole body wagging. Reaching his target, the Lab shoves his greying golden snout into Shona's hands, demanding a fuss.

Cal opens his arms and pulls Shona close; the way her curves fit to his is like muscle memory. A few moments in her presence makes him so much stronger and he already feels a million times better.

'It's so good to be home. Today has been crazy.' She shrugs off her coat and Cal reaches for it, taking it to the line of hooks by the back door.

When he turns back, Shona has opened the fridge and reaches for a bottle of wine, holding it up in question. He groans in agreement.

'I need that.'

Laughing, she wraps her arms around his waist while he works on the bottle, pressing her cheek to his back. The cork makes a satisfying pop as the neck releases it.

She takes her wine from him and he holds his glass against hers, meeting her blue eyes and finding them certain and steady as always. He feels an overwhelming rush of love for this woman: the anchor holding him.

'How's your mum doing?'

'I spoke to Spencer and she's the same. I don't know what to do – I need to work and be here and yet I feel so guilty leaving her. Most of her friends are gone now, or can't visit her in the home. She's all alone. But I can't move her. It would kill her.'

Shona sets her glass down and squeezes his arm.

'You're doing everything you can. She's well cared for and you're visiting as much as possible as well as packing up the house and dealing with the estate agents and solicitors. It's a lot. You're a good son, Cal. She refused to plan for this stage, remember?'

He presses his forehead against hers, feeling the burden loosen.

'It makes me miss *her*, as well,' he says. 'Ridiculous.'

Shona doesn't need to ask who he's talking about. She knows the grief of being an only child rears its head at significant moments. Margot's loss overshadows everything.

'Not ridiculous,' she murmurs. 'Not at all.'

They stay like that for a moment. Then Cal stands tall and pushes back the encroaching darkness.

-

It's late when they finish eating and clearing up, then settle in front of the fire. Cal helps Rocket onto the sofa. The dog can get his front paws up but needs help with his spindly back legs so he can rest his head on their laps.

As Rocket circles to find the best position then grumbles contentedly when he flops down, Cal is acutely aware that the hound is old and tired and isn't going to be around forever. The idea of losing him is intolerable. He's less prepared for that moment than his mum's death.

'Something happened today,' he says as Shona squeezes in next to him and rests her head on his chest, toying with Rocket's velvet ears.

She listens quietly as he recounts Bella's visit. Her body stills when he mentions Barr, but otherwise she doesn't react, waiting until he's spilled the whole story out, including Sarah's surprise reaction.

'The worst thing is that Allegra is one of the names Naomi Barr claimed Jason used to mutter in his sleep. But, it's a coincidence,' he says. 'Right? It has to be.'

Shona lifts her head from his chest and her gaze pins him with its clarity.

'I'm not sure I believe in coincidences. But there may be another explanation.'

The swirling anxiety in his chest is back.

'Like what?'

'I don't know… it's a horrible crime. Luckily there actually aren't that many people capable of that sort of thing so it's inevitable names will be linked, or… I don't know.' She trails off, sounding less and less certain as she speaks.

'Some would say the MO is completely different. A family targeted in the middle of nowhere, not women leaving nightclubs and walking home.'

'It's not that dissimilar to what happened to Margot though,' she says.

Shona doesn't doubt for a second that Barr killed his sister. Cal feels the warmth that comes from being believed. Then a pulse of guilt that this wasn't something he was able to do for Bella today.

'Lachlan Merrick has never protested his innocence. Not once,' he tells her.

'Then the chances are the right man is in prison and Bella's mistaken.'

'She looked so betrayed when I suggested that. I felt awful. I want nothing more than a reason to put him away, but I looked into this case and it all seemed above board.'

'What do you want to do?'

'What I *want* to do is run away, hide in a hole and never hear the name Jason Barr again.'

Cal stares into the fire in front of them, hypnotised by the undulating movements of the flames.

'You're not going to do that, though, are you?'

She knows him better than he knows himself.

'No,' he sighs, shaking his head, thinking of Sarah's desperation for a new case. 'I don't think I am.'

CHAPTER NINE

EPISODE ONE: WHO WAS ALLEGRA CARLO?

The name Allegra Carlo is unusual and beautiful – it rolls off the tongue like a melody. And yet these words have come to evoke horror. Allegra's murder is one of such brutality that even saying her name makes people shudder.

What kind of monster would see a mother taking a walk to a river on an unusually hot day in Scotland's Strathmore Valley, with three young daughters in tow, and think of them as prey? Even hardened criminals have lines they will not cross.

The fact that Isabella survived is pure chance. In the chaos after the event it was initially thought she was dead and her father was told it was one of her sisters who was still alive. When he arrived home, his middle child came back from the dead before his eyes – and he was hit by the loss of the youngest.

The cold-blooded killing of Allegra and two of her three children has overshadowed her life and who she was. By all accounts, Allegra was an incredible mother, now famous for making valiant attempts to protect her daughters. But she was a person beyond that – smart and sparky and feminist. She had a PhD on river topography and was fascinated by the natural world. For the time, marriage and parenthood came later for Allegra and Dominic and were cherished all the more for it.

Allegra's remaining daughter wants this podcast to honour the person her mother was as well as focusing on the crime that cost them so much.

'I don't remember Mum's face clearly, but I have so many snippets of memory. Her reading to us, or combing our hair, or kicking the football in the garden, shouting at the dog for stealing the ball, but I never grew up to know her, to know who she was. My father doesn't like to talk about her so in many ways she's a mystery to me.'

It was Allegra who pushed for the move to the Scottish borders, close to the wilds she adored. She saw the isolated farmhouse as a perfect project for her and her architect husband, Dominic, to get their teeth into and a wonderful rural life for the girls.

Neighbour Lynn befriended Allegra when she moved to the area.

'Her youngest was the same age as my little girl so we used to get them together from time to time.'

'What was Allegra like?'

'She was fun – laid back – more laid back than me anyway. She didn't mind the girls making a mess, getting all the toys out or building dens with all the sofa cushions. But she was smart too – her mind was always going at something or other. She'd take a little container and a magnifying glass into the garden and show the girls bugs or leaves… aye but it's a long time ago. Sorry. Thinking about it makes me emotional.'

'Do you think she was settling into the area?'

'Aye. I think it was harder than she realised being away from town and the shops with three bairns. But she liked it here and she was determined to stay and make a go of it. Gail liked her school and Izzy was due to go there in the autumn.'

'What about her husband, Dominic?'

'He was a nice enough guy. His family were from Glasgow, so he'd grown up in Scotland and met Allegra at university. He wasn't around much because of work. People said all sorts of things about him when they were found, mind.'

'What sort of things?'

'Well, you know. I don't like to repeat gossip but it's always the husband, isn't it?'

Except when it isn't.

This is Finding Justice *and I am your host, Cal Lovett.*

CHAPTER TEN

CAL

Cal doesn't like ambushing people, but no one at advocate Jeremy Fishpool's Edinburgh stables is getting back to him and he likes being ignored even less. He's sick of being told that the KC is in court today so he should call back. Instead, he waits outside Edinburgh's High Court, watching Fishpool shake hands with a client on the steps and stride towards the street, his arm already raised to hail a cab. The advocate is tall and thin, his long handsome face one that juries and judges trust. This man in his immaculate suit and scarlet tie can literally help you get away with murder. He does it every day.

'Jeremy!' Cal steps forward and the advocate barely turns, so he has to call again.

He sees a hastily concealed flicker of recognition when he gives his name. Fishpool doesn't break stride, however, moving down the street, irritation crossing his face as he searches in vain for a cab to swoop in and save him from this conversation.

'You'll need to contact my clerk. We're not making any comment before the verdict.'

He thinks Cal's here for his latest case – a footballer charged with strangling a woman in a sexual 'game' he claims was consensual. Cal has only seconds to make an impression.

'Actually, that's not why I'm here.'

'If you want to cover the application to the bench then you need to go through my office.'

'Application? To become a judge?'

Irritation crosses Fishpool's face and he quickens his pace.

'A Senator of the College of Justice,' he corrects Cal.

'Oh,' Cal says. 'Actually, I want to talk to you about Lachlan Merrick.'

Surprise causes Fishpool to come to a halt. People part round him, continuing their flow of movement as he frowns at Cal.

'Merrick? Why?'

'Let me buy you a drink?'

'I don't think so.'

'I don't want to operate on misinformation.' Cal steps back, holding his hands up as if it doesn't matter either way. 'But if you're too busy, I can ask around.'

The advocate frowns at him and Cal keeps retreating slowly, calling his bluff. Fishpool stretches his arm out and shucks his sleeve up to see the time. It's as ostentatious a movement as the watch on his wrist. He sighs.

'Very well. A quick one.'

Cal is ready to suggest the pub on the corner, but Fishpool leads him to a small side street and they plunge through a door and behind a heavy brocade curtain into a restaurant that looks more like a gentlemen's club. In the late afternoon, it is half-empty and the advocate makes immediately for a corner table that is clothed in a thick white tablecloth.

'James – the usual please, two glasses,' Fishpool says as a man emerges from behind the bar to whisk his coat and briefcase away. 'This gentleman is paying.'

Cal swallows at the thought of how much this is going to set him back and what Sarah might have to say about the expenses. At least he's managed to get Fishpool to himself for a moment. The lawyer is old school and has fought his way to the top by taking the toughest cases with the most heinous defendants. Thankfully, he has not defended Jason Barr.

'Well?'

The glasses are barely on the table.

'I've been speaking to Allegra's surviving daughter. We're doing a podcast,' Cal says. The man's hawk-like expression barely softens but from the twitch of his jaw Cal can see he remembers.

'Isabella.'

'You remember her name.'

'We're not all cold-hearted vultures, Mr Lovett,' he says. 'That case made a big impression on me. I've never forgotten it.'

'And you were on the team representing Merrick.'

'I was. Though if it's details you're looking for, I might have to disappoint you. I pretty much got the coffee in those days.'

The man sits back, an arm draped casually on the table, the glass of wine in his hand, raising the ruby liquid to his lips. Always playing a game. Cal has to hand it to him, he's a smart player. Giving the impression of helpfulness, all the while closing him down. There's no way he was just getting the coffee, even back then. There's no way he'd admit to it if he was. Why is he minimising his role? It's not exactly on brand.

'Tell me what Merrick was like.' Cal slides his phone onto the table, pressing record. 'You don't mind, do you?'

He slugs at the wine and is immediately hit with the layers of history and flavour contained in the glass. So good it's almost worth the expenses form headache he's going to have.

Fishpool's eyes narrow but he doesn't protest.

'He was a violent drug addict.'

'But what was he like?'

'Doesn't that tell you everything you need to know?' He sounds bored, like he sees this every day and to be fair he does. 'Left school at thirteen, a charge sheet as long as your arm littered with petty thefts and assaults, usually while under the influence. Violent towards his partner, obsessed with the beautiful woman in the house at the end of the lane where he worked.'

'Did he admit to that? Being obsessed with Allegra?'

'After the initial admission, which happened before he asked for a brief, he didn't say much of anything. Sat there in silence most of the time. It used to infuriate us, I can tell you. He gave us nothing to go on.'

'Is that normal? For someone accused of such a serious crime to say nothing even when their lawyer wants them to talk?'

Fishpool shrugs. 'Nothing in this line of work is ever 'normal', Mr Lovett. I'd be bored if it was.'

Cal waits.

'But no, usually they talk. Try and talk themselves out of it, cry, beg, apologise. Merrick was different. But then the crime was too.'

'How so?'

Fishpool sets his wine on the table, dropping the affable man about town act for a moment. His eyes are serious as he speaks.

'You've read the file, the coverage. You know the details. I've rarely seen a crime more senseless and bloody. Allegra was unrecognisable by the time he finished with her. And to target the girls…' He swallows and turns his head so Cal can't see the emotion in his eyes. 'That's just not cricket, is it?'

Cal doesn't know where to begin. Fishpool's turn of phrase makes him shudder, but he swallows it down with the expensive wine. Across the restaurant, the waiter is lighting tealights and setting them in glass holders. The red light from them is cast onto the tablecloths like drops of blood.

'Did he ever say why?' he asks. 'Make any comment on what happened that day?'

'No,' Fishpool says, signalling to the waiter for the bill. 'The case was cut and dried, unbelievably brutal. And, when it came to sentencing, I did advise him to keep his mouth shut. Trust me, he wasn't going to do himself any favours in front of a judge. At least he had the common sense to do as he was told.'

'You didn't suggest he plead innocent?'

Fishpool lets loose a guffaw.

'It was patently obvious that he'd done it. There was the confession, the fingerprints, the bloody shirt, the pattern of behaviour and the motive. The whole thing was practically gift wrapped for the prosecution.'

The KC swigs at the wine before continuing, Cal's surprised it isn't running down his chin.

'No, the best we could do for him was to use his co-operation to ensure he one day sees the light of day again. He must be due for parole soon – and that's down to me.'

Cal chooses not to point out that Fishpool was 'getting the coffee' back then. He watches as the advocate leaves the restaurant, not even glancing back.

Whoever's direction it was, Lachlan Merrick certainly did do as he was told. When it comes to the Carlos, he's kept his mouth shut ever since.

CHAPTER ELEVEN

CAL

Cal drives to a neat estate of executive houses on the edge of Perth. The driveways are all immaculate, cars parked straight and shining, the hills a gorgeous backdrop in the distance. The development ends in lush fields, as if it has simply been dropped into a cleft in the landscape while trying not to impact anything around it.

Doorstepping people isn't Cal's favourite part of the job, but sometimes that first reaction is the most valuable and the chance to crack open the story. Wiping his palms on his trousers, he gets out of the car, conscious of a watchful atmosphere as he slams the door.

It's Saturday morning. Early enough that it's not yet busy, but late enough to be decent, he hopes. Setting the recording going, he takes the path to the front door and rings the bell, nervous but trying to smile, to look approachable. A few moments later, a woman opens the door, her hair wet and her face friendly, devoid of suspicion. She's wearing expensive leisure wear that he suspects is made of cashmere and her bare toes have gleaming red polish on them.

'I'm sorry,' she says, gesturing at her head. 'I'm not long out of the shower.'

'Are you Fiona Selkirk?'

'Yes… well that was my maiden name. How can I…?'

She trails away, premonition perhaps telling her she doesn't want to know. The smile gradually lessens, until it vanishes altogether. There's a hardness behind the veneer, a knowing.

'I'm Cal Lovett,' he tells her quickly, used to talking fast when the door might be closed on him at any moment. 'I'm a podcaster doing an investigation into an old case. I think you might be able to help me.'

Her face has already fallen, the ghost of the past flitting into her eyes as dread, her jaw set at a defensive angle, as if he's going to punch her instead of talk to her. She knows, of course, and he wishes he could leave her in peace, but if unearthing her old pain is going to help Bella then it has to be done.

'I'm not sure what you…'

'It's about Lachlan Merrick,' he says. 'I think you used to know him.'

A spasm across her face now.

'Oh.' She stares at Cal. 'My husband is out,' she says. 'He goes to the gym on a Saturday morning. He knows some things, but he doesn't know… everything.'

'I understand,' he says. 'Could I come in? Maybe we could have a cup of tea and a quick chat?'

'I'm not sure…'

'Might be better while he's not here?'

Fiona nods and he follows her down the hallway into a bright luxurious kitchen. On the far wall, bespoke shelves are filled with plants and the sun shines onto gleaming surfaces through a massive skylight.

The fridge carries a carefully styled display of family photos.

'Are these your children?'

He points to a picture of two boys digging on a beach, hoping this will disarm her. Fiona smiles tightly at the image and he sees a snatch of pride on her face along with the anxiety.

'Ross has finished his PhD now and Ollie's doing well at his Edinburgh law firm, wants to be a partner one day.'

The fridge is covered in photographs, several of the boys with a young woman – perhaps an au pair or nanny. Some of them surfing, and one of the family on safari together, arms wrapped around each other in front of a four-by-four vehicle, an elephant in the far distance, faces brown and happy. So much light after earlier dark. Fiona Selkirk escaped the monster. The deaths of Allegra and her daughters made that happen. He thinks of Bella and her sons, the dark legacy of the crime still cascading through the generations.

He watches Fiona carefully, noticing the tremor in her hands as she squeezes the teabag against the side of the cup. Her head is bowed over the task, delaying looking at him until she has to. Only when they're sitting at the kitchen table does she meet his gaze.

'I'm sorry,' he says. 'I know you probably don't want to remember.'

'I can't be long. I don't want to do this when Gary is here. Please.'

He nods.

'I just wanted to ask about what happened back then. I understand that you called the police?'

Fiona stares into her tea.

'Yes, I called the tips line.'

'What made you do that?'

She shrugs. 'We had a volatile relationship. Lachlan used to be… obsessive. He worked in this warehouse on some farmland and he talked about this woman who lived nearby a couple of times. It made me uncomfortable.'

'In what way?' He keeps his voice soft, trying not to bring her out of the memories she's clearly drifting into. Her voice is monotone and her guard is up now. If she'd been like this when he rang the doorbell, he doesn't think he'd have got over the threshold.

Fiona shrugs. 'He just kept bringing her up. Said she was snobby and thought she was too good for normal people. But, I don't know. It wasn't what he said so much as the way he said it. He would use it to wind me up at first, but then later it seemed almost like he couldn't help talking about her, like he was in love with her or something. It drove me mad. We were on and off and arguing all the time and…' She heaves a big sigh of disgust. 'I don't know what I saw in him.'

'Did you think he was capable of that kind of violence? Was he violent towards you?'

She shrugs, her eyes sliding away from him. 'He used to get mad when he was drunk. We both did. Sometimes he could be sweet but he could change so fast and I… I would rile him up and I knew what I was doing but it was almost easier if he hit me. Do you understand?'

No, he thinks, but he's trying to build rapport, so he doesn't say it. It's alarming how such toxicity can seem normal to the people within a relationship, their view of love twisted and warped by time and power.

She keeps talking, words falling over themselves now.

'I'd hit him back too. We used to call the polis on each other. Fucked up.' For a moment Fiona seems almost affectionate in her reminiscence. 'Did I ever think he could do that… no. But you never really know people, do you? And he changed.'

'How so?'

She looks up at him, clear grey eyes heavy with resentment.

'We'd had a massive row the day before it happened. After that, he was different.' She swallows. 'When I saw the news I realised it was near the farm where he worked so I went round because… I wanted the inside track. Everybody was speaking about it.'

'What was he like when you went round?'

'Awful. All the curtains were drawn and he was in the dark in his bedroom. The place stank and he stank. His eyes were all bloodshot like he'd been crying. I thought it was because of our row. But something didn't add up. He'd never been like that before. Moody, yes, but this was more like he was devastated.'

'But you didn't call the police right away?'

She shakes her head, slowly.

'It didn't occur to me at first and when it did, we were getting back together. He owed me money and I wanted it back.' Fiona looks down at her hands, fingers twisted tight together and her jaw set at a defiant angle. She clearly doesn't want to think about those days.

'So what made you get in touch with the police in the end?'

She scowls.

'We had another row a couple of weeks later – a really big one – and I guess I… Look, I'm not proud of this, but I guess I wanted to punish him.'

Fiona's hair is drying in a soft expensively dyed bob around her face. The effect is sophisticated and Cal is finding it hard to reconcile two very different images of her. The suburban fifty-something mother doesn't tally with the sordid drug-taking and arguments that featured in her relationship with Lachlan Merrick. But then, he'd wager Merrick is different now, too. More than thirty years in jail will do that to you.

'What happened when you reported Lachlan?'

'They raided his flat the next day. I didn't expect that to happen. We were in bed and the door went at three in the morning and then it was being rammed, and these men were in the room shouting at us to get up. It was awful. I was half asleep and I wasn't wearing anything and they made me stand there with my hands on my head while they grabbed Lachlan and took him away, all these officers just staring at me. I was shouting at them to give me a dressing gown or something and they took their time over it.'

'Then what happened?' he asks softly, sickened by her description of the experience, though he can easily imagine 1980s police officers being less than delicate, shaming her for the thrill of it. It's also incredible to him that she'd willingly carried on sleeping with a man she'd shopped to the police for a triple murder. Every word she says is laden with the chaos of her life back then.

'They took me to the station too. Made me get dressed and shoved me in the back of a police car. Asked me questions all day and into the night. They treated me like I was dirt, like I'd done what he did. I mind they wouldn't give me my fags. My hands were pure shaking.'

'This was while they were searching the flat?'

She nods. 'They came in and said they'd found some clothes with blood on them and asked were they mine.'

'Had you seen the clothes while you were there?'

She shakes her head. 'No. That place was always a midden – food left everywhere, clothes a foot deep on the floor. You could never find anything.'

Cal shifts in his seat – it's an eerie sensation watching Fiona lost in the past.

'And so what were you thinking right then, about whether he was guilty?'

Her exclamation is bitter.

'I must have known, mustn't I? I mean, I called the police, so subconsciously I must have known. But honestly, at the time, I just thought it was all a big mistake and they'd let him go and he'd be sorry for hitting me and we'd make up. But, it wasn't like that…'

'It must have been a huge shock to you.'

'I really didn't think he was capable of that. He could be a bit of a headcase, but *that*?'

'When did you next see him?'

Fiona takes a moment to answer.

'I haven't seen him since that day. It was a wake-up call for me. I went back and lived with my parents in Fife and went to college and got a decent job. A few years later, I met Gary and we had the boys.' She sits up taller, looking almost defiant. 'I didn't want any memory of that time of my life. It wasn't me. I burned everything – my old clothes, letters, anything from that time. Started again.' Fiona runs her hands through her hair. 'I haven't had a fag in ten years, but I could do with one now. It makes me feel dirty just thinking about it.'

'I understand.'

'It could have been me, that's what my mum said later. It could have been me stabbed.' She shudders. 'I think you should go. I don't have anything else to tell you.'

'Before I go. I wondered… did Lachlan have a friend called Jason back then?'

Fiona frowns. 'I don't think so, no.'

He slides his hand into his pocket and takes out a photo of Barr from those days. He hopes she won't link it to the actual man – this image hasn't been widely published and he looks different. He's decided just to take the risk. Fiona studies it and then shakes her head.

'No, never seen him.'

Cal exhales slowly, trying not to convey his disappointment. That would really have been a little too easy.

'Right. Well.' She glances towards the front of the house.

Cal takes the hint and pushes back his chair, lifting his cup and setting it beside the sink. 'I won't take up any more of your time.' He nods to the fridge. 'You have a lovely family. I'm glad it's worked out for you.'

Fiona sniffs, her arms folded.

She leads him down the hall to the door and he says his goodbyes, handing over his card in case she thinks of anything else, but she closes the door while he's still on the mat so he doesn't expect to be getting a call. He walks to his car, feeling unsettled by her. She didn't once express sadness for Allegra or the girls, didn't ask how Bella and Dominic are doing all these years later. As awful as she says she feels about the events of that summer, Cal's impression is that Fiona feels more sorry for herself.

CHAPTER TWELVE

BELLA

Gail had watched their little sister while Izzy lifted the plastic boxes of picnic food into the bag Mummy would carry and gathered her swim things and Philly's armbands. A towel for each of them, crisp apples and strawberry jam sandwiches.

Then the four of them had set off, the day like a bleached memory now of golden sunshine and yellow oilseed rape in the field behind the house, bright cabbage-smelling flowers. Jet running into the crops, knowing they were heading for the river, crouching and waiting for them, Philly in those little red wellies that she loved so much, fat thighs visible between boots and shorts. Izzy remembers feeling a burst of love for her little sister, taking her pudgy hand and swinging it as they kicked their way along the edge of the field. Tiny fingers, sticky and soft.

At one point, Mummy stopped and shaded her eyes, scanning the horizon.

'What is it?' Izzy asked her.

'Nothing sweetheart. Just a car in the distance, I think.'

Her skin thirsted with the need for the cool water, splashing rainbow sprays like fairy light.

There it was in front of them: the curve of the thin path that threaded through a copse of trees to a quiet pool in a bend of the river. Squealing, dropping Philly's hand and running ahead, too desperate to wait for the others. Izzy remembers her mother's voice, calling out to her not to go into the water yet. That was one of the final moments of unbridled, pure happiness in her life.

Sometimes now when she's going to sleep, she takes the memory and holds it gently in her mind, like a bird's egg, precious and fragile. Eyes closed, on the cusp of sleep, she tries to transplant herself back into that day, to feel the way the dappled light hit her skin, sense the smell of the hot pungent crop and the clouds of insects that billowed up around her. Sometimes, she almost manages, but it is fragile and tears so easily if she tries to force her way inside. She worries that the memory is finite and she can deplete it by overuse, that it will shatter forever at some point and she can never have it back.

–

Bella has to tell her father about the podcast but she doesn't know how. The deaths of his wife and daughters broke him. He isn't the same Dad she had as a small child. Instead of living in her full, fun and chaotic house in the countryside, she was parented in a new city, Aberdeen, by a tortured man. He did his best – they both did, cleaving to each other – but it was a matter of survival for them both.

She picks a night when Noah is taking the boys to the football and invites her father for dinner, just the two of them.

Bella sets their plates down on the table – the salmon dish with pine nuts and a cream sauce that he favours, a dish heaped with vegetables and buttered potatoes. She waits while he fusses with the bottle of white wine he's brought with him, pouring the ice-cold Reisling into the glasses she and Noah were given for their wedding eighteen years ago.

'Dad,' she says when he sets down the bottle. 'There's something I need to tell you.'

He stops, giving her his full attention, serious, expectant. For a second, she sees the young version of him through the grey.

Her voice trembles when she speaks.

'I've spoken to a podcaster, Dad, about what happened to Mum and Gail and Philly. I should have told you first and I didn't. I'm so sorry...'

His face creases in pain and her heart stutters as she watches him rearrange it. He clears his throat.

'It's your story to tell, Bella. That was always going to be your choice.'

She's shaking her head, trying to formulate the sentences.

'That's not it, not all of it. I... I remembered something. A voice from that day.'

'What?'

Her father's hand jerks and his knife clatters to the floor. Neither of them moves to retrieve it. When she looks at his face, his skin is grey and his eyes are sunken with horror.

'You remember?'

'Not all of it.'

'Bella, I don't understand what you're saying.'

This is the last moment to turn back.

'I don't think it was him, Dad. Lachlan Merrick.' He winces at the name. 'I think someone else killed them.'

'Bella. No. You mustn't torment yourself. It was *him.* It was. There's no mystery about that. It's the one saving grace of the whole horrible thing. They caught him and he's behind bars and he can never do that to anyone ever again.'

His voice is fierce. She can see now, what it is that's holding him to the earth, the thread by which he is tethered. It's justice. And she's about to take it away.

'There's a man,' she says. 'Jason Barr. He's been convicted of other things… I heard him on television, Dad. I heard him and I just knew.'

He shakes his head and Bella quails inside. She wasn't prepared for this, for him to not believe her. On their untouched plates, the butter is congealing, the sauce hardening over cooling pieces of salmon.

Her dad's tone drops to conciliatory now. She feels trapped inside the cage of his equanimity and their inability to argue with each other.

'You're the same age she was then, you know? You're so like her. She'd be proud of you. Don't let this consume you, Bella. It was him. He confessed and he's rotting in jail and we deserve to live. Please, don't do this to yourself. Don't do this to…'

Me, he doesn't say.

'I'm as certain as I have ever been about anything ever. Jason Barr was there that day. I know he was.'

Her father's gaze drops to his plate. He lifts his napkin and sets it on the table beside it. Neither of them is going to eat now, the tablecloth is stained with the condensation dripping down their glasses. From outside she can hear the faint sound of a neighbour's dog barking, the hum of a car passing. He clears his throat again.

'Dad?'

He pushes back his chair. Sad, slow, quiet.

'I think maybe I'd better go. We can talk in the morning, or… Maybe you should speak to Noah.'

As if Noah is a voice of reason, someone who can make all of this go away.

'Dad, please.'

She sounds like a child, like a little girl. Victim Izzy again, not survivor Bella. He shakes his head and holds a hand up to her in apology. Then he is gone. She hears the click of the latch and the engine starting and him pulling slowly away and she can't bear it.

Bella can't stop herself from sobbing loudly, not even at the thought that the neighbours will hear her. She crawls up the stairs to the darkness of her bedroom and burrows beneath the covers. As she cries, her words come out long and low as cattle moans. She hasn't called for her mother for decades but it's the word that comes to her now, pointless and instinctive. *Mum*.

Mum. Mum. Mum.

CHAPTER THIRTEEN

EPISODE TWO: CONFESSION

The man police eventually pulled into the station to interview for the murders of Allegra, Gail and Philippa Carlo and the attempted murder of Isabella, was thin and pale. He scratched repeatedly at sores on his arms, his hands apparently red and raw from over-washing and his mind obviously addled by the strong weed he'd been smoking. His skin reeked of it.

Lachlan Merrick had been working for several years as a labourer for the farm and a quarry in the area where Allegra lived, but wasn't initially connected to the crime as a suspect. Only when his behaviour deteriorated after the murders and he became increasingly erratic, did one of his colleagues phone the police tips line with the suspicion that Merrick was involved. With the line overwhelmed by calls, this initial tip was not fully followed up on until a second call came in naming Merrick – this time from his girlfriend.

At the same time, it emerged that Allegra had been bothered by a local man in the weeks and months before her death. Washing had gone missing from the line, the man had come to the door with flowers and she'd been followed when out walking.

Despite her fears, Allegra had downplayed the incidents, omitting to tell her husband Dominic, who often worked away.

'She did tell me about this guy who was watching her sometimes.'

That's Lorna, a close friend of Allegra's from their university days.

'I had no idea she hadn't even told Dominic about it.'

'Why do you think that was?'

'I don't know. Dominic hadn't wanted to move to the farmhouse – he thought it was too rural with him away on projects so much. Allegra had twisted his arm to buy that house and she desperately wanted to raise the girls there. Maybe she didn't see it as serious enough to worry him. I should have said something…'

'You weren't to know – none of you were.'

'Allegra was beautiful. It wasn't the first time she'd been on the receiving end of unwanted attention from men… I think it pissed her off – the idea of changing her life to avoid them. She had three girls and she wanted to be strong and show them they could go where they wanted, do what they wanted… she had such dreams for them.'

The audio recording of the following police interview is crackly and poor quality. We won't play the whole thing for you – it's long and mostly unintelligible. But there are some significant moments.

'I'm tired.'

'Aye, and you can have a break really soon, maybe something to eat? You'd like that, wouldn't you, Lachlan?'

'Just tell us. Did you know Allegra Carlo?'

'I told you. I don't know who you're speaking about.'

'I think you do, Lachlan. *Allegra Carlo*. Lived along the road from where you used to work? Three wee ones, a collie dog? Nice-looking woman. Moved up fae down south. Been all over the news the last couple of weeks.'

'For the benefit of the tape, the suspect is shaking his head.'

'We have witnesses who say you did know her. They say you were harassing Mrs Carlo. That you'd been bothering her for a while.'

'You need to answer, Lachlan. You're in very serious trouble. You're looking at a long stretch, pal.'

'It was nothing. I didn't mean any harm!'

'So you did know her, then?'

'For the tape, Lachlan.'

[Muffled] 'Aye.'

This questioning continues for a long while and into the next day. By the time the following part of the conversation takes place, Merrick has been questioned for eleven hours.

'Did you hurt Allegra, Lachlan?'

'I want to go. How long are you keeping me here, like?'

'Come on laddie, stop wasting our time.'

[Mumbles] 'Didn't hurt her.'

'We know that's not true. What were you doing on the 30th of June? Between twelve and two?'

'Don't know. Nothing.'

'Come on Lachlan pal, that's not true, is it? For the benefit of the tape, DS Giles is now showing the suspect a blue T-shirt.'

'Do you recognise this? Know whose it is?'

[whimpering sounds]

'No!'

'It's yours Lachlan. We found it in your wardrobe at the back in a plastic bag.'

'No…'

'Do you know what these stains are?'

'For the benefit of the tape, Lachlan is shaking his head.'

'They're bloodstains. From when you stabbed Allegra.'

'No. No. I woke up and it was there… I didnae!'

'Come off it. You killed Allegra and her wee lassies, didn't you, Lachlan? Killed those kiddies. It was a wicked thing. You'll feel better when you tell us the truth. Tell us that you did it, put her family out of their misery, they need to know. Come on Lachlan, it's time to tell us the truth. We can help you then. You can have a nice long sleep and a feed and it will all be better when you just tell us. Okay? Come on.'

[Moaning]

'What was that, Lachlan? We need you to say it for the tape. Then we can stop. That's right, that's it. You can do it. You killed Allegra, didn't you Lachlan? And Gail. And little baby Philippa. Didn't you? Didn't you?'

[Sobbing]

'Come on. When we do a bad thing we need to take responsibility. That's the right thing to do. Be a man, Lachlan. Tell us what you did. You liked her, didn't you? Aye, you wanted her. Fine-looking woman. We've seen the pictures, we know, Lachlan. You wanted her and she turned you down and you got mad. You wanted her so bad, didn't you? If you're responsible you should say so. Don't you think the man that did this should be punished? It's your fault she's dead, isn't it?'

[Anguished cry]

'Aye.' [Sobs] 'Aye. It is.'

CHAPTER FOURTEEN

CAL

Cal presses a button on a silver panel next to the gate. He's tired after the long drive south to Birmingham. Ahead of him, up a sweeping gravel driveway with a fountain in the middle, is a modern pastiche of an old manor house. An executive home that contains a confusion of deception and illusion.

He hasn't been inside before, though he has watched the occupants, almost stalked them here at the height of his obsession. He's not proud of that descent into madness. Until recently, this was Jason Barr's home. The intercom crackles but no one speaks and the gate swings open. He steps onto the gravel, noticing the beauty of the flowers poking over the borders everywhere he looks: dense clumps of daffodils, the yellow blossom of a forsythia and pink cherry tree confetti.

The front door opens before he reaches it and Naomi Barr stands in front of him. Now fifty, she seems to have aged a decade in the last year. The previously immaculate dyed hair and fuchsia lipstick has given way to more muted tones. Her face is lined and she's letting the grey mingle with ash blonde, overtaking it like the plants in the driveway are doing to the pathway. Naomi escaped Jason Barr alive, but not unscathed.

Cal feels itchy and uncomfortable being here. Theirs is not an easy truce, and it is one that comes loaded with mistakes. Naomi's in marrying a convicted criminal and supporting his defence, Cal's for ignoring her cries for help when she realised her husband truly was the monster Cal said he was. She has never been an easy person to talk to.

'Come in.'

He follows her into a white tiled hallway, freshly grouted. He wonders if this is where the police found spatters of her blood after her ex-husband assaulted her. The smell of fresh paint lingers in his nostrils, perhaps she has simply been trying to erase her memories of sharing her home with him. There isn't a speck of dust anywhere.

He watches, silently, perched on an uncomfortable stool at the breakfast bar, as she makes tea in china mugs.

'How are you, Naomi?'

Loneliness floats on the air between them.

'My friends avoid me.' She shrugs, though he sees the pain beneath the dismissal. 'I got to keep the house. The divorce comes through next month. It could be worse.'

'It could. But I'm sorry all the same. You could move, you know. Start again somewhere new. People forget.'

She shakes her head. 'No. I'm staying here. I have my garden, my cat. That's all I need.'

Cal sips his drink, scalding his mouth but unsure what to say in response. Naomi had a thriving social life and an amicable divorce and settlement from her first husband. She threw it all away when she fell in love with her prison pen-pal Jason Barr. He finds it hard to feel truly sorry for her when he remembers the positive impact she had on his image. Again, the fire inside him flares at the thought of his sister's stolen justice.

'Maybe one day we could do a podcast,' he suggests. 'About why women fall for dangerous men.'

Naomi just stares at him.

'I never thanked you properly,' she says eventually.

'It's not necessary.'

'When I called you I was one step away from… doing something stupid.'

She brushes tears from her eyes and Cal remembers the broken woman he drove to collect from the isolated holiday cottage on the west coast of Scotland after she fled her violent husband. Once loud and vivacious, she barely spoke as he drove her south to Detective Inspector Foulds.

'Naomi, I need to talk to you about something you once told me.' She peers at him, her expression morphing to one more calculating and wary, now that she knows he wants something from her. 'You told me that Jason used to say the names of women in his sleep.'

She looks away from him, out of the window to where a ginger cat is washing his paws on the lawn.

'I don't like to think about that.'

'I know,' he persists, 'but I really need you to try and remember the names he said. I wouldn't ask if it wasn't important.'

'Why?'

He hates having to come to her cap in hand.

'I'm looking into other crimes Jason might have committed.'

'Which crimes?'

Cal shrugs. 'None in particular.'

Naomi stares at him. It's cold in the house, the atmosphere mausoleum-like. This, he thinks, is where Jason Barr sat and ate – he touched these surfaces, this chair, this mug. It makes him want to run. Naomi exudes unhappiness from every pore, she always has. He's sure the predator Barr scented it and targeted her as a result.

As he has aged, Jason Barr turned his youthful violent impulses into a manipulative and calculating kind of violence, slower and more insidious. Naomi is incredibly lucky to be alive. While some are sceptical that Barr could be guilty of a range of different crimes and victim profiles, Cal doesn't find it a stretch. The sheer hatred of women displayed is the common denominator and acts like a smoke signal to him – the man's adaptability and cleverness has convinced so many people.

'Why should I help you?'

He sighs, never able to fathom Naomi's inability to do anything for anyone unless there's something in it for her. She has no altruism – or any comprehension of the debt she owes to the people who searched for her when she was missing.

'If you don't help, I'll let it be known that you refused. I'm sure Detective Inspector Foulds will also be prepared to give a few quotes about wasting police time and it'll make a fascinating episode…'

'Okay!' She holds up a hand. 'But there's not much I can tell you.'

'Anything is helpful.'

'He said women's names. "Joyce, Katie…"'

She's watching him, shrewd assessment in her eyes. Cal keeps his face mask-like.

'Any others?'

'Allegra.'

'That's what I thought you said, before.' His tone is conversational, but Cal can see the interest in her eyes.

'He didn't say anything else? About any of these women? Surnames? Locations? Details?'

'I don't know!' She puts her hands over her ears, trying to press out the world in a way that seems more suited to a small child than a grown woman. Switching persona so quickly. 'I don't want to know.'

He understands that at least. She shared her bed with Barr and heard him muttering about his past crimes. But he doesn't believe that's all she knows. Something made her realise. Something finally penetrated her delusional romantic bubble and made her run from him.

'Naomi,' he says, when she emerges. 'Anything you can remember will help me piece things together.'

Her face draws tighter, her lips thin.

'Stop it crying,' she says, quietly. 'He said: "Stop that brat crying or I'll stop it for you."'

CHAPTER FIFTEEN

CAL

Cal is rattled by Naomi's words. His mind can't help but turn to Philippa – a gorgeous bundle of energy, according to all who knew the toddler. Was it her? The idea of what this could mean and the dehumanisation of those words make him feel ill with horror. Sick and dirty at being in this home where Barr lived.

'I just want him out of my life,' Naomi says, breaking him out of the unpleasant reverie. 'I want to pretend it never happened, any of it.'

'You can't pretend that,' he says gently, trying to mask the utter frustration he often feels when dealing with the woman. Apart from brief moments of insight and repentance, she barely takes responsibility for anything.

'He's still got things in my house. I want them out of here, but he can hardly come and get them, can he? What am I supposed to do?'

Cal stills, a tremor inside him at her words.

'What things?'

She shrugs. 'Some boxes of stuff he had in storage that he brought here. They're in the loft and they're too heavy for me to lift down. I don't like to go up there.' She fixes her gaze on him. Calculating. 'You could move them for me…'

Cal grimaces. He isn't going to get anywhere with Naomi if he doesn't play along. Would it be totally immoral to do what he's thinking? Probably.

'Of course,' he says. 'Show me where the access is.'

He follows her up one side of the curved double staircase to the landing, where she points to a hatch above. He uses the pole she provides to reach the hook on the trapdoor and a ladder slides effortlessly down with it.

'There's a light switch on the side,' Naomi calls up as he takes the steps, coughing a little at the stale air and dust that have been unleashed.

His senses humming, Cal flicks the switch and sees a tangle of boxes, some empty, others spilling over with possessions, a far cry from the immaculate show home below him. He's curious about Barr's belongings, though the police searched the house when Naomi went missing last year so it's unlikely there would be anything that interesting or significant.

'They're the boxes at the back,' Naomi calls from below. 'Can you see them?'

Cal makes his way fully into the attic space. It's close and warm up here and he can't quite breathe properly. As he weaves his way through the debris, he's moving away from the light into the gloom. Pulling out his phone, he turns on the torch app and holds it in front of him. Most of the boxes up here are new – marked with the logo of a removals company. But at the back there is a cluster of older boxes, their sides worn and creased, lids folded in to keep them closed. Propping the torch next to him, Cal eases open the flaps of the nearest.

The box is filled with paperwork and photographs. He lifts the top of the pile out and holds it closer to the light. Leafing through them, he sees they are letters to Jason, mixed with what look like receipts and old childhood pictures. He throws them back in the box, scalded by the shock of holding something so intimate. This man killed his sister. Cal does not want to humanise him.

His breathing feels shallow and his forehead clammy with sweat and the overwhelming sense that he's doing something very wrong. Jason Barr would never give him permission to look through his things. And yet. He owes Barr nothing. What if the treasure trove of information here holds clues to the person Barr is? The police can't have gone through all of this carefully… they took laptops and phones, searched for bodies and blood. They weren't looking to get into the psyche of a monster.

Cal waits, vaguely aware of Naomi's protesting cries from below. What should he do? After a couple of minutes, he moves towards the hatch – her face is upturned and frowning.

'There you are. Didn't you hear me?'

'Sorry,' he lies. 'Things are very muffled up here.'

'Well, did you find them?'

'Yes, I think so. Shall I bring them down?'

'That's what I asked you to do,' she snaps.

Cal returns to the boxes and hefts them to the lip of the hole, then moves to the ladder and ferries them down one by one. He's sweating and his hands are dirty by the time he finishes and seals up the hatch.

Naomi is looking at them in distaste.

'I don't want them in my house,' she says.

'Well…' He tries to sound casual. 'I suppose I could maybe…'

'What?'

'I could take them, if you want. If it's helpful. Dispose of things.'

He holds his breath and waits, sure he's gone too far in his naked desire to see what's in these boxes. There is no way Naomi will give him her ex-husband's possessions, even if she does now hate the man.

But Naomi looks from the boxes to Cal.

'On one condition,' she says, hands on her hips.

He sees now that she does know what she's doing.

'What's that?'

'I want to be free. I don't want you coming back here. I want you to leave me alone. Stop checking on me, phoning me. After this we're done forever.'

Cal looks down at the innocuous and dusty boxes, feeling the conflicting pulls of curiosity and disgust. Why would he want to delve any deeper into Barr's mind than he already has? *To get more answers*, the small voice at the back of his brain needles.

Is it morally wrong? Does he care?

He holds out his hand, entering this Faustian pact.

'Done.'

CHAPTER SIXTEEN

CAL

Cal drives his toxic cargo back to his mother's empty house. Carrying the boxes into the place he and his sister grew up, the last place he saw Margot alive, is the ultimate betrayal. He is bringing pieces of Barr into his life, playing a dangerous game. But he has to hope that his sister would understand that he's doing this to get the answers they need, the answers Bella needs.

He sets them down in the corner of the living room. Outside, evening is setting in and he's tired from the day. Talking to Naomi always has this effect on him. He should be using this time to make progress on the house, but he can't bring himself to. Neither can he bring himself to wade through Barr's boxes and the detritus of his life, not now.

Instead, Cal showers and gets dressed in clean clothes, then he grabs his car keys and heads to see his mother.

When he arrives at the home, the smells of dinner greet him, making his stomach rumble and reminding him he hasn't eaten since breakfast. The tinny sounds of televisions echo around him as he walks along the corridors, wondering how she will be when he sees her. He reaches her door and taps softly on it, venturing into the space, not wanting to wake her if she is sleeping.

His mother is in bed, propped up on a couple of pillows. She looks diminished and frail – her bones show through and her hair has thinned to strands. At first, he thinks she is asleep, but when he sits down, her eyes open a little, scanning for him.

'It's me, Cal,' he says, drawing closer, taking one of her hands in his.

Touching her feels strange – she was never a particularly physically demonstrative person and when his sister died she curled in on herself even more. From the age of nine he hasn't really experienced the hugs and love that exist between him and his daughter. His experience of how to be like that came from his older sister and the care she showed him. Cal still marvels that Margot knew how to be that way, growing up in their emotional desert of a home.

Now, he wonders if his touch comforts or repulses his mother. Her skin is cold even though the room is sweltering, so he grabs a blanket from the foot of her bed and lays it across her.

'How are you doing, Mum?'

Her eyes rest on him. He thinks she makes a brief nod. Can't be sure, though.

'The weather's getting better, I think,' he says, at a loss for what to say. 'Cherry blossom is out now.'

Then her head turns and she's trying to say something, her lips moving. He leans in to listen to the hoarse whisper.

'When's Margot coming?'

The question winds him. When he catches his breath, Cal opens his mouth to remind her and then decides against it. What is the point in re-traumatising her now?

'Soon, Mum,' he says. 'Maybe tomorrow.'

She turns back and her eyes fix on the silent television screen in the corner, a soap playing that she would never have watched at home. Cal sits beside her, feeling helpless, until her head droops and her mouth slackens. He lifts his hand from hers and steps slowly backwards and away, not wanting to wake her, fighting the urge to run.

-

When he gets home, the boxes are in his mother's living room, taunting him. As a distraction he moves into a frenzy of sorting and cataloguing everything there is left. He piles kitchen crockery in boxes for the charity shop, loading old blenders and worthless paraphernalia into the boot for the tip. He sorts through paperwork and knick-knacks, ruthlessly binning and boxing the past.

It hurts. Every time he comes across an item that sparks a memory of his sister and his parents in happier times, he pushes down the emotion and redoubles his efforts.

He's been putting it off, but now he enters his parents' bedroom and starts on their drawers and cupboards. Anything to avoid the pulsing presence of the boxes downstairs. Some of his father's clothes still hang there, though the man himself is long gone. He doesn't like thinking about his father because it leads back to the fractious and occasionally violent relationship his dad had with his sister and the remorse and sadness that must have contributed to his early death. There is little new in this space – all things carefully taken care of and repaired through the years.

He hadn't expected to find a box of jewellery in the wardrobe. His mother never really wore much – just a simple gold chain and her wedding ring. There's a brooch on the dresser that he remembers her pinning to her scarf on special occasions. Not that she ever allowed herself happiness after his sister vanished – or before, if he's honest. Inside the box, a clutch of black-and-white pictures sits on top. He flips them over to see neat calligraphy names on the reverse. *Vivian and Johnny*.

His mother as a child: pulling a wooden horse across the lawn, a smile splitting her face. Pure joy. The image confounds Cal. He's never seen this, nor has he ever seen his mother that carefree. It brings a lump to his throat, seeing her there. After a moment of staring, he sets the picture carefully to one side and continues his sorting. At the bottom, he finds a small box containing a ring – what looks like a diamond flanked by sapphires. The stones aren't small and despite their lacklustre home, they sparkle in the light that drops through the window.

The ring is far more lavish than any of the other items. It was his grandmother's, he thinks. Intended one day for his sister Margot. Lying on his palm, it almost bewitches him. He wishes he could have seen this on his sister's finger, that she would have pulled it off and set it by the sink to do the washing-up, that it would have glinted at him as she held a glass of wine across the table in a restaurant, chastising him, perhaps, in her sisterly way. These are all fantasies. He never got to know her as an adult, so he only has his childish recollections of the woman she was becoming.

Cal tucks the ring back into the box but instead of putting it with the rest of the jewellery, he slides it into his work bag. It deserves to be cleaned and made new again.

–

‘I’m worried about you,’ Shona tells him on the phone that evening. ‘Do you want me to come down and help?’

‘I’m almost there,’ he says. ‘It’s the final push and I’ve booked the estate agent to come tomorrow.’

‘How are you feeling?’

‘Numb,’ he admits. ‘I just want to come home. You and Graham must have done this for your parents?’

‘Yes, but there were two of us and it was less… loaded.’

He glances across the room at the boxes. He hasn’t told Shona what he took from Naomi’s house. It feels wrong, like he’s stolen something.

When they say goodnight, Cal dumps his phone on the sofa and forces himself to his feet. He treks to the almost-empty fridge and reaches for a beer, cracking the top off the bottle and taking a long swig to try and swallow down the dread.

Back in the lounge, he sets his beer on the glass coffee table and drags the boxes away from the wall. Perching on the edge of the sofa, he pulls back the flaps on the first box and, after a brief second’s hesitation, plunges into the world of Jason Barr.

On the top of the box is fabric – what looks like a lace doily, twisted with the desiccated remains of spiders that have fallen into the gap and died in the darkness. Gradually, he draws out a pile of towels and sheets, the old linen leaking an unpleasant musty odour into the living room, mingling with the smell of home. There seems to be nothing significant here, perhaps some of it is from his childhood, but why Barr has kept this makes no sense to him.

Cal draws out a sampler from the bottom, beneath a patterned towel that is stiff with age. Tiny stitches of flowers, butterflies and bees adorn the words *Home Sweet*

Home. His mother's handiwork? Something sentimental? Beneath it: a soft knitted baby blanket. Was Jason Barr swaddled in this once upon a time? What hopes did the person who held him have for her child? He feels another unpleasant lurch of empathy and drops the whole lot back into the box as if it could burn his fingers.

The next box is filled with photographs and letters, all mashed together in no particular order. Either Jason Barr paid little heed to his past, or the police were extremely careless. Photographs are crushed and dog-eared. Cal sees familiar images near the top. There is one of Barr as a child holding a kitten. Though the child is smiling, the image makes Cal shudder, and fearful for the cat. He hates this picture. It was used as part of the rehabilitation campaign that helped acquit Barr a couple of years ago.

There are pictures of the killer as a small boy, in shorts and a little shirt, shiny shoes, squinting unsmiling into the sunshine. As he leafs through the bunch, Cal notices there are no pictures where Barr looks truly happy. The same is true of his mother. He pushes away the thought of what this means, his stomach stirring at these cloying notions of sympathy. He refuses to feel that for this man. No matter what he does, Cal is consumed by hatred for him.

There is only one photograph of Jason Barr's father – a figure reputed to have been violent and unpleasant. In the image, Barr senior is stripped to the waist, hands on hips, his muscles beefy and a cigarette hanging from his lips. The man's leer is intimidating and there's an angry scar across his chest. Beside him, Barr at three or four years old, blank-faced and dark-eyed, hands on his hips in a mirror of the father.

Sighing, Cal digs further into the box. Nothing in it is ordered and so now he comes across later images – Barr with friends, girlfriends. He sorts the images of Barr with women into a separate pile and keeps the ones of friends as well. Maybe he can find some of these people. In one black-and-white picture, Barr, maybe twenty years old, and an unsmiling young woman lean against a car. Barr's hand is around her, but his fingers are clenched at her neck – he looks like he's in control of a puppet.

Cal studies the picture more closely. This woman, barely more than a girl, must have been with Barr before the series of assaults he was jailed for. Women were struck over the head when walking from pubs and clubs in the early hours of the morning. It took years to find the culprit. Maybe he can speak to this woman. But how to put a name to the face? Unsettled by the innocence in the woman's eyes, Cal sits back, sullied by the traces of the past that he is rifling through.

It's almost midnight. His neck is stiff and store and his childhood home creaks around him – the familiar sounds of the heating system wheezing and the radiators ticking. All of them need bleeding. None of this will be his problem, soon. The stack of letters sits, taunting him. He cannot face them tonight. Exhausted, he piles the pictures to one side and stands, his bones creaking as much as the house.

But, as he takes the stairs, the phantoms follow him. One, in particular, walks by his side.

'I'm trying, Margot,' he tells the air. 'I'm still trying.'

CHAPTER SEVENTEEN

EPISODE THREE: PLAYING WITH FIRE

Aliyah was a dancer at FIRE nightclub where Jason Barr worked in the 1980s and 1990s. She's still too frightened to speak openly about what happened there. We've protected her identity and the voice you're about to hear is an actor.

'I worked in the bar for a couple of years in the evenings, mainly washing glasses. It was a horrible place to work but I needed the money.'

'What was horrible about it?'

'It wasn't safe for girls. The punters used to take a lot of liberties and no one stepped in to stop them. The bouncers were even worse. The club owner was a guy called Wayne – all he cared about was money.'

'It sounds stressful.'

'They felt they had a right to you. It was all couched in playful terms but it was serious underneath. One of my friends dated one of the security team and he knocked her about. She was too frightened to leave him, so it went on and on. She moved away in the end. Then there was the other business run from there.'

'What was that?'

'Cocaine.'

'Do you think the owners of the club knew about it?'

'I don't know, but I think they must have done. It was a big operation. There were cellar rooms they kept it in that we

weren't allowed into. I made a mistake once going into the wrong doorway and I saw them unloading shrink-wrapped blocks into a hole under the floor. One of them saw me and he went mental. He threw me against the wall. I thought they were going to kill me. Someone followed me home. He said he'd come and see me if I talked to anyone about it. So I never did.'

'Do you know where they were going to get these packages?'

'There were rumours. I don't know if they were true. I tried not to hear.'

'Where did the rumours say they came from?'

'Somewhere over the border. In Scotland.'

CHAPTER EIGHTEEN

BELLA

It's a grey and ordinary day, only a smattering of rain on the windshield, when Cal and Bella drive south from Aberdeen to the Strathmore Valley area. Passing Stonehaven, they have the thrashing steeliness of the North Sea to their left. Bella is quiet as the roads scroll away beneath them. Cal knows she hasn't been back to the area since she and her dad moved to Aberdeen.

'You don't have to do this,' Cal says when they stop to buy a coffee. 'If you change your mind, that's fine.'

A wind has whipped up and is sending rubbish scudding across the car park of the uninspiring service station. It's blowing Bella's hair back off her face so he can clearly see her determination.

'I'm not backing out now.'

As they near their destination, the tension in the car thickens. They leave the dual carriageway, passing through villages and out into open fields. It is a place filled with small roads and twisting turns. Polytunnels cover some of the sloping fields, ragged carcasses flapping in the wind. There is no mobile reception in several spots and Cal hopes they can find what they're looking for.

He needn't have worried. The closer they get, the further forward Bella leans in anticipation.

'I recognise it,' she says in tearful wonder. 'There! Look!'

Cal draws the car to the side of the road opposite a stone house surrounded by a wall and a beautiful garden.

'It's so much smaller than I remember it.'

They wait for a moment while Bella drinks in the view. Then she sits back in her seat with a sigh, wiping her eyes with the tissue Cal passes her.

'Ready?'

She nods.

He follows the road along another five hundred yards. Fields stretch around them and in the distance are the farm and industrial buildings where Lachlan Merrick worked all those years ago. Cal parks the car on the verge and points to the field to their right. A footpath runs along the side of the stubble, claggy with mud.

'That's it there,' he says, glancing over at the startling green of the tree line, young leaves vibrant with frequent rainfall.

Bella is transfixed. She unclips her seat belt and Cal does the same, determined to follow her lead, one step behind so he isn't pushing her.

'I can turn it off at any point,' he reminds her as he passes her a wireless microphone to clip to her jacket. 'Or we can come back if it's too much.'

Bella doesn't seem to hear him. She opens the car door hurriedly. They climb a stile and drop down into the field.

'This wasn't here,' Bella says, her hand on the wooden post. 'There was just an opening beside the gate.'

Cal stays silent. Bella is in a reverie, her voice smaller and more vulnerable, stripping back the layers of adulthood to reclaim the kernel of the child inside her. He keeps pace as she steps into the field, following a path down the side, fallow mud and course stubble to their left. Above them, grey clouds laced with black threaten rainfall. He's conscious of the crunch of their feet, the sound of their breathing in the stillness.

'It was hot that day, wasn't it?'

Bella nods. 'The sky was blue and the crop was as tall as me. I couldn't see over the top of it. Jet used to go in there. Mummy used to leave the buggy by the road, hidden by the hedge – she always said there was no one to steal it. That it was safe here.'

Her hand flies out as if she's seeing it all in front of her, feeling the rare phenomenon of the gentle Scottish sun baking her head and her back. Cal can imagine the excited chatter, the dog circling them, the family unaware of what lay ahead.

They're approaching the cluster of trees. It is thought Allegra and the children passed them without event on the way to the river, but this is where their bodies were later recovered. Cal watches Bella anxiously, his mouth dry with apprehension. She comes to an abrupt halt, as if a force field is stopping her going further. Then she steps back and shakes her head.

'I'm not sure I'm ready.'

'That's fine. Totally fine.'

She stares at the line of trees at the far edge of the field, yearning in her eyes.

'I wish I could see the river.'

'We could cross the field and go round that way, if you like.'

Cal points to show her the direction he means, away from the trees.

'Yes.' Bella sounds breathless with longing.

Cal narrates for the recording that they're moving out into the fallow field, skirting the trees and then heading back onto the path and towards the wood, which is fairytale-like, filled with undulating twists, green mosses and infant ferns.

'It's exactly the same,' she whispers. 'This is it. Oh God. It's so wrong to be happy to see it.'

'No. This was a happy place for you. And for them, too. Don't let him take that.'

Bella swipes at her face and plunges into the wood, her movements fierce and determined.

A few hundred metres in, they find it: the sinuous waters of a small river, wider at this point on the bend, where a gravelly beach forms a natural swimming point. Today the tea-coloured water seems opaque and it's hard to imagine wanting to plunge in, but Cal can see that in the hot sunshine it would be welcome. A rope hangs from the bough of a tree, its frayed end hanging in the flow like hair.

'That wasn't here before,' Bella says, taking it in. 'This is the rock I always lay on.'

She kneels on the flat platform above the water, running her hands over the stone in wonder. 'It's just the same.'

She wriggles round so she's sitting on the rock. 'I still fit.'

Bella closes her eyes and he watches the contours of her face soften.

'I think I remember,' she murmurs. 'I remember that day. I'm sitting here on my towel and I'm warm and my hair is dripping down my back. Mummy's on the beach wrapping Philly in her little frog towel with the hood.

She's holding out Gail's towel and telling her to get out of the water but she won't.'

Eyes still closed, Bella laughs. When she opens them, there is a raw nakedness that is so strong it makes Cal step back.

'Sorry,' she says. 'I just need to sit here for a bit.'

'That's fine. I can explore,' he says softly. 'I won't be far away, just call if you need me.'

He walks a short way along the side of the river – until it bursts back out into the fields again, where it becomes a drinking hole for cattle, judging by the mud and cowpats beside it. The farm and its buildings seem a little closer from here. He'd like to take a look if he can, because he isn't sure if you'd be able to see the family crossing the field from that vantage point, though it seems likely that you would. As much as he hates to admit it, Cal finds it increasingly plausible that Merrick was indeed the aggressor. It feels like a local crime – one that needed intimate knowledge of the place. What would Jason Barr have been doing here? The man had no known connections to this area. It seems utterly impossible that he would happen upon the Carlos that day.

'Damn,' he whispers to the silent river.

The truth is that he has exhausted all avenues of connection between Barr and Merrick, can find no evidence that they knew each other. Is it just his anger at Barr that makes him want it to be true?

The sound of Bella calling shakes him from musing and he starts back along the path.

'Here,' he calls. 'I'm right here.'

When he reaches the pebbly beach, he sees a different woman. A trick of the light makes her seem almost suffused with calm and he steps closer, to see her glowing with emotion, smiling despite the fact her eyes are brimming with tears.

'I feel closer to them. I feel like I can grieve.'

They stay a while longer. Bella gathers leaves and floats them down the river, something she says Philly used to love doing, and she draws a heart in the ground with a stick.

'I remember Gail doing this that last day. She got dirt on her things.'

A rumble of thunder sounds in the sky – away in the far distance – but it reminds Cal that the weather seems to be closing in.

'Ready? We don't have to go back that way.'

Bella squares her shoulders. 'No,' she says. 'I want to. Let's do it.'

When they reach the edge of the wood, she stops.

'Would you mind if I hold onto you?'

Cal offers his arm and she hooks hers through it. He can feel her shaking.

As they near the trees, Bella's pace quickens. They're almost in the shadow of them when she stops abruptly. Her hand flies to her mouth, suppressing a cry.

'Oh. I'd forgotten.'

'What?'

'We used to love these trees. Gail…' Her voice shakes. 'Gail called them the halfway point. She would run ahead and wait for us here, hide behind the tallest one.'

She looks at Cal, her gaze beseeching.

'You're doing really well.'

He's opening his mouth to suggest they leave it there today when she speaks.

'Hiding.' She takes a step forward. 'He was hiding in the field. He was lying down. That's why we didn't see him until it was too late.'

A tingle runs through Cal. This information doesn't appear in any of the files he's read.

His eyes sting as he pictures the family's final steps, small legs heading for home. Perhaps Allegra was carrying Philly in her arms. One woman with three children. She couldn't run; he can see that. It was too far and she would never leave them.

'Will you tell me,' she says, 'exactly where they were found?'

Bella's eyes are glittering in a way he finds disturbing but who is he to deny her the detail if she needs it? He can easily see the largest tree, huge roots bulging out from its base. It's distinctive and recognisable from the police photographs. The ground all round it was stained with blood.

'Here,' he says. 'Your mother and Gail were found against this tree.'

'Together?' Her voice is ragged.

'Yes.'

'Where was Philly?'

'She was covered up, over here.' He paces towards the hedgerow bordering the field, taking Bella with him as their arms are still anchored together. 'There was a towel over her.'

'She would have hated being away from mum,' Bella sobs. 'All on her own.'

'I know,' is all Cal can think to say. 'I know.'

'Where was Izzy?'

He notes the drop into her old name – needing to put distance between her, now, and the child she used to be.

Cal points to a small dip in the land, almost a ditch, close to the tree where her mother and older sister lay.

'In there. Izzy was in there.'

Bella drops his arm and walks towards the hole where she was left for dead. Police believe she was knocked unconscious and that's how she survived. When they found her, she was covered in blood from a head wound, hollow-eyed and almost catatonic.

She lets out a heart-wrenching cry and spins to face him.

'She told us to run. Me and Gail. She told us to run.'

Bella's whole body is shaking.

'We tried. But we couldn't leave them. We tried but then we stopped and went back. We didn't know what to do.'

She looks at Cal in horror, the memory jerked from the deepest recesses of her brain like a fish on a hook, writhing.

'If we'd done what she said…'

He hears the unspoken words. *Gail might still be alive.*

'Can you see him?' Cal asks. 'The man?'

Bella closes her eyes.

'No… there's just a space.'

Without warning, she lets go of him and claps her hands over her ears, dropping into a crouch. Cal sinks down beside her, fearful that this is too much, regretting the decision to come, no matter what the therapist they consulted said about taking control being good for Bella. He pats her on the back, awkward and inadequate.

'Bella, I'm here. You're safe. You're safe.'

He says it like a mantra, as much for himself as her.

'I can hear him,' she moans, drawing back and fixing him with wild horse eyes. 'I can hear what he's saying.'

Cal holds his breath, his gaze bolted to hers.

'What can you hear?'

'He's saying "Stop that brat crying or I'll do it for you."'

Bella's face is pale, her eyes wide with terror. All Cal hears is the echo of Naomi in her voice. Everything he thought he learned this afternoon, everything he's been telling himself about the perpetrator having to be Lachlan Merrick, vanishes in a second.

CHAPTER NINETEEN

CAL

Cal takes Bella's arm as they return to the car. Her feet catch on the uneven ground and she seems dazed. He opens the passenger side door and helps her in, noticing how chilled her fingers are. When they're both inside, he takes off his coat and lays it across her lap, turning the engine on and heat up full blast.

'Here,' he says, pouring her a cup of tea from the thermos and unwrapping a bar of chocolate, 'eat this.'

Bella complies, wordlessly cupping her hands around the lid of the thermos and accepting the pieces of chocolate he breaks off for her, like a child. For a moment back there she *was* a child again.

They sit quietly for a while and he passes her a sandwich from his bag, relieved to see the colour back in her cheeks as she eats and digests what's happened. He unhooks the little microphone and stows it carefully.

'I'm sorry,' she says finally. 'If I scared you.'

Cal shakes his head. 'I'm sorry if it was too much for you. You couldn't have known the reaction you would have.'

She leans her head back against the headrest.

'If I'm honest, I knew there was going to be something today. It's been building inside me for a while now.'

'Since you heard his voice.'

'Yes.'

'Coming here today has been confusing. Until just now I had convinced myself that Merrick must be the one who did it, Bella. I can't imagine how Jason Barr would know about this place – he doesn't seem to have any link to the area. It's so out of the way.'

'So you don't believe me?'

She bolts upright, stricken, and Cal holds out a hand to placate her.

'Yes, yes of course I do.' Does he? In truth, Cal feels more confused than ever.

Bella relaxes back into her seat.

'What do we do?'

Cal looks out of the windscreen. Directly ahead of them lie the hulking silhouettes of industrial buildings.

'I want to go there at some point,' he says. 'Have a scout around where Merrick was working. It feels like he's related to this somehow. He has to be. But I can do that another day. You've been through enough and you must be exhausted.'

'No.' Bella grips his arm. 'Please. Let's do it. I feel like all of this is opening up and I need to know.'

Cal studies her. Common sense is telling him this is madness and he should pull back, but the itch of the story and Bella's naked need for the truth has infected him too. He sighs, knowing he's going to crumple.

'Are you sure?'

When she nods emphatically, he starts the engine and pulls the car onto the road.

–

As they get closer, the few buildings loom higher and it becomes clear that there are more of them than it appeared from the horizon – almost a rabbit warren of barn-type structures. A sign announces that it is private land but, with misgivings, he ignores it and bumps the car down a short track to what seems to be the front of the complex.

A German shepherd dog tethered to the wall by a rope is barking frantically, baring its teeth. A craggy-looking man appears at the door behind it and stares at the car, hostility written across his face. He moves creakily, and Cal guesses he must be in his sixties.

'What do we do?'

'You stay here,' he tells Bella, pressing down the urge to turn tail and leave.

Slowly, he opens the car door. The boiler-suited man moves forward, his walk lurching and bow-legged.

'This is private,' he shouts. 'You're in the wrong place and you need to clear aff.'

Reminding himself that the dog is tied up and can't do anything more than make noise, Cal advances slowly, holding both hands in as friendly a gesture of surrender as possible, trying to smile.

'I'm sorry to be a bother,' he says. 'But I'm making a podcast and I just wondered if I could talk to you?'

'Are you hard of hearing? You need to get te fuck. We're no interested.'

'We really aren't trying to cause trouble.'

'If you don't leave right now, I'm going to let this dug off. Dinnae push me, son – he's got a hell of a bite.'

'Okay, okay, I'm going.'

Cal backs away slowly, knowing when a situation is too far over the edge to be pulled back. There's no way he can get through to this man, clearly. It's gutting because he's old enough to have been around when the murders happened. But then another voice rings out.

'Wait! Please.'

He startles, unaware that Bella had left the car. She steps towards the man, her movements calm and determined. The dog redoubles his barking, leaping in the air and jerking the rope in a frenzied manner. The shadow of a second man is visible inside the building and the hairs on Cal's arms prickle, all his instincts telling him things are turning and they need to leave, now.

'Bella,' he says. 'Come on, let's go. It's not a good time.'

The older man makes a move towards the dog. Cal doesn't want to cross him. He looks both wasted and strong, as if he survives on Embassy smokes and weight-lifting.

'I've told your pal here that you need to fuck off.'

The man from the shadows behind emerges and strides for Bella. He's younger and moves more quickly.

Cal doesn't like the aggression in his eyes and darts forward, but before he can get between them, Bella takes another step, her eyes fixed on the older man. She's quiet but unflinching; he can see a core of steel running through her that he didn't know she possessed.

'I'm Izzy,' she says. 'Izzy Carlo.'

Her words have an instant effect. His arm drops from the dog's collar, the aggression on his face replaced with shock.

'What?'

The dog is still creating a racket, its maw a slavering mess of sharp teeth. Cal waits, heart going fast, unsure now where this stands. The man straightens.

'Leroy, quiet!'

A welcome silence takes hold, ringing in Cal's ears. Now that it's quiet, he can hear that distant rumble of thunder.

'You're no having me on, are you lass?'

Bella shakes her head. 'We're making a podcast about Mum and the girls.' She points to the field. 'We've just been visiting the place where...'

'Aye,' he says. 'We saw the car on the road. Thought it was just rubberneckers, like.'

'Do you get a lot of them?' Cal asks, stepping forward, trying to consolidate the disarmament.

The man shrugs. 'From time to time. We always send them on their way.'

'I can see that,' Cal says, nodding at Leroy.

'Ach, he wouldn't hurt a fly but he makes a good noise. You can give him a clap if you like.'

Cal eyes the dog sceptically, but Bella holds a hand out and advances towards the animal, which is now wagging its tail in anticipation of attention. 'Hello, boy. Good dog.'

His muscles release the ramrod tension that had run through them.

'What is it you're after, then?'

The man is watching Bella with naked curiosity and sympathy.

'We know Lachlan Merrick worked somewhere round here,' she says, rising from where she's crouched to stroke the now-prone dog's belly. 'I guess I'm just trying to understand what happened and how.' She shrugs. 'I was so little. I don't really remember.'

'He did work here,' the man says. 'I remember him. Out of his heid a lot of the time. There was a man who used to rent the buildings down the way and he worked for him.' He gestures towards two warehouses at the end.

They look sunken and derelict – the roof of one has fallen in and stone is crumbling from the walls. 'Between you and me, there were some dodgy deliveries going on but we stayed out of all that. They're long gone, thank goodness. All the polis scared them away. No one ever came back to them.'

'And you remember Lachlan?'

The man shrugs, looking around as if having met Merrick makes him guilty and he doesn't want to admit to passing the time of day with a triple murderer.

'I saw him around. If we'd have known what he was going to do… me and the boys would have torn him apart.' The man's looking at Bella, awestruck and emotional. 'You were just a bairn. You and your wee sisters.' He sets his jaw.

'Thanks,' she says, and it's strange watching her engage with this calloused man on the basis of his proximity to the crime. The horror it evoked was universal, Cal knows that. It's only now that he can see it in the flesh.

He glances over into the distance. From here you can almost see the copse of trees where they died.

'You have a look around,' the man says to them both, interrupting his train of thought. 'If you like.'

'Do you know who owns the land?'

The man shakes his head. 'It was all parcelled up, I think… long time ago.'

Cal makes a mental note to double-check as the man scratches the now-friendly Leroy on the head.

'Thanks for your help.'

'Take as long as you like. We won't let anyone bother you.' He inclines his head to the inside of the barn where the other man has retreated and the sound of a welder has started up, sparks flying into the darkness. Cal thinks he feels the first drops of rain, like imagination.

'Course,' the man adds. 'It's not like you'll find anything. Place is falling doon now. The polis took this place to pieces. I reckon anything dodgy had been moved out well before. They questioned us all over and over, about your mum, that day, the car…'

Bella isn't listening, already drifting further along the lane, transfixed by the collapsing buildings at the end, as if they hold some sort of key or solution to the problem.

'Wait,' Cal says, taking in the words and turning back. 'What car?'

'The one some of the lads saw. That day. Parked up the other side of the river through the woods. A yellow estate or summat. Don't think they could ever agree on what model it was, like. The cops said we shouldn't talk to the press about anything, that it might stop them catching the right person if they yabbered aboot it. And then in the end it was him onyway. I've no thought about that car in a while. Probably some couple having it away without her old man finding out. Mind you, one of the lads said it had been in here as well… I'm no sure.'

He shrugs. Cal waves to the man but inside his thoughts are teeming. He's sure he's never heard mention of a car. Jogging to catch up with Bella, his steps hit the dusty ground with the beat of the first fat raindrops.

'We're going to get soaked,' he says. 'Are you okay? Bella?' He touches her arm and she turns, glassy-eyed. 'I think we should go. You don't look well.'

Her skin has a greenish tinge and the rain is getting heavier now.

'Just a quick look,' she pleads.

Cal hesitates. He wants to see the warehouses too.

'Sure, but let's be quick.'

But when they reach them there is nothing to see. The buildings are old and broken down. Cal rattles the chain on the door and the fat, rusted lock squeals in protest. He peers through a cracked pane of glass by the side of the doors, but there is nothing except dark emptiness and piles of bird droppings. Whatever happened here is long gone.

They jog back to the road, past the old buildings where the man and the dog are nowhere to be seen, the pair of them chased away by the rain. Thick drops hit the ground like fists and bounce up again, striking their legs. By the time Cal and Bella reach the car, they are soaked and breathless, slamming the doors behind them just as lightning flashes in the sky and the windscreen is obscured by hammering water. There are no more answers for them here.

CHAPTER TWENTY

CAL

Bella falls asleep on the drive back. He sets the radio on low and focuses hard on the road, passing lorries that are sending up fizzing clouds of wet spray, the car's wipers flipping back and forth without cease. An hour from Aberdeen, the storm relents, though the road is still waterlogged and difficult to navigate in the dark.

While he drives, Cal's mind flicks between the problem of managing his mother's demise and the events of the day. His emotions at seeing the place Allegra and the girls died are so close to the surface it's hard to step back and be objective. He thinks of Margot, Allegra, Gail, Philly, armies of women and girls taken by senseless violence and rage. It makes him sick and tired. A never-ending cycle of pain.

The question of what to do next is bothering him. How do you make a breakthrough if you aren't even sure there's one to make? This case is so frustrating and he can't shake the thought that the modus operandi is different. Would Barr really be cruising remote parts of Scotland looking for women and children to kill in the same time period he was stalking and attacking women leaving bars and nightclubs in Birmingham? Was he in the area for whatever was happening in that warehouse? Did he just happen to see Allegra and take the opportunity? Or is Cal clutching at straws because if he can't get Barr for Margot's murder then the next best thing is to send him down for these ones?

Cal becomes lost in his thoughts, wondering how to find the warehouse owners and if Companies House will have a name he can track down. When Bella stirs, he pulls himself into the present and focuses on the approaching headlights, trying not to be hypnotised by the glare.

'Thanks for making the trip with me,' she says after a moment.

'Bella, the man at the barn said something that struck me. Just as we left him, he mentioned a car that some of the men had seen that day. A yellow car. Do you ever remember hearing about that?'

'No. I don't think so. But then, I've spent half my life avoiding the news about the case. Do you not remember reading about it, then?'

Cal shakes his head. 'No. Nothing I've read mentioned it. Maybe he's mistaken…'

'But you don't think so.'

She's sitting up straighter now. He can feel her gaze on his face.

'He seemed pretty sure. And he knew exactly who you were so he's clearly familiar with the details.'

'Did Merrick have a yellow car?'

'No. He drove a blue van. But that doesn't mean he didn't have access to one.'

'What about Jason Barr?'

Her tone is light but he feels the weight of her question. The same one is nagging at him.

'Not as far as I know, but I can do some more checking.'

He thinks back to the nightclub, the chain of jobs and people surrounding it – the whole thing happened so long ago that it's hard to pick apart.

Bella looks out of the window, her face turned away from him in the darkness.

'Do you think we're mad?' she asks eventually. 'That we might be chasing something that never happened?'

'Like a collective delusion?'

That makes her laugh.

'I'll be honest with you, Bella. I'm not going to give up and I will chase every lead we find, but I'm just not sure we'll ever be able to prove this.'

She sighs. 'I know.'

'I'll keep trying, though.'

'What are you going to do next?'

Cal and Sarah have been pursuing a meeting with Lachlan Merrick, trying to get him to agree to talk to them. Now, more than ever, he wants to question the man, to try and find the missing links.

'I'm going to try and talk to Merrick.'

A boy racer in a glossy red sports car shoots past them, wheels aquaplaning a moment before he regains control. Cal slows automatically, holding his breath until the danger has passed. Bella barely seems to notice.

'I want to come with you.'

'What? No,' he says, stunned. 'I don't think that's a good idea.'

For Bella to walk into the prison, sit across the table from her mother and sisters' murderer and tell him she thinks he didn't do it, would be pure insanity. But he can tell by the tone of her voice that she's determined.

'It might be the thing that gets him to talk.'

Cal swallows. How does he begin to explain to her that the common rules of emotion, guilt and decency really don't apply to people like Lachlan Merrick. His thoughts jump to an interview he did once with serial murderer Marc Dubois. A killer who got his kicks from toying with Cal. But then it nudges at him that Dubois is the person who unlocked Margot's case. In messing with Cal, Barr's ex-cellmate revealed the details that led to her body. Could it be the same for Bella?

'Look,' he says. 'There may come a moment when that makes sense, having the two of you face to face. But we need to keep our powder dry. We don't yet know how approachable he's going to be and having you there is as likely to make him clam up as it is to help.'

Bella makes a noise of frustration.

'I know you want to confront him,' he says, more softly. 'But we need to do this carefully if you're going to get the answers you're looking for.'

'I just want to do something, I need to.'

'If you really want to help then I need you to talk to your father.'

He glances across, sees the dread lodged in her face.

'I tried. He won't return my calls. This has never happened before.'

Cal wonders what must be going through Dominic Carlo's mind. He's been wrenched back into a living nightmare.

'I'm sorry Bella. Look, we don't have to…'

'Don't say it.'

He indicates and pulls into the outside lane.

'All I'm saying is…'

'I know,' she cuts in. 'But we *do* have to keep going. No matter the cost.'

CHAPTER TWENTY-ONE

EPISODE FOUR: LIVING AROUND THE LOSS

'Thank you for speaking to us today, Dominic. I know that keeping your silence has been important for you and the last thing we want to do is distress you by making you relive this tragedy. Can I ask why you've never given an interview about what happened, and why you're doing so now?'

'I guess, maybe it's time. Our grief – Bella's and mine – was so strong that if I didn't use every scrap of energy I had to keep us afloat, to re-imagine our lives, then I didn't think we were going to make it. Does that make sense?'

'Perfect sense. And it worked, didn't it? Bella has a successful career and a lovely family, you live close to each other, you managed to continue designing beautiful buildings. These achievements are not to be underestimated.'

'Yes. Although it will never be possible to be whole again, we have grown around the void. I was able to give Bella as normal a childhood as was possible in the circumstances.'

'And you never remarried?'

'Allegra was the love of my life. I have never wanted anyone else.'

'So why are you here now?'

'Well, for two reasons. I'm doing this for Bella, my daughter. I've always sheltered her from what happened. I know that seems

crazy because she was there that day. How do you protect someone from something they witnessed, something so awful?'

'No, I understand. Izzy became Bella. Bella didn't remember.'

'That's it. But now, she wants to know things – she needs to. She is the same age her mother was when she died. I did not immediately understand her need to pursue this, but I have always respected it and I support her.'

'What was Bella like before and after that day?'

'She changed. Izzy was different. Izzy was our wild child, Allegra and I used to say. She was so chaotic and messy. She had all these ideas and was like a whirlwind – we loved that about her. All three of our girls had such distinct personalities and we loved them all so much. I love Bella still, of course, but she did change. She stopped being spontaneous and carefree. She became neat and organised. It is another grief for me that she had to do that. Though, maybe that would have happened anyway… we will never know.'

'You said there were two reasons for doing this?'

'Yes. I cannot bear the thought that someone might not have been punished for what they did to my wife and children. The sort of man who would do this is not the sort of man we want walking the streets. I would like to have peace of mind, one way or the other. My daughter believes another man was there in the field. I know we cannot currently say who that person is, but I like the thought that he is afraid. That he knows you are coming for him.'

CHAPTER TWENTY-TWO

CAL

Cal waits with the families of other prisoners in the rounded entrance building at HMP Shotts, the only prison in Scotland to cater solely to long-term male inmates. There is a bite in the air this morning and outside, the ground is cold and hard, a gang of crows shrieking as they fight over some rubbish in the car park.

When his ID has been checked and he has passed through security, Cal takes the stairs to the visitor centre, leaving his phone and keys in a locker. With the others, he waits for the doors to be opened to the main visiting room and for more searches to take place, then he takes his seat, ready for Lachlan Merrick to be brought through from the cells.

He knows what Merrick used to look like – a lanky, awkward young man with a pronounced jaw and a mop of unruly sandy-coloured hair – but the pictures he's seen are thirty years old. Before his arrest for the murders, Lachlan Merrick had a string of petty thefts and domestic violence incidents behind him, but nothing that indicated the escalation would be so rapid and severe. Another thing that doesn't fit about the case.

Cal has interviewed men in prison before, and his mind snaps back to Marc Dubois in particular, the serial killer who knew details about his sister Margot's disappearance. The man's knowledge, gleaned on the inside from Jason Barr, blew open her case and Cal's fruitless obsession with understanding him tore wide the holes that already existed in his marriage. He wonders what Dubois would think if he knew he was indirectly responsible for progress on Margot's case, for the recovery of her body and the family's chance to have a funeral. He can't ask: Dubois was found hanged from the door of his cell only weeks after their last conversation.

As the men file in, he returns to the present and scans their faces, trying to identify the one he needs. Merrick is last through the door and delayed enough that Cal thinks he must not be coming. Every other table is now occupied, so at least he is confident this is his man, even though only traces of the younger version remain. Directed by a guard, Merrick threads his way through the tables towards him.

Merrick is not what Cal expected. There's a nothingness about him – you could easily pass him on the street and never know his infamy. Long stays in prison generally change people, making them harder and tougher so they can survive, but there is no evidence that Merrick frequents the prison gym. The young-man lankiness he saw in the pictures has altered in the prisoner shuffling towards him, head down, shoulders hunched. Merrick has gone to seed, his waistline thick and his skin pasty. He wears a long-sleeved T-shirt and baggy joggers that look like they might fall from the soft pale flesh at any moment. When he sits on the chair opposite and looks up, Cal swallows at the sight of grey-blue glassy eyes beneath a mop of sandy hair. There's a hopelessness to him. He's looking into eyes that expect nothing.

Two of Merrick's teeth are missing and he grunts as he scratches at his head, sending flakes of dandruff onto the floor. No one in the room has recoiled, there is no nervousness at his presence or other evidence that this is a violent, brutal man. He looks like a run-down accountant.

'Thank you for seeing me.'

Merrick shrugs, barely making eye contact.

'I wanted to talk to you about your case, if you don't mind?'

He keeps his voice low, leaning across the table. This doesn't feel like the right place to be talking about such carnage – a toddler is playing on the floor only a few feet away, a grubby toy train clenched in his fist while his parents whisper urgently to each other. Bile swims into Cal's throat at the thought of what Merrick was convicted of doing to Philly – the youngest Carlo was a similar age to this little boy when she was dashed against a tree.

Any sense of life in Merrick's deadened expression disappears completely at his words. It's like watching a shutter come down across his face.

'I've nothing to say. If that's why you're here then you've wasted the journey. You shouldn't have bothered. I don't want to rake over it all.'

And yet, Cal thinks, Merrick agreed to this meeting. He's here. If it's such a waste of time, then why?

Merrick shifts forward in his chair, making to stand, and Cal sees he has only seconds to capture the prisoner's attention before he walks away.

'No,' he says. 'You don't understand. I'm here because I've been approached by someone who thinks you're innocent.'

The man stills. The whites of his eyes are yellow and bloodshot, like he hasn't had a good sleep in decades. The room around them fades into the background, all Cal's attention on Merrick's blanched face.

'What are you talking about? Who?' His words are barely more than a whisper. Merrick jerks his head from side to side, looking around as if afraid they will be overheard, and Cal sees a momentary glimpse of what looks like fear. In that second of naked vulnerability, his tongue flickers nervously across cracked lips. 'I pleaded guilty. Back at the trial.'

'I listened to your police interview, Lachlan. They pushed you pretty hard.'

Impenetrable thoughts cross the doughy face. Merrick seems agitated at the thought that someone might be willing to stand up for him. The conversation is slippery; Cal can't grasp it.

'Has your solicitor suggested putting in appeals over the years?'

Merrick shakes his head, his voice deadened.

'People like me don't appeal.'

But this isn't true. Cal frowns. Are they wrong? Is Merrick the killer? And a remorseful one? Why wouldn't he grasp any opportunity to be free?

'Did you do it, Lachlan? Did you kill them?'

'I said I did, didn't I? In court. Why did you come here?'

Merrick's voice has risen. Cal sees the nearest guard twitch, his eyes on them, hand straying briefly towards the radio on his belt.

'I might be able to help you, if you didn't, that's all.'

Cal feels desperate and sordid. Is he offering a killer redemption or an innocent man a lifeline?

'You don't know what you're talking about.'

'Can we just talk about what happened?'

'No one in their right mind thinks I'm innocent. Not even me.'

'Izzy.'

Merrick's eyes fix on Cal's, boring into them. His brow wrinkles in confusion and anger.

'You asked who. Izzy Carlo. Allegra's middle daughter. She doesn't think it was you, Lachlan. *She's* the one who doesn't think you killed them.'

There's only the briefest second where Cal sees what looks like surprise before thin lips close tight, as if he is in pain.

'I didn't think she remembered.'

'What do you mean?'

'Tell her I'm sorry.'

Cal feels the frustration building at these impenetrable answers.

'What happened in the barn where you worked, Lachlan? There were deliveries...'

Merrick's eyes jerk to Cal's. He looks sweaty, ill under the artificial lights.

'I don't know what you're talking about.'

'I think you do. What about a man called Jason Barr? Do you remember him?'

The blood drains from Merrick's already washed-out face. Abruptly, he pushes back his chair and lifts himself from it, turning on his heel and striding away. There isn't even a split second of hush or reaction. The babble around him simply continues and Cal watches as the man reaches the guard and the doorway then vanishes from view.

CHAPTER TWENTY-THREE

CAL

Cal heads for the exit, disappointed with himself for failing to make a breakthrough with Merrick and rattled by his reactions. He's sure they're onto something but if Merrick won't talk he'll have to find the evidence somewhere else.

'You've been to see Lachlan.'

A man stands outside the door to the visitor hall, leaning against the wall, arms folded. He pushes away from the brick and steps forward. Cal halts, alarmed at the scrutiny, though this is a prison and so someone must always be watching. He studies this man, who is a world away from Merrick, healthy and defined, but softened by bookish black-rimmed glasses and a tweedy jacket, a line of pens in the top pocket.

The man reaches out a hand. 'Tariq. I'm the prison counsellor.'

They shake and Cal senses that Tariq has lain in wait for him. It's an intriguing thought. He waits for him to speak.

'Lachlan doesn't get many visitors.'

'I can imagine. He's been here…'

'Thirty-eight years. He's one of our longest residents.'

'There aren't many people who've been inside that long. Shouldn't he have been released by now?'

'He was in trouble when he was first imprisoned. I understand there were severe drug-addiction issues and he was targeted by the other inmates given the nature of his crime. He stabbed a cellmate and years were added to his sentence. His crime means leniency is never an option. But he has kept his nose clean for a long time now.'

Cal hesitates, struck by the intense feeling that Tariq wants to tell him something.

'Do you have time to talk to me about the role you do here? Can I buy you a coffee?'

Tariq laughs. 'There's not a plethora of coffee shops in these parts. I could rustle us up a couple of machine coffees though if you can bear it? I always like to talk about our work. People have very fixed and outdated ideas of prisons. We try to break down the barriers when we can.'

Cal follows the counsellor down the corridor and through two sets of gates. He waits while the man jabs the buttons on an ancient vending machine and chats about the way they work with prisoners to change their response to conflict and prepare them for an eventual return to society. When the machine has groaned into action, Tariq passes him a plastic cup that feels too flimsy for its cargo then leads Cal into a cupboard-sized office, stacked with files and boasting no natural light.

'I don't spend a lot of time in here,' he says, clearing a pile of files off the spare chair so Cal can sit. 'I'm usually with the men, either in groups or individually. This is just a bolt hole and filing cabinet.'

'Have you known Merrick… Lachlan… for a long time?'

'I've been here for thirteen years and we have had several sessions, but he's not a regular customer. Keeps himself to himself.'

'Has he discussed the case with you? If I'm allowed to ask?'

Tariq smiles. 'You're allowed to ask, but I wouldn't be able to tell you anything if he had. But no, our sessions have been much more around how Lachlan will acclimatise to the outside world if he is released.'

'Do you think that will happen?'

Tariq shakes his head. 'Couldn't call it. I wouldn't say I was jaded, but I've been around long enough to know that what's logical doesn't necessarily happen. There are always political considerations above my pay grade, so we try and prepare our clients for all eventualities.'

'But you think he should be?'

'That's not for me to say. I don't believe Lachlan Merrick poses any threat to society, for what it's worth.'

'And do you think he's paid the price?'

Tariq's eyes are brown pools that darken at the question. 'Thirty-eight years is a long time.'

Cal notes the lack of answer.

'It is. But a lot of people think they should have thrown away the key.'

His mind returns to the field, the ditch where Izzy was discarded and left for dead with the bodies of her mother and sisters.

The counsellor shrugs. 'I am not one of those.'

'You believe in rehabilitation.'

'I wouldn't be here if I didn't. You don't agree?'

Thoughts of Barr barge their way into his mind, shoving the Carlos aside. Tariq's view seems so simple to him now, almost idealistic. Maybe the counsellor isn't jaded, but Cal certainly feels that way. Chewed and spat out by the justice system too many times. He considers himself mild, liberal, kind, until it comes to Jason Barr.

'I do. Generally. But I think there are exceptions to the rule. People who are beyond saving.'

Tariq regards him, wordless and apparently without judgement. Cal feels the desire to spill his thoughts and fears. No wonder the man is in the role he's in. He sets the coffee cup on the table in front of him.

'Why did you want to talk to me?'

Tariq shrugs, as if it is nothing. 'I've listened to your podcast. I know you are thorough, fair. But I suppose I want to see that all sides are represented. You should talk to other people about Merrick. Not just those who detest him.'

'I'm struggling to find anyone who knows him.'

Another shrug and a neutral smile.

'Perhaps there are other people who visit him. Maybe they could help you.'

Cal stills. 'I suppose it would be too much for me to ask you to share their names?'

Tariq throws his head back and lets free a deep throaty laugh.

'That wouldn't be investigative journalism at work now, would it?'

'I suppose not.' Cal stands to leave. 'Thank you – I should go and leave you to your work.'

Tariq leads him to where he can reclaim his mobile phone from the staff at the entrance and Cal turns to say goodbye.

'I'll walk you to your car,' Tariq announces, smiling at the security staff and pushing his way out of the prison, striding away from the doors towards the car park. When he catches up with him, Cal can see complex emotions rolling across the counsellor's face.

'It must be very difficult to keep to the lines and also do what is best for your clients,' he says carefully.

Tariq nods. His hands on his hips, he paces up and down, seemingly engaged in internal debate.

'I hope you understand,' he says finally, stepping backwards in a retreat from Cal. His eyes are intent, his gaze unbroken. 'I really do want to help you. It's just that it isn't my place to talk about Lachlan's daughter.'

With that, he turns and jogs back to the building, tweedy jacket disappearing in through the sliding doors, leaving Cal with a thousand questions on his lips.

CHAPTER TWENTY-FOUR

CAL

Cal calls Jeremy Fishpool. The man's clerk tries to fob him off but he refuses to be placated and eventually the line is connected to the annoyed-sounding advocate.

'I really don't have time to chat, Mr Lovett. What with my legal work and the consideration of my judgeship, things are exceptionally tight.'

'I'll get to the point. Merrick has a daughter.'

'What?'

'Lachlan Merrick is visited in prison by a daughter. Who is she?'

'I don't recall. Why do you care?'

'I'm trying to understand him, understand what happened back then.'

'Well then, that's your mistake. He's a brutal triple murderer. Understanding him isn't going to get you anywhere.'

'The girlfriend Merrick had at the time was called Fiona Selwin. I talked to her and she didn't mention a daughter. Could it be hers? Did she come to the trial? Was she in the public gallery supporting him?'

'I don't remember.'

Cal's mind spins back to the pristine house on the neat estate in Perth. What was he missing? It's on the edge of his consciousness, but he can't make it come into view. Frustrated, he takes a deep breath and tries to stop his mind nagging at the problem. That's when it clicks into place. He has seen Merrick's daughter. She was right in front of his face.

He hangs up abruptly, ignoring the sound of Fishpool remonstrating with him, not caring if he annoys the pompous advocate. Fiona Selwin lied to him – by omission, yes, but it still rankles.

–

Instead of calling, Cal makes the drive from Aberdeenshire to Perth to see Fiona, riled up and needing to look her in the eye to be sure of the truth. How is any of this relevant to his quest to implicate Barr? He's not sure that it is, just that he needs to untangle these relationships and understand what's going on if he stands any chance of getting close to Lachlan Merrick.

This time, her husband opens the door. He can see at a glance that the man takes pride in his appearance. He must be a bit younger than his wife: a tight white T-shirt shows off bulging biceps and either he takes a lot of holidays or is a fan of the fake tan bottle. His hair is gelled in regimented spikes and his smile is as white as the T-shirt.

'Is Fiona in?'

Cal crosses his fingers behind his back.

'Who's asking?'

'My name's Cal Lovett. I spoke to her a little while ago for a podcast I'm making. Maybe she mentioned me.'

His voice is stronger and sterner than it naturally is, his veins pumping with anger that Fiona has played games with him. As if her privacy is so much more important than the questions Bella has and the cloud of grief she lives beneath.

Gary frowns, then recovers himself.

'Oh aye, right.'

Before he can explain, Fiona calls down the hallway.

'Who is it? You've been…'

The words trail away when she sees Cal. Her face closes again but he's had enough.

'I need to talk to you about your daughter, Fiona.'

He watches her lips purse stubbornly, her eyes flickering to her husband in panic before she capitulates.

'You'd best come in.'

He's shown into the living room this time, left waiting on the soft pile carpet, a canvas of the couple and their sons looking down at him from above the electric fireplace. He wonders what Fiona's daughter thinks about her place in the family, if she even has one. Fiona and her husband are in the kitchen. Their whispers stretch to him, but he cannot decipher the words.

Eventually, Fiona appears at the door, her face pale and frozen in a kind of anger that shows the hard edges she used to have haven't really been smoothed away, just polished.

'This isn't fair,' she says. 'I've built a life. We have friends, jobs, standing.'

His lip curls at the word. The number of ills he has seen that idea used to conceal is breathtaking. No one ever wants to fall back down when they've clawed their way out of the hole they were in.

'Why didn't you tell me about her when we spoke?'

Her gaze is one of flint and stone.

'We don't speak much.'

'Why?'

'She's difficult. Always has been. Compared to her, the boys were easy.'

Cal feels immediate empathy for this girl.

'The pictures on the fridge. The older girl – that's her, isn't it? I thought she must be an au pair because she isn't in any on her own, only in the background.'

Fiona glares at him, defensive. And what if he is judging? He glances at the huge canvas of Fiona, her husband and the boys, the movement involuntarily.

'Tell me about her.'

'Why? It's not relevant. She doesn't know her father. She was born after he went to prison and I was careful never to talk about him.'

'Does Lachlan know about her?'

She shrugs.

'Aye, but he's a triple murderer, he wasn't exactly going to be involved, was he? She's in her thirties now and he's still in prison. He missed it all. It was better for her not to know.'

It's hard to argue with that. Cal can see how difficult it would have been for a child to be saddled with that.

'What's her name?' he asks, softly.

The question seems to surprise her, as if she's forgotten her firstborn is a person.

'Melissa.'

'Where does she live?'

Fiona shrugs, seeming irritated by the question.

'Somewhere near Edinburgh. I've got the address somewhere. Look, we don't get on, okay. She was an ungrateful teenager, total nightmare. Maybe it was in the blood.'

Cal struggles to conceal his distaste. It's breathtaking, this woman's dislike for her daughter.

'How does she get on with the boys? Her brothers?'

As they've been speaking, Fiona has gradually pivoted away from him, so her eyes are on the giant canvas. The woman shrugs, interested only in the images of the three men.

'Fine.'

'When did you last see her?'

Another shrug.

'A couple of years, I think.'

It's hard to know what to say to that. Cal can't imagine being estranged from Chrissie. He takes a breath, digging into his reserves.

'It must have been difficult for you when she was small?'

'Aye. It was. I was on my own. I had to move away from where I was living – getting clean was a bloody nightmare but my parents said it was a condition of me living there and I had to for the baby. We got through it. Then I met Gary and had the boys and life's been good since then.'

'How old was Melissa when you had them?'

'A teenager.'

'That must have been hard for her, adjusting?'

Fiona snorts.

'Hard for her? She had it bloody easy compared with me. My parents doted on her. Were never like that with me when I was a bairn.'

'But you told her about Lachlan eventually? She knows now?'

Fiona's nostrils flare.

'Never. She has no idea.' She rounds on him. 'Why are you here? So what if I never told you about her? It was a long time ago and I've moved on. I don't want to be dragged back there. And how do you know about her anyway?'

The heat has risen to form two pink spots on her cheeks.

'She's been visiting Lachlan in prison, Fiona.'

'What?'

Shock silences the woman.

Gary appears at the door, moving to stand beside his wife and putting a hand on her shoulder. His previously amiable expression is now cold and threatening.

'I think you should leave.'

Perhaps it's just memories of being an invisible child, but Fiona's treatment of her daughter has triggered something in Cal. This house is making him claustrophobic – everything so perfect on the surface but rotten underneath.

CHAPTER TWENTY-FIVE

EPISODE FIVE: FALSE CONFESSIONS

It's hard to fathom that someone would confess to something as hideous as the slaughter of Allegra Carlo and her daughters if they weren't responsible. Surely, no one in their right mind would take responsibility for a crime this abhorrent if they didn't have to? In fact, recent research has shown that false confessions aren't as uncommon as we would all like to believe.

Professor Edgar Reeves works at the University of Cambridge in the Institute of Criminology. Over the past decade, he's been conducting research into false confessions, speaking both to convicted individuals and the police officers who interviewed them. In all of these cases, evidence subsequently came to light that showed that those convicted could not have committed the crimes for which they were incarcerated, though they admitted everything in interview.

Reeves says there are factors common to many of the cases.

'People always think false confessions are impossible, or one in a million, but really this isn't true. What we're talking about is the amount of strain, both internal and external, placed on a person during the interview process. At the point of a false confession, they are likely to be stressed, tired and confused. Saying they did it becomes the easy option.

'What we've seen time and time again in police interviews where false confessions have happened is that the suspect is backed

into a corner, usually after many hours of interviewing – days, even. There is a point at which it seems like they will never be able to get out of this situation – no one believes them. This leads to a person's absolute despair. And then what happens? Someone comes along and offers them an "out".

'Often, this is "good cop" – someone taking a kind approach following long periods of hostile questioning. Police interviewers can be incredibly skilled at making suspects feel the only way out is to admit to the crime: help me to help you, I understand you didn't mean to hurt them, I can see how this happened, etcetera. *And that's remarkably effective if they're wearing down a guilty person. But, what we've discovered is that it's also remarkably effective at wearing down the innocent.'*

'And have you had a chance to review the tape we have of Lachlan Merrick's confession?'

'I have. It's not ideal because the footage is audio only and it would be more helpful to see the body language in the interview and how the police and Lachlan were presenting. However, it is possible to form certain conclusions from what we do have.'

'And what are those?'

'Lachlan Merrick was exhausted, stressed and possibly coming down from drugs or alcohol. You can hear him slurring his words on the tape. We know he was a long-term drug user, so that fits with his general profile. The officers interviewing Merrick are extremely persistent and very hostile – they'd seen some awful things at that crime scene so wanted to make sure they nailed the culprit, and were under extreme pressure from government, media and public to do so.

'After many hours of this, Merrick would almost certainly have felt there was no way out. Even when his legal representation arrives, he doesn't step in effectively at points I would have expected intervention. For example, he doesn't ask for breaks when his client is clearly distressed. That's surprising to me and

perhaps again a reflection of how the case was viewed at the time. Merrick was already abhorrent to them and less than human.'

'And what about the confession itself?'

'You'll see that Lachlan Merrick has been gradually broken down. They ask him questions he can admit to – about being attracted to Allegra. They make it seem a reasonable emotion and an understandable step to the crime. They open a door behind which there is rest, approval, help, and he walks through it.'

'But surely, some people would resist that? People who were innocent would fight tooth and nail to prove it?'

'It depends on the person and their inner resources as well as their understanding of the legal system. But everyone has their breaking point.'

'Having listened to the tape, do you think Lachlan Merrick is guilty or innocent?'

'I couldn't say one way or the other. What I can say is that not once on the extended version of the tape does Lachlan give unprompted details of the crime scene. In fact, there are several times when he gets details wrong and is almost corrected by the officers. They ask leading questions and make it clear when they are pleased or displeased with him. It would have been clear to him what they wanted him to say.'

'So, on that basis…'

'On that basis, I'd want much stronger evidence before moving to a conviction. It's my personal opinion that this confession cannot be relied upon.'

CHAPTER TWENTY-SIX

CAL

Melissa works as a practice manager in a GP surgery in Edinburgh's Leith. She has two young children. It's striking that there wasn't a single picture of them in her mother's home. She is guarded but open to having a conversation, so he arranges to meet her in the coffee shop next to the clinic where she works.

It's lunchtime when he arrives. Cal is early so he sits and watches the people coming in and out, several of them in scrubs. Then there's a woman at the door, rounded and pretty – he can see traces of her mother in her, but she's different to Fiona – the harshness is absent. She looks flustered, her eyes finding the stranger watching her.

'I'm nervous,' she tells him when they've said hello.

'Please, don't be. This can all be off the record for now. Why don't you grab a seat while I go and order?'

She seems uncomfortable with him paying but he insists and buys sandwiches and coffee, taking a punt on a couple of slices of cake as well.

'You don't have to eat it,' he smiles, apologetically, 'but I couldn't resist.'

Melissa laughs. There is more colour in her cheeks and she seems calmer, settling at their table, though her fingers are clasped tightly in front of her, like she's at a job interview.

'What is your podcast about?'

'Well. It's a long story and I'm nervous about confusing or complicating things for you, but I was contacted by Isabella Carlo, the little girl who survived the attack in the 1980s.'

Melissa's face pales and her tentative smile vanishes completely.

'Oh God. That poor woman. And her father.'

'She's doing really well considering what happened. They'll always be grieving but they've kept going.'

She is loved, he thinks, but doesn't say.

'We see so many people in the surgery with trauma. I just can't imagine...'

Cal studies Melissa, trying to consider how much detail to give her. He'd expected a more hostile discussion and this has disarmed him. In the end, he opts for the bare bones so he doesn't say anything that can't be taken back.

'The thing is, she is convinced that there was another man there that day.'

'Someone else? With my father?' Her voice drops to a whisper.

Melissa sits back as the server brings their sandwiches, her eyes wide and fixed on Cal.

When the woman has gone back to the till, she leans in to listen to him. He can see the fear in her and wishes he didn't have to inflict this.

'She remembers a voice and she says it wasn't your father's. So I've agreed to take a look back at the case.'

'Oh. But...'

He watches the ripples of confusion on her face.

'It's okay. You can ask me.'

'Well. I just wonder… How can she be sure it's not him, not Lachlan, I mean? It was more than thirty years ago. She was a child.'

Cal takes a breath.

'She heard the voice again.'

Melissa freezes. 'Who?'

'It's going to be going out on the podcast soon but we're still putting it together so I can't name him yet, until the lawyers have seen everything. I can tell you that it's a person who has been convicted of other crimes.'

She stares ahead, thoughts passing across her face like clouds.

'And does he have a connection to my… to Lachlan?'

'It's possible. But I haven't found it yet.'

'So this is why you wanted to talk to him?'

He nods. 'Can I ask about your relationship with Lachlan?'

Melissa toys with a crisp from the garnish on her plate then sets it back down.

'I don't really know how to categorise it. I didn't know who he was until I was in my twenties. My grandparents told me and I wished I'd never asked. But… well, I'm not sure I mean that.' Her eyes fill with tears that she swipes at furiously. 'God, this is so stupid.'

'It isn't,' Cal says, passing her a napkin.

'I suppose it helps explain my mother a bit.'

'I've met her,' he says, trying to telegraph understanding. Melissa's body language has changed as she talks about Fiona: she's folding in on herself.

Her laugh is hollow.

'Lucky you. What did you think of her?'

He sits back, unsure how honest to be and how she might take it. But when she speaks her tone is flat.

'It's okay. You won't shock or upset me.'

Cal doesn't really know what's about to come out of his mouth until he starts speaking.

'I have a very difficult mother,' he says. 'My sister was murdered when I was quite young and she sort of shut down after that, was never really there for me again. It's incredibly difficult not to feel that there's something wrong with you… something fundamentally unlovable, I guess.'

He shrugs, afraid he's shared too much, but Melissa is watching him, entranced, her shoulders moving back into a relaxed posture.

'That's how I feel. Do you have other siblings?'

'No. Just me and Margot, my sister who died. You have two half-brothers?'

Melissa nods. 'They had a very different experience of her. She loves them.'

She says it simply, and yet Cal feels the waves of pain striking him full in the chest.

'There is nothing wrong with you,' he says softly.

'Thank you for saying that. I just have to try and believe it.'

They sit for a moment, chewing their sandwiches in silence. It's comfortable, like the aftermath of a storm.

'When did you meet Lachlan?'

'Not that long ago. Maybe five or six years. It took me that long to come to terms with what he did, and also I wouldn't have tried to contact him while my grandparents were still alive. I think it would have upset them, though they never would have said that.'

'I had the impression from your mother that they played a big role in your life?'

She nods. 'They were more like parents than she was. It was hard before she met Gary but after… she didn't want me around. I was an awkward moody teenager and it didn't fit with the perfect family she was building. She worked hard to get there, I know she did.'

'You don't need to be reasonable about it.'

Melissa smiles at him.

'I think I'm hard-wired to make excuses for her. People expect you to be close to your mother, to love her. If I say anything critical it's like I'm a monster.'

'I know,' he says, simply, his mind on his ailing mother and the conflicting emotions he has to surf whenever he is with her.

'I'm afraid I don't think I can help you. I don't talk to Lachlan about the crime. I wrestle with seeing him at all. I don't know who he was then, all I know is the man I've met now. I thought maybe we would have a connection – how desperate is that?'

'It's not. It's understandable.'

Melissa smiles. 'That's nice of you to say. But I'm aware of how pathetic it is. Trying to form some sort of connection with a murderer just because we share the same blood. But now he seems so grateful to see me that I can't stop.'

'I recognise the people-pleasing tendencies.'

In fact, it's so like looking in an emotional mirror that it's uncomfortable.

'It's a mess. Honestly. But then, sometimes I think maybe there is something there, some sort of affinity. That makes me feel even worse. What if I'm like that?'

Cal holds up a hand to stop her. 'I can tell you right now that you're nothing like that. Nothing.'

She nods, grateful and tearful again. 'I think I know that really, but it's in there… thoughts that taunt me when I can't sleep at night.'

'Look, I'll be honest. Your… Lachlan didn't want to talk to me about Allegra and her daughters. He got up and walked away. He's also never sought any appeals or protested his innocence from jail. I find it very strange. Most people, guilty or innocent, would jump at the chance of securing their freedom and there I was suggesting he might not have done it, but… nothing.'

'Perhaps he just feels he deserves to be there,' Melissa says.

'Do you think that's it?'

'I assume so. He has promised me he will take full responsibility before the parole board next year.' She shifts in her seat. 'To be honest, I made it a condition of meeting him. We wrote for a year before I plucked up the courage.'

Cal finds it so strange being here with Melissa – she's younger than Bella, but he thinks they'd get on well in another life. He can see how much pain there is inside her when it comes to her family, but as the hour races past they chat about her work as a practice manager at the surgery and he can see how kind, efficient and impressive she is.

But as they talk, his mind is also whirring. Lachlan Merrick was almost frightened of talking to him, as if he had something left to lose. If Merrick opens the door to claims of innocence, it could arrest the parole board progress and delay any chance he has of meeting his grandchildren. Even if he isn't afraid of Jason Barr, maybe he's finally got something worth hanging onto. The more Cal talks to Melissa, the more he thinks that might be the case.

CHAPTER TWENTY-SEVEN

CAL

Sarah has finally managed to get hold of the police files from the Merrick case after Bella made an official request as daughter and sister of the victims. When she sends the files across in a transfer there are hundreds of pages: interviews with local people, notes from the detectives manning the tips line, forensics, and yet no mention of a yellow car.

'Maybe the man you and Bella spoke to at the farm was wrong? Misremembering?' Sarah suggests.

'It's possible but he sounded so sure. I don't think it's something you just make up. What would be the point?'

'There are notes from two officers who were sent to the farm: PC Wallace and…' she laughs, 'DC Dick. Maybe you can speak to them, jog some memories?'

He spends the rest of the morning googling and making calls about the two officers. It takes a while because Police Scotland won't divulge personal information, but he does eventually find pictures of a retirement party for a DCI Hamish Wallace on Facebook. An hour later, he's in the car heading south towards Dundee.

–

DCI Wallace has the sort of institutionalised confidence of the long-serving police officer, but he's open and friendly, which gives Cal pause from his initial judgement. The man seems to be enjoying his retirement, apparently spending all his free time in the hills biking as well as volunteering with various local organisations to 'keep out of Sylvia's way'.

Wallace is fixing a mountain bike when he arrives, the frame upended on an immaculate driveway on the outskirts of Broughty Ferry, which is lined with regimented bedding plants, not a speck of mud in sight. Two cars are parked in front of a garage, each one gleaming. Cal feels inadequate by comparison, wishing he'd parked his battered and dusty Volvo round the corner.

'I'd offer to shake your hand, but...' Wallace holds up his oily fingers.

'No worries,' Cal says. 'Thanks for agreeing to speak to me.'

While Wallace energetically attacks the workings of the bike with an Allen key, he outlines the aims of the podcast, emphasising Bella's involvement while steering clear of any suggestion that the police might have got things wrong back then. The ex-officer agrees to be recorded as long as Cal runs any quotes past him before using them.

'I didn't sit in on any of the interviews, I was new to the force and far too junior,' Wallace tells him. 'But it was quite the case then and now. I've worked on some horrible things in my time but never anything like that, thank God. The slaughter.'

He sets the spanner on the floor and lifts one end of the bike, spinning the wheel. Cal's not sure what he's doing. Has always been useless with bikes.

'You did go out and do some interviews though?' he asks, casually. 'I think I've seen your name on the files?'

'Aye, I went out with the officer I was shadowing. We did door to door in the area. It was rural though so hardly anyone nearby.'

'DC Dick?' Cal inwardly congratulates himself for managing to say this with a straight face.

'That's the one.' Wallace shakes his head. 'Dick by name and dick by nature, I'm afraid. No way he'd be on the force these days but it was different back then. He's dead now.'

'Right. That answers my next question. Has he been dead long?'

'A few years now. I only heard that on the grapevine. He left the job about ten years ago. Between you and me, there were some issues with drink and he retired under a cloud. I was terrified of him when I started out, but he was a sad old bastard in the end.'

Wallace straightens and surveys his tidy domain, gleaming toolbox on the ground beside the cleanest bike Cal's ever seen.

'I just wanted to ask you about the people you interviewed at the industrial buildings over the fields from the crime scene, where Merrick worked.'

'Oh right. Fine.'

Cal watches for any kind of evasion but Wallace betrays nothing so he carries on.

'Do you remember one of them mentioning a car that had been seen in the area? A yellow one?'

Wallace scratches his head.

'Maybe, yes. That rings a bell. But it was a long time ago so I can't swear to it.'

'It's just… that's not in your notes. There's no mention of it.'

'Oh.' Now there is guilt on Wallace's face, and a sort of bodily alertness creeps in. Subtle, but there.

'Why would that be?'

'Now you've jogged my memory. We went out there right before Merrick was arrested. By the time we came to write it all up, it was pointless. They had him and he'd confessed. Dick told me not to bother with extraneous detail when we were doing the notes for the file. I didn't know better – it was my first few weeks in the job. But that was like him, always cutting corners. It got him in the end.'

'But you didn't worry about it at the time?'

'No, I mean, the case was cut and dried, plus Merrick didn't own a yellow car so it definitely wasn't relevant to his conviction. Don't get me wrong. That sort of shortcut bollocks is definitely not okay and when I knew better I'd never have indulged in it, but in this case, it would only have been relevant if it wasn't Merrick who killed them, so no harm done.'

Cal lets his words hang in the silence for a moment.

Wallace turns slowly to face him, his previous confident contentment vanishing.

'Tell me again why you're doing this podcast?'

CHAPTER TWENTY-EIGHT

CAL

It's the middle of the night when he remembers. Cal sits bolt upright in bed, his heart thudding like he's waking from a nightmare. It takes a moment for his senses to click in; there is a strange dislocation in such a sudden awakening.

Cal swings his legs out of bed and grabs a T-shirt, pulling it over his head as he leaves Shona sleeping. In the open-plan kitchen-living room, he ruffles the dog's head and flicks the lights on, the naked windows' dark eyes watching him. Cal sees his reflection – his hair wild and face a ghostly blur. He shivers in the early morning chill.

The boxes he took from Naomi Barr are sitting in the corner like guilt or shame. Something he hasn't wanted to face.

Sinking to his knees, Cal drags them towards him. He has to try a couple before he finds the one with the photographs, his impatience making him rough and awkward. When he does find it, he tears open the flaps and looks down at the mess inside, pausing a moment with a sheen of sweat on his forehead and a thudding inside him. Rocket has padded over to him and snuffles at the cardboard, sneezing three times. Cal tugs him away and the old dog flops down next to him.

Taking a breath, he plunges his hands into the musty box, rifling through the piles clumsily in his urgency and this disorientating sudden wakefulness. But he can't find what he's looking for. Swearing, he tips the box on its side and the pictures cascade onto the floor. A kind of madness has come over him. The heat of his hatred of Barr is burning strong tonight.

'Slow down,' he imagines his sister saying, her cool amusement so easy to conjure in his mind. He closes his eyes and tries to summon his memories of her.

She's right. If it's here, he'll find it.

Taking a deep breath, he starts stacking the pictures in a pile, checking each one as he gathers up the mess he's made. He is himself again, as if whatever dervish was inside him has spun away. But what if he's wrong? Has he imagined it?

He just needs to be methodical, he tells himself, stacking one pile back in the box and crawling across the floor to retrieve more. Then he sinks back on his haunches. Finally. There it is. That black-and-white image of Jason Barr and a woman he doesn't recognise. Barr's arm is fixed around her in a possessive way that sends chills through Cal. The pair of them leaning against a car. The picture is black and white, that's the problem. So he can't tell, but it's a light-coloured car. He stares at it as if he can will it into colour. Could it be yellow? It's possible.

Then he flips the picture over. It confirms his worst fears and hopes in one. Written on the back, a heart drawn clumsily around the words: Daisy and Jason. Cal feels his throat close. The house seems to breathe around him. What if Barr had access to this vehicle when Allegra and her daughters were killed? What if he *was* in the area? It's an incredible stretch, he knows it is, but something was going on at the nightclub and the old warehouse so it's possible. Bella heard his voice.

When he finally stands, his knees scream from being on the hard floor. He bundles the rest of the photographs into the box and takes the black-and-white image over to the kitchen with him. Its presence pulses in his mind as he turns on the coffee machine. Rocket lets out a dramatic sigh from his sleeping position.

Cal sits with his coffee and stares at the picture, scrutinising every inch and committing it to memory. He needs to send this to Foulds and see if she can help identify 'Daisy' so they can date it. He can't be sure, but he thinks he can see a tiny chink of metal in Barr's hand that could be a car key. As he studies the picture, it's not only the Carlos he's thinking of. He can't hide from the thought that Margot went missing that same year. They've never found the car Jason Barr was driving when he killed her.

CHAPTER TWENTY-NINE

CAL

When it gets light, he photographs the picture and sends it to DI Lorna Foulds, the only officer he's ever found who is as invested in bringing Jason Barr to justice as he is. He types the barest details into a message and waits. It doesn't take long for her to call.

She sounds out of breath. He presses the phone to his ear, concerned.

'Are you okay?'

'I'm out for a run. So, no. I'm not okay. Fucking medical coming up.'

He glances at the window. It's seven a.m. and there's a steady drizzle coating the world and misting the air.

'I wondered if you'd come across a Daisy in your investigations? Or that car?'

'She sort of looks familiar, so it's possible. Where did you get this picture?'

He decides to be economical with the truth.

'Naomi Barr gave it to me.'

Foulds huffs. She hasn't forgiven Naomi for her time-wasting vanishing act last year. He fills her in on the intel from the farm workers and that Wallace confirmed there was a sighting of a yellow car in the woods close to where Allegra and the girls were killed.

'It's a very long shot,' he apologises.

But Foulds sounds more intrigued than deterred.

'Sometimes cases are built on long shots.'

'Does this mean you believe Bella?'

'I don't know what I think, but anything that fucks with Jason Barr is good enough for me.'

Cal smiles. 'Thank you.'

'I'm going into the station this morning. I'll see what we can do with working out the identity of the woman. The fact that there's a first name on the picture will narrow things down. I'll also ask some of the car nerds we call on if they can work out the make of the car from the bit we can see.'

When she hangs up, Cal sits in the kitchen for a long time, his feet ice blocks on the floor, goose pimples on his bare arms. He should get going, have a shower, call Bella, call Sarah, but for some reason he just can't move. He keeps picturing his sister, crammed into the boot of a car the colour of sunshine. Dead or dying.

-

The darkness of his thoughts is interrupted by Shona coming into the kitchen, tousled and yawning. Even the maelstrom of emotions inside him can't stop the rush of adoration for her. It's a marvel to Cal that his love for Shona keeps deepening and expanding. He's never felt as safe and understood with anyone as he does with her.

'You're up early.' She swivels to take in the scene of carnage behind him, the sleeping labrador in the midst of the boxes and photos. 'Ah.'

'I found this.' He brandishes the photo and she leans in to take a better look.

'Is that Jason Barr?'

'Yes. But it's the car I'm more interested in. If it's yellow…'

He lets the thought hang. Shona rubs circles on his back.

'Have you called Foulds?'

'She's on it. I'll talk to Bella and Sarah today as well – do some digging and see if I can find a Daisy.'

Shona frowns. 'Maybe you should get some sleep too?'

'I'll try. I just keep thinking about Margot. I didn't expect this case to stir everything up for me, but it really has.'

'Do you want me to stay? I could cancel the conference.'

He stands and wraps his arms around her. More than anything he wants to be with her right now, but he makes his voice light.

'No love. You've worked hard on this presentation. Go and wow those white coats… we'll be fine, won't we Rocket?'

They both look over to the dog – the Lab lifts his head fractionally and then flops back down with a huff.

Cal laughs. 'He's in charge of sleeping.'

-

The day passes in a blur of jitters, partly caused by the case and partly the copious amounts of coffee he drinks while searching the internet for Daisy. It's a needle in a haystack type search – doomed to end in frustration. Eventually he manages to fall asleep on the sofa and wakes up disorientated, the sky dark and the dog nosing him for his dinner.

Rocket fed and walked, Cal realises he is supposed to have food shopped – the cupboards are bare and Shona is away for the night. A takeaway is tempting, but he's trying to be healthier since he had his cholesterol tested, so he drives to the 24-hour superstore and dashes in for essentials. The shop is bright with artificial light, but the aisles are mercifully clear, only a few scattered shelf stackers with vast pallets to navigate and a bored assistant on one of the checkouts.

It's bitter outside, so he grabs the bags and dashes to the car, yawning and desperate to get back home. He's just lifting the shopping into the boot when he smells an alien odour: something medicinal and overpowering. Out of place in this deserted lot.

He doesn't even have time to straighten properly, his head is still bent over the groceries, loops of the bag handles sticking up where he has released them. Then another set of hands, these clamped over his mouth, the medicinal smell nauseating and a brief flash of terror as he realises he's in big trouble.

CHAPTER THIRTY

EPISODE SIX: THE BLOODY SHIRT

In the last episode of Finding Justice *we heard from a false confession expert that Merrick's confession bears some of the hallmarks of others that have turned out to be unsafe. While we can't be certain that Lachlan Merrick made a false confession, and the man himself refuses to be questioned on the subject, there was other evidence that led police to Lachlan. Today, we'll be looking at the forensic evidence from the crime.*

So what evidence was there? Glasgow University forensic expert Leah Abimbola is here to explain.

'There were two key pieces of evidence that tied Lachlan Merrick to the crime scene. While the police were alerted to Merrick's suspicious disintegration in the weeks after the murders, there was nothing conclusive until they secured a warrant to search his home and found the bloodied T-shirt stuffed in a carrier bag at the back of his wardrobe, along with underwear that we believe Merrick stole from the Carlos on a separate occasion.

'Initially, however, forensic work concentrated on the scene and the bodies of Allegra, Gail and Philippa, conducting the postmortems of the three victims, examining their clothes and the bags and items they were carrying with them, and undertaking fingertip searches of the field.

'The family's beach-style bag had been ransacked, with one of the girls' swimming costumes used to bind Allegra's wrists. In

the bag was a Tupperware container with a bloody fingerprint on the lid. That fingerprint matched those later taken by police. The smoking gun, so to speak.'

'That and the bloodstained shirt?'

'When they tested the shirt found in his wardrobe, that blood type was Allegra's. The T-shirt matched the one she was wearing that day.'

'I mean, this all sounds pretty conclusive? I can see why the police would be certain they had their man.'

'Well, yes and no. As with all forensics, it's important not to jump to conclusions. Yes, Allegra's shirt covered in blood was in Merrick's wardrobe. Yes, his fingerprint was on the picnic box. But what do those facts actually tell us?'

'That he touched the box and someone, likely him, put the shirt in the wardrobe.'

'Exactly. While it's useful evidence, it doesn't categorically tell us what happened that day and you also need to consider what evidence wasn't there.'

'What do you mean? Are you referring to the murder weapon?'

'Correct. Postmortem analysis of the victims suggested the weapon was a large kitchen knife. However, that weapon was never recovered.'

'So we don't know whose fingerprints were on it?'

'Precisely. It has always bothered me that Merrick supposedly managed to dispose of a murder weapon so skilfully it was never found, and yet left a bloodstained shirt where it could easily be located.'

'It doesn't make sense.'

'The prosecution would argue, if they had ever needed to, that Merrick was under the influence of drugs when he carried out the crime. So these irregularities of behaviour could be explained.'

'Do you buy that?'

'I don't "buy" anything, Mr Lovett. I deal in cold hard facts and these questions remain.'

'None of Merrick's blood was found at the scene, was it?'

'No – more missing evidence. It's possible that Allegra was stunned in the initial stage of the attack and didn't have time to fight back, but the evidence collected at the scene suggested she had crawled towards one of her daughters.'

'But none of these issues were ever debated at trial, were they?'

'There was no need. Lachlan Merrick pleaded guilty.'

CHAPTER THIRTY-ONE

CAL

When he wakes, Cal is being manhandled across a room to another door, the world swimming around him. He gags and one of the men dragging him swears. His head is throbbing and there's a strange taste in his mouth – probably whatever they gave him to knock him out, he realises, panic rising. What's behind that door? What's going to happen next? He thinks of Chrissie, of Shona, Rocket. He needs to see them again.

When the door swings back, he is shoved hard into the dark mouth of the black room, a strong hand between his shoulder blades, sending him stumbling forwards so he hits the floor and pain fires through his knees. Before he even manages to turn, the door slams shut behind them, leaving him alone and unable to see. He hears the click of the key in the lock.

Cal's heart fireworks inside his chest and panic chases its way up his throat, blotches blurring what little vision he has in this prison. He can't breathe, can't think or feel. Agonising moments later, Cal realises the assailants have gone. Dragging air into closed lungs, he forces the breath to bring reason back into his body, great noisy lungfuls of air that remind him of Shona doing yoga in their living room.

Faint objects rise out of the gloom around him. He is in another office, this one deserted, and the corner in front of him is piled high with broken furniture and old desks, a cracked computer monitor. He turns on the spot, peering into the dusk as his eyes adjust, frantically looking for an exit, a clue to where he is, but there is nothing. The place is infuriating in its blandness.

Even the smell doesn't help – the acrid tang of cheap air freshener fills the air, pushing its way down his throat, sticky and cloying. He takes a moment to stretch his stiff arms and legs, forcing himself to stop and make sense of what's happening.

These men, what do they want from him? Is he being held for money? He's a podcaster, with no power or leverage. Why would anyone kidnap him? He thinks of Shona, away on her conference, Chrissie at university in Edinburgh – there is no one to raise the alarm. This is the perfect time to abduct him – were they lucky, or did they know that? The thought sets him adrift. He's read too many case files, knows far too many dark stories of final moments. Are these his?

To distract himself, Cal makes a careful sweep of the room, tentatively running his fingers over breeze block walls and the occasional pin board, finding them empty of paper and pins. Every time he comes up short, he has to fight the panic. Even a tack would have felt like a comforting weapon right now, though he knows it wouldn't get him far.

There are no external windows, the only light coming from a small high pane of glass on one side of the room, but even that is weak. Gradually, Cal's eyes adjust to the darkness and he makes inventory of the wrecked office furniture, wondering if he can break something up to use as a weapon. He finds a desk with a wobbly leg but after wrenching and working it for ten minutes, he's still no closer to dismantling it and all he has to show is a sheen of sweat and a woozy sickness that must be due to whatever they used to knock him out.

He tries shouting, though his voice is a detached rasp and he cannot make it loud enough. He is frightened that they will hear and come and yet he needs to try. It makes no difference. No one comes. He is simply exhausting himself, screaming into a void.

Next he goes silent and still, pressing his ear to the door and listening. Closing his eyes he reduces all his senses to this one, straining for the faintest sense of movement or conversation. Maybe he will hear them talking and be able to work out what they want from him? Is anyone there? He pictures a man on the other side, pressed to the door, listening right back and has to fight down nausea. But, no matter how long he listens, there isn't so much as the slide of a shoe on the carpet squares. Is it better or worse to be alone? What if they never come back? He takes the handle of the door and rattles it, harder and harder. It barely shifts in the frame.

'Fuck!'

The frustration bursts out of him, but he doesn't have the energy to sustain it.

Depleted, Cal sinks to the floor, his mouth dry, reducing the scope of his wishes to a bottle of water or a cold can of Coke for now. Anything to take his mind away from the darker thoughts. He just needs to close his eyes for a moment. Only, a moment becomes hours, drifting in and out of sleep on twisted dreams. He chases his daughter down winding streets, or is it Margot? Barely a flick of her red hair is visible as she rounds the endless corners, always just out of reach.

When he wakes again it is properly dark and there is no noise – not even the distant hum of a road. He waves a hand in front of his face but sees nothing. He could have fallen off the face of the earth. What do these people want with him? He rakes through his past cases, racking his brains for someone this aggrieved and organised, but comes up short. Maybe they've contacted Sarah, maybe they have demands and right now she's on the phone to Foulds, making a plan to come rescue him. He just needs to hang on. Or maybe they're coming back here to kill him. He'll fight, he decides, his daughter's face in his mind's eye. To the last breath.

The room is cold and Cal starts to shiver, finding the noise of his teeth chattering oddly frightening. Torn between moving for warmth and succumbing to the bone deep exhaustion, he curls in a foetal ball as far from the door as possible, praying for morning to come and afraid of it, too.

CHAPTER THIRTY-TWO

BELLA

The podcast has unleashed an obsession. Bella has read everything she can about Merrick, which is less than she would have expected. How can there be so little information about a man in jail for triple murder, the man accused of plunging his hands into the heart of her family and tearing it apart? She itches with the desire to visit him, even though she has promised not to.

Every day, she has been checking her phone and email repeatedly – it's been so long since she heard from Cal and waiting for news is torture, but she can't bring herself to break the silence by contacting him. It's a superstitious feeling. If there was good news, or some sort of development, he would contact her, so this lack must mean the best she can hope for is stasis. Is he out of touch because he can't break something to her? She is too afraid to ask.

At work she has been distracted and slow. Her manager called her into his office to ask if she needed anything and if she maybe wants to take some time. Bella has never been close to being reprimanded at work before, no matter that this is a gentle enquiry. She'd left his office red-faced, vowing to herself that she would concentrate and, for a day or so, it worked but then she found her gaze on the window and her thoughts on Jason Barr and Lachlan Merrick, the arguments circling in her mind.

At home, Bella has been just as absentminded, forgetting to go to the shops when she has promised she will pick up bits for the boys' lunches, stirring a boiling pasta sauce as it over bubbles, or not hearing one of her sons until he has asked the same question four or five times. Her family has been tiptoeing around her: Noah gently took the wooden spoon from her hand earlier and suggested she put her feet up while he finished off; he sent one of the boys to the shop at the end of their road for the bread rolls; he answered their mundane questions. She has only half heard the whispered conversations between them, barely realising that there is a quiet agreement among her boys to pick up the slack, not to complain. Occasionally, she has been able to raise her head from her thoughts and see that they are watching her, trying to smile.

'I'm sorry,' she says to Noah every night on repeat. 'I'm sorry.'

'No need to be sorry, love,' he murmurs these words like a mantra, whispering them into her hair as he holds her. 'No need to be sorry.'

There is every need.

Now it has been almost two weeks since she heard from Cal and she feels petulant and angry. She has been snapping at the boys, bursting into tears for no reason. She knows from the look on her father's face when she answers the door, and the bunch of her favourite yellow tulips in his hands, that her husband has told him something is wrong.

'Noah called you.'

He hands her the flowers and kisses her on the cheeks twice, Italian-style like always.

'You're scaring them.'

They make their way to the kitchen and she busies herself putting the flowers in a mason jar. Ben comes in the back door and drops his football kit by the washing machine.

'Looking good, Granddad.' He high-fives Dominic and grabs a bag of crisps from the cupboard before dashing upstairs.

'You'll ruin your…' she starts, but finds she can't be bothered to shout up after him. And it's not true. The crisps won't ruin his dinner. He's unfillable – always hungry and yet thin as a rake from all the sport he does, the perpetual motion of today's teenage life.

'I haven't heard from him, Dad, from Cal. What's taking him so long?'

'He's not a miracle worker.'

While she reaches for cups and teabags, Dominic bundles up the cellophane from the flowers, separating the paper and tucking them both in the recycling bin.

'I know that, I just want…' She stops. What does she want? Then she turns and looks at her father. The one person who can understand more than anyone. 'I want to be *sure*. One way or the other.'

He sighs. 'Bella…'

'Please don't tell me we never can be,' she whispers. 'I can't bear it.'

Dominic shakes his head. He lifts his immaculate jacket from where he has carefully laid it on one of the high breakfast bar chairs. He shakes it loose and reaches into the inside pocket, drawing out a slip of paper.

'I want you to think carefully before you use this.'

'What is it?'

'Promise me, first. Once you do this it cannot be undone.'

She fights her impatience and the urge to wrench the piece of paper from him.

'I promise.'

'This is the number of a man who contacted me many years ago. He worked with Lachlan Merrick in prison.'

Her father never says the name of the man incarcerated for killing her mother and sisters. It sounds like he has a mouthful of sawdust and it might choke him.

'*Worked* with him?'

'Well. Some sort of counsellor. He wanted me to meet Merrick and talk to him, a sort of mediation process. I declined.'

Bella reaches for the paper and tugs it from his fingers. It does not come easily.

'And you think I should contact him?'

Dominic sighs again. 'No. That is the last thing I want. But you are not yourself Bella, and maybe he will have some answers or be able to help you. You cannot just rely on a podcaster. You have to look for your own truth.'

Bella stares at the paper in her hand. An unfamiliar name in her father's elegant cursive scrawl. It is faded and creased, as if it was screwed up and thrown in the bin then reconsidered and smoothed out again.

'Thank you,' she whispers.

'But Bella.' His voice sharpens, a tone she remembers from when she was a teenager, though she barely caused enough trouble for him to have to use it. 'You must not let your life get sucked down this drain of wondering. You are forgetting the people around you. The ones who need you, who are alive. We had to make a decision all those years ago, you and I. We had to decide to live. That we were not going to let one man ruin everything. That is not what your mother would have wanted. It's not what we fought for, you and I.'

Tears fill her eyes as she looks at him. She tries to imagine losing her boys, losing Noah, and persevering as he has done. She cannot speak, but she nods, dropping the paper on the counter and pressing her index fingers to her eyes to hold in the tears.

'That applies whether the right man is in jail or not,' he says. 'Understand?'

'Yes,' she says when she can speak again. But she's not sure she's telling the truth.

CHAPTER THIRTY-THREE

CAL

When he wakes, it is a jerk into consciousness from a black void of nothing. How long has he been out? Cal's head is splitting, like an axe has been swung into his skull. As his eyes adjust, he remembers the events of the previous evening, finds he is still lying on the floor in this nondescript office. What's woken him? His head lurches as he tries to sit up, breath racing, his chest tight with panic.

'I'd stay still for a moment if I were you.'

The voice is calm, dangerously so. Cal startles and twists to find the speaker, but the man is behind him and he doesn't yet have the co-ordination to rise.

'Drink that.' There is a bottle of water next to Cal. 'You'll feel okay soon, bit of a headache maybe.'

Cal's already twisting off the plastic bottle top, his fingers weak with relief.

'What do you want?'

The man strides to the door. 'There's a bathroom at the end of the corridor. Don't try and run. There's nowhere to go. We'll wait for you in the next room.'

Cal can barely take in the words, his head is tilted back and he's chugging the sweet lukewarm water, trickles running from the sides of his mouth and down his chin.

When he looks up, the shadow of the man has vanished from the room.

He drains the bottle and stumbles to his feet, groaning at the stiffness in his limbs, the pain in his back from a night on the cold and miserable carpet tiles. He blinks as he moves into the corridor, unused to even this diffuse light. It's amazing how fast his ability to resist has crumpled. Now, putting one foot in front of the next is confounding enough. He peers down the narrow hallway. There is nothing of note. Nothing to use as a weapon and no obvious escape route. As Cal makes his way along the corridor, he keeps an anchor hand on the wall, trailing it along as if he's in a maze trying to find his way out.

He uses the bathroom, which is windowless, rank and stinking but welcome nonetheless. He washes his hands and splashes brackish water from the rusty tap on his face, trying to regain some measure of mental agility, though the headache still pulses inside his skull. Eventually, he cannot delay any longer. He wipes his hands on his jeans and pushes back the bolt on the door, retracing his steps along the hall and shuddering as he passes his overnight prison.

When he opens the door to the other room, he is immediately grabbed by thick fingers – a man waiting behind the door. The contact is rough and so unexpected that Cal cries out in shock. He is punched to the ground before hands guide him to an office chair and he is shoved into it, the wheels spinning and jolting him across the floor with the impact.

Blood fills Cal's vision. He can't see the man properly and his ears are ringing from the impact.

'What I'm about to say doesn't leave this room.'

There is a man across the desk from him, pushed back into the shadows on his own chair. It is the voice from before but even as he wipes the blood from his face and blinks, the man remains a mystery, concealed beneath a balaclava. He dimly takes in a stocky frame and hears a southern accent but the room spins around him.

'I'm about to offer you the thing you've always wanted.'

'How would you know what I've always wanted?'

Cal is tired, in pain and furious at the presumption. He tries to push away from them and make a break for freedom, lurching pathetically, but hands grip the chair from behind, holding it steady. He shoves the floor with his feet, trying to turn, but he's going nowhere.

'You want Jason Barr dead.'

Involuntarily, Cal stops pushing.

'What? Why would you offer me that?'

'Maybe I'd be willing to make a trade.'

There is cotton wool in his head. Cal can't make the words make sense. He sniffs and blood trickles down the back of his throat.

'Who are you?'

The man's chuckle sends shivers through him.

'You could just think of us as a group of concerned citizens with some good connections and a desire to improve society by ridding it of scum like Barr.'

One of the men behind him barks a sharp laugh.

Cal scrambles for thoughts, more confused than ever. What do they want from him?

'Jason Barr is in prison.'

'Well, let's just say that access doesn't pose a problem for us.'

His heart thumps and his spinning head won't let him fully digest the words.

'What are you saying? I don't understand.'

'Oh I think you do. It's quite simple. We can make him go away. Forever.'

The strangest sensations: joy and fear spiral inside him, followed by sharp disgust at himself. He's not allowed to want that, is he? That's his deepest darkest desire. A socially unacceptable one. It's supposed to stay locked inside, not be exposed in this dingy office in God knows where.

'You want to kill Jason Barr?'

'Go to the top of the class.'

'It's hardly like you need my permission.' Cal meets the man's sarcasm with his own.

'Ah but I do. There's just one condition to this offer, Mr Lovett. If we deal with Jason Barr for you, we will need something in return.'

His stomach drops. He's so confused. Hungry, thirsty and broken. Most likely just how they want him. Though at least now he knows they aren't planning to kill him today.

'What do you want?' His voice cracks as the words break free.

'We need you to drop this investigation you've started into Lachlan Merrick.'

'The Carlo case? Why are you interested in that?'

'All you need to know is that it's not in the public interest to have that particular can of worms opened up. We'll deal with Jason Barr and you can get on with your life – find some other rocks to turn over. Capisce?'

Cal thinks of Bella, of her anguish and her search for the truth. They'll kill Jason Barr if he walks away from her. Margot would be avenged.

The slick smooth voice continues.

'Mr Merrick will not be granted parole next year. As far as we are concerned, the right man is in prison and it's best that he remain there.'

But Cal is struggling to focus on Merrick. Instead, his mind is teeming with conflicting thoughts about Barr. He wants Barr to pay for what he's done to Margot and to everyone else he's hurt. His dream has always been for the man to spend the rest of his life in jail. But. If he was gone from the world, that would be even better, wouldn't it? Freedom. Absolute freedom from the background noise of where he is, what he's doing and if he ever feels the slightest bit of remorse.

Cal rubs his face, his eyes gritty and his mouth dry. He can't think straight. If Barr dies then he also gets away with it, doesn't he? No pain and remorse, just blissful nothingness for a brutal man who should be suffering. And, it's wrong. That's not what we do in a civilised society. He's against the death penalty, once worked on a documentary about inmates on death row in a Texas jail, and so he knows things are never straightforward, never black and white.

Except when it comes to Jason Barr.

'Right,' the smooth voice is now saying, backing away from him, drifting from the room. 'My colleagues will drop you back. Do what we suggest and everything will be fine. Oh and it should go without saying: talk to no one about it. We will know if you do.'

Before he can reply, a rough strip of cloth is looped over Cal's face, the world again going dark, his breathing heavy and his ears straining to understand what's happening. Hands, as meaty and strong as Jason Barr's, are lifting him, standing him on his feet. More hands, pushing him. He stumbles, his arms out before him in protection, confused and disorientated. One thought running through his head: what if this is the answer to everything?

CHAPTER THIRTY-FOUR

BELLA

Bella waits until the next day to call the number on the slip of paper. She picks it up several times and turns it over in her hands, staring at the number until she has memorised it. *Patrick Greaves. The Reconciliation Project.* That's not what she wants, is it? Reconciliation. Such an impossible word to encompass the acres of pain inside her. She wants the truth. Retribution. Merrick can give one of those to her at least.

Finally, she can bear it no longer. When the rest of the family have left for work and school, she presses the number into her phone and waits, dry-mouthed, to be put through to this Greaves. There is no going back after this, that's what her father said, isn't it? Bella's finger hovers over the screen. What is she starting? Her life was so sorted and perfect. Now she's blowing it all up on a fruitless quest.

However, the voice on the other end is kind, almost beleaguered, and it disarms her, bringing to mind the image of a bearded geography teacher, one the kids like and can have a joke with, who has been round the block and can't be intimidated.

'Mr Greaves, thank you for…'

'Pat. Call me Pat.'

'Right… Pat…' She takes a deep breath, alarmed at how tongue-tied she is. Her phone slips a little in her clammy hand.

'Take your time,' he says, clearly sensing her disquiet.

'My father passed on your number. You gave it to him some years ago.'

'I remember,' he says. 'Dominic.'

He probably looked it up but, even so, she's impressed that he cared enough to do that.

'You told him he could speak to Lachlan Merrick?'

'Well… yes, that could have been part of a mediation process I was working on a pilot for. We had explored using your family's case as a test but, I have to be honest with you, neither party was open to pursuing it, so we didn't get very far along that route.'

'You mean, he didn't want to talk to my dad either?'

Bella feels affronted, angry even, at the slight. How dare Lachlan Merrick get to choose?

She waits, every muscle in her arm clenched and her fingers tight around the handset.

'At the time I was working with Lachlan Merrick, he wasn't really sure what he wanted. I worked as a counsellor in the prison he was remanded to and we had started this pilot programme with some government funding. I had hoped this opportunity might be a step that would help him come to terms with his offending and fully admit to himself what he had done. Back then, there was a theory that families of victims find speaking to a remorseful offender helpful in giving them closure and control – something that's been backed up since then – so we made that offer. It's understandable that your dad didn't want to take us up on it. I'm not sure I would have wanted to in his position, even doing what I do.'

'I see.' Bella swallows. 'But what if *I* wanted to meet him? Now.'

There is a long pause. So long that she lifts the phone from her ear to check they are still connected.

'I'll be honest with you, I think it's unlikely you could do that through a mediation programme.'

'Why?' She sounds like the child she was when they were killed.

'The pilot I was running back then was not taken forward. Victim-offender mediation does happen now, but it is carefully controlled and only offered in certain circumstances, often with a younger offender as a way of rehabilitating and reducing sentence length. With Lachlan Merrick at the end of his term and shortly eligible for parole, this wouldn't fit that requirement.'

'I see.'

Bella doesn't know what to say. She'd pinned her hopes on this chance – the thought that she could look Merrick in the face and find the truth in his eyes. Perhaps it would trigger her memories further. Now the idea is being taken away as quickly as it was planted.

'Can I ask why you'd like to meet him? Is there a particular reason you want to now?'

Bella sighs.

'I remembered something. I'm working with a podcaster to look back at the case. He's great, but I just think we don't know everything about that day. I need some answers.'

'I do understand. Look, maybe I shouldn't say this, but if you really want to speak to him, we could request that you be put on Lachlan Merrick's visitor list at the prison. It's a long shot but it could work if he's open to the conversation. I have contacts there who might make an approach for you.'

'Really? We can do that?'

'Yes. But… I have to warn you, unless things have changed since I worked with him, I really don't think he's going to be able to help you. Even if he decides he wants to.'

'Why is that?'

Bella presses her ear to the phone, every muscle tense.

'When I knew him, Lachlan Merrick told me that he wasn't sure what happened. He said he didn't remember that day at all.'

CHAPTER THIRTY-FIVE

CAL

Fresh air and light hit Cal's face and he drinks them in, feeling his nausea subside, though the blindfold is still tight and pinching. His stomach growls. Hands shove him across rough ground and he stumbles, guided until he hears a car door open in front of them. They set him in what feels like the back. There is someone next to him.

Cal cannot speak. Can only listen to the engine and attempt to count the twists and turns in the road, but it's impossible to keep up and soon he is lost, still dehydrated and confused. After what could be ten minutes or twenty, the car slows and bumps onto the side of the road. It strikes him that they may have changed their minds. Maybe they're going to kill him.

When the door opens and arms reach for him, he shies away, suddenly convinced this is it. The man swears and wrenches him out, letting him fall to the ground, his arm scraping along what feels like tarmac. He is pulled to his feet and dragged, moaning and grazed. Then another car door opens and he is shoved in the back.

There is the clink of keys, the door is slammed shut behind him and it sounds like they are walking away. Inside the vehicle, there is silence. Slowly it dawns on him that the smell is familiar. A moment later, he hears the sound of the other car drawing away, leaving him shivering in the total quiet. What is he supposed to do?

Cal waits a long time, too afraid to move. How can he be sure they really have gone? Is this a trick? Eventually, with shaking hands he works the tight knot of the blindfold at the back of his head, loosening it so it slides down around his neck and he can adjust, blinking into the brightness of the world. He lets out the breath he has been holding.

He's in his own car, on a country road, only fields and woodland around him. It looks like Aberdeenshire – familiar scenery of rolling fields and dry-stone walls, the sky huge above – though it feels he's been to another country or planet. Even so, he can't quite get his bearings. Where is he? The urge to flee overtakes him and his hands shake with delayed shock.

Swivelling in his seat to double-check no one is there, Cal confirms that he is alone but cannot banish the feeling of threat. He climbs between the seats into the front and locks the car, noticing his phone is on the seat beside him – dead. There is no choice but to drive and try to find his way. His fingers fumble for the starting button, then he pulls out onto the road and eases slowly onto it, unsure of his reactions and cognition. Now that he is free, he feels tearful. He cannot think about the ultimatum the man brandished in front of him, not yet.

After a few miles there is a turning and a slightly bigger road. He recognises it somehow and turns right out of instinct, catching up with and following a tractor. Soon enough, another sharp bend and he sees the A96, the main road between Aberdeen and Inverness. He is only ten miles from home. His heart is still thundering and his eyes return repeatedly to the mirror, trying to see if he's being followed.

The journey feels interminably long but it is a relief to see his own house coming into view, to bump along the track to their converted barn. He abandons the vehicle, racing to the door and shoving his key into the lock. Rocket barrels into him, wagging his entire body and whimpering with delight. Cal drops to his knees and buries his head in the dog's fur, feeling worse for the pet's clear delight at seeing him.

'I'm sorry, boy. I'm sorry.'

'Cal! Yoo hoo!'

He turns and sees Mary – their closest neighbour – walking down the drive at a clip. She moves surprisingly quickly despite her eighty years and the gnarled walking stick she carries. Rocket bounds to meet her, knowing she will have a pocketful of treats. Cal follows, guilt at the dog's abandonment throbbing inside him.

'I wanted to catch you – I popped in and fed this wee man last night as I couldn't see your car and I thought maybe you'd forgotten to ask me.'

She peers at him – her disapproval tangible. Cal feels the emotion choke his throat. He wants to hug her.

'That's so kind of you Mary. I had an… emergency and there was some confusion over who was going to be around.' The explanation feels hideously inadequate. He and Shona lead chaotic and busy lives, but they would never forget Rocket, never. 'I'm so grateful to you for looking out for him.'

'Aye, well,' she softens at his obvious distress. 'He's a good boy.'

Rocket dances at her feet and she reaches for a treat, waiting until he sits before opening her palm.

'It wasn't your mother was it?' Mary asks, suddenly.

'No,' Cal says, 'she's still hanging in there.'

Mary nods. 'Well, I'll be off.'

Cal watches as she heads back along the track, walking her trademark lopsided pace. She never comes in for a cup of tea, though they've asked her many times, only ever to feed and collect the dog. Shona says Mary's only happy when she's doing things and he thinks probably that's what keeps her so fit and young for her years. As Rocket returns to his side, he makes a mental note to buy her a huge bunch of flowers and some of the York Fruits jelly sweets she likes.

When she's gone, Cal feels uneasy, conscious that *they* may be watching. All of a sudden, nothing feels safe. His last bit of normality was when he was at the supermarket last night. Remembering the shopping, he crunches over the gravel to the car and opens the boot. His bags of groceries are there, though they have spilled and he has to gather the scattered items. The yogurt and mince will have to go straight in the bin.

Safe out here in the middle of nowhere, he and Shona have only ever bothered to lock up at bedtime, but when Cal carries in the shopping and calls the dog to come for more food, he shuts and bolts the door firmly behind him, then goes round checking the locks on all the windows and other doors. Ravenous, he makes scrambled eggs for himself and gives Rocket a second breakfast.

Plugged in, his phone screen comes back to life, and messages ping in from Shona. He replies with an apology about his phone not being charged – which is at least the truth. Then he hits the button to call Sarah. Are *they* listening to this? Have they tapped his phone?

'I'll explain later, but do you remember that man I interviewed in Castleford, once?'

'Yes, you mean…'

'Don't say his name.'

'Cal, what's going on?'

'I'm fine. I can't explain now. But can you email me his details, please? I need his services.'

He hangs up before she can argue and logs into his email account. Paranoid, he changes the password. Moments later, the contact is in his email with a line of question marks. He will have to come up with a plausible excuse later. Sarah will never let this go. For now, he messages the security consultant, asking him if he has a local recommendation for someone who can sweep a house and car for bugs and trackers. It feels ridiculous, like a spy novel rather than his life.

That done, Cal sits back on the sofa. In a moment he will shower and change, think about what he needs to do next, what any of this means. He wishes someone could tell him last night was a figment of his imagination and not a sick reality. But the medicinal taste is still in his mouth. His eyes slide closed and he's only vaguely aware of the warm bulk of Rocket settling beside him as he sinks into sleep.

CHAPTER THIRTY-SIX

CAL

The door being unlocked startles Cal from the deepest sleep he's had for years. Alarmed, he leaps from the sofa, frightening the dog, who starts barking loudly. He's so confused and bleary that he's still casting around the room for a possible weapon when the door swings back to reveal Shona, the look of amusement on her face rapidly turning to shock when she sees him brandishing the fire poker.

'Cal? What's going on?'

The roar of adrenaline inside him is so powerful he can barely hear her and it takes a moment for Cal to persuade his body to relax the stance it has taken so instinctively. His fingers release and the poker tumbles from his hand, landing on the rug with a soft thud.

He forces a laugh.

'Shona, you frightened me. I'm such an idiot, I was asleep and…'

He steps forward and takes her in his arms, partly to conceal his fear, holding on tight.

'I missed you.'

His heart is beating so forcefully he's sure she must be able to feel it.

'Cal, what's happening? Are you sick or something?'

The words are on his lips, he's planning to tell her everything: his abduction in the late evening, the unseen man with the terrible threats and the unsettling offer. He has learned his lesson when it comes to Shona – keeping things from her only drives a wedge between them. But then… something inside stops him.

A little voice whispers insistently.

What if he wants to stay quiet?

That's ridiculous. He doesn't mean it, not at all. He just needs time, to take a moment and think it all through, that's all. He can do that over the next few days, doesn't need to act now. His mind is stupid with sleep and the aftereffects of whatever they gave him.

He'll tell her, he's going to tell her, absolutely. But not yet. Because he knows what she will say. She'll want to know why he hasn't called the police immediately. She'll suggest picking up the phone to Foulds right now. And though he knows that's probably the most sensible, rational thing to do, he can't quite bring himself to. He's tired, that's all. It was a shock and so he just needs a moment or two to think.

So he plasters a smile over the cracks in his equanimity and kisses her.

'Maybe I am coming down with something. Couldn't keep my eyes open. I think I was having a really weird dream. I was so deeply asleep.'

He laughs again, hopefully more convincingly this time, and walks over to the doorway to turn on the lights as dusk has crept up on him, a whole day lost to recovery. He's starving, he realises.

'How was the conference? Hang on…'

While Shona goes into the kitchen, he dashes into the hallway and turns the key in the door. When he spins back, she's standing there, watching him.

'What are you doing?'

He can feel heat searing his face. 'I thought I heard something last night. I thought maybe we should be better on home security for a little while.'

'Oh.' Shona's eyebrows knit together. 'Is that why you're acting so strangely?'

'I was thinking of getting one of those camera doorbells.'

She's watching him carefully and he knows she's trying to figure him out. They are so closely aligned that when he is even a little bit off the rails she feels it. He needs to pull himself together. They'd discussed the camera doorbell a while ago and decided it was pointless out here in their peaceful isolation. It's hard enough to get the postman to the door, there is no passing traffic or opportunistic crime. Someone would have to target us, he thinks now with a shudder, would have to know we were here.

'I think maybe you're coming down with something,' Shona says, laying a cool hand on his forehead, experimentally. 'You're not quite yourself.'

'Maybe,' he agrees, following her through the house to act as sous chef because, despite the lack of ingredients caused by the ruined shop, she will manage to spin something out of nothing – a stew with crusty bread softened in the oven, a glass of wine and an escape from the world is exactly what he needs right now.

But all evening, he can't shake the phantoms in his head. The voice echoes inside him. *The thing you've always wanted.* That's not true. Yes, his hatred for Barr runs bone deep, but that's not who he is. So why is he hesitating?

When they go to bed, he waits until Shona falls asleep and then he lies there and gives into the fantasy – Jason Barr dead. He wonders how they will do it, what the papers will say, if anyone will mourn him. The evil he has obsessed over for so long – a solution to that pain is in touching distance.

When the world is still so very dark outside, he can admit to himself that yes, the idea of Barr taking the ultimate punishment appeals to the darkest parts of him. If someone can offer it to him on a platter, no strings attached except one very small condition, why shouldn't he take it? Why shouldn't he sleep peacefully at night knowing the man who slaughtered his precious sister, a young woman with her whole life ahead of her, is gone for good?

Barr's past threats loom in his mind, along with the knowledge that the killer will be free in only a few years. The easiest thing is for Cal to just stop what he's doing. To pause the investigation into Allegra's case. Pave the way for the ultimate cleansing. All he needs to do is nothing.

He thinks of Sarah and how much his producer has poured into this podcast, how her career is only just back on track after the threat of redundancy last year and now the new owners are thinking of canning them. Delaying the series could do real damage, but he knows she would do it for him. His mother is sick, he could tell Bella that he needs to take a break for a few weeks. She would understand that. It makes sense. And then when Jason Barr was gone, that would be it. The moment these people, whoever they are, strike and take him out, it would be a moot point. Cal and Bella wouldn't ever have to worry about Jason Barr again. The world would unquestionably be a better place without that man in it.

After a couple of hours of tossing and turning, Cal gets up and walks a confused Rocket round the field beside their house, hoping to soothe or exhaust himself. The countryside is perfectly quiet. Above him, the moon is pregnant with light, craters clearly visible on her pitted surface. From the other side of the field, he stares at the house where Shona is sleeping, a glow of orange light from the full-length window on the end of the old barn. The dog huffs and flops to the ground at Cal's feet, tongue hanging.

'I know, boy,' he says, ruffling the fur on Rocket's head. 'It's late. We'll go back now.'

But as he stares at the house, he finds himself anchored in place, seeing his life from a different angle. For the first time, he takes in the true cost of doing nothing. If he drops the podcast in return for Barr's removal then there will be a barrier between him and the people he loves. He could never tell them. Never tell Chrissie, Shona, Foulds… anyone. The dangerous fantasy that's entranced him starts to tarnish.

Unsettled, Cal whistles low to the dog and Rocket lumbers to his feet. As they move off, he glances back at the house and his heart leaps. A black shadow passes across the window. Cal freezes, the hairs on his arms standing to attention as he stares at the building. Surely not. He becomes aware of his breath, the blood pumping in his body. He stares at the house, until his vision blurs. Nothing moves.

Sighing, Cal yawns and clicks his fingers to Rocket. He's going to make himself ill.

'Bedtime, boy.'

Back at the barn, Cal makes his way around the house, checking that all of the doors and windows are secure, reassured by the fact that the dog is not barking. It's his imagination, that's all. When he rounds the last corner, the driveway is still deserted.

Quietly, he crawls into bed next to Shona, Rocket on the floor beside him. As he struggles to sleep, he realises the questions he hasn't given enough thought to, of course, are who these people are and why *they* want Barr dead. His brain has stepped over the logic, the obvious. They don't just want Barr dead. They wouldn't need Cal's acquiescence for that. They want him to stop looking into the Lachlan Merrick case.

There is something wrong with the case. And if he keeps going, Cal is probably going to find it. That's the real truth of the matter.

CHAPTER THIRTY-SEVEN

BELLA

Bella hasn't been able to stop thinking about what the counsellor said. For the sake of Noah and the boys, she's pulled herself together, but she's living life in parallel, one part of her brain focusing on daily tasks, work, chatting to her family, and the other on the idea of visiting him.

The thought makes her feel cold and terrified. She dismisses it several times but keeps coming back to it. What if this is the only way to get the information they need? Maybe she needs to face it properly. These buried memories are bobbing to the surface, full of noxious emotions, and hiding away from them isn't working.

The only person who really seems to see what's going on inside her head is her dad. Or maybe it's just that he's been waiting for this moment ever since she was a child. For her to rebel against the way he has chosen to deal with the crime. It's not that she wants to wallow, Bella tells herself. Or that his was the wrong way of dealing with things. He was submerged in grief with a traumatised five-year-old child in his arms, the only thing to do was to kick to the surface. No, it's more that now she wants to confront. She's ready to look it in the eye.

She sees her father watching her, though he pretends not to be, looking away quickly when she catches him.

'How are you?' he asks often.

'I'm fine, Dad, fine,' she repeats, the burden of reassurance tugging her down.

There is no word from Cal. Bella takes leave from work, unable to focus, and spends time walking, pounding the pavements for hours, seeking answers and finding none, only sore feet and an increasingly gaunt appearance. She shuns friends and ignores invitations out. The world is closing in on her.

Her younger son becomes increasingly clingy. More sensitive than his older brother, Ricky is like a barometer, picking up on her changing moods. One evening, he makes the voyage from his gaming station in his room and snuggles next to her on the sofa, pressing close like he used to do when he was small and fit so neatly with her, like a little jigsaw piece.

'Want to watch something?' He holds the remote out. 'You choose?'

Bella swims out of her fug for a moment, staring into the concerned face of her fourteen-year-old. She never hears her mother's voice but she does now, slipping into her thoughts. *Come on Izzy. Look at what matters.* Tears spring to her eyes and she swallows, forcing a smile.

'Why not. You decide though. I don't mind, lovely.'

She reaches out and tousles his hair, awed at the proximity of him and the little pockets of affection that they still find with these awkward and growing boys. Ricky puts on the latest episode of a long-running zombie series and she settles in beside him, but she can't relax – the past is closer to the front of her mind than the present. He doesn't deserve this, none of them do.

The next morning, she phones Pat.

'I want to try and see if he'll talk to me,' she says. 'I think it's time.'

CHAPTER THIRTY-EIGHT

CAL

Shona opens her eyes and stretches, yawning so he sees the pink inside of her mouth. Cal bends and kisses her, drawing her close and keeping his arms tight around her.

'Are you watching me sleep?' she mumbles, tucking her head into his neck. 'That's creepy.'

'You don't know the half of it,' he says, softly.

He tells her over breakfast, taking her hand and sitting her down at the table, speaking haltingly at first until the words come out in a great torrent.

She waits for him to finish. He can see her calibrating and assessing, deciding what to say. He can't bear the suspense.

'Please, say something.'

'The reason you didn't tell me what happened to you…'

He feels his stomach falling away. The hardest question to answer. Cal hates himself for this, but he can't lie to her.

'I was almost tempted by what they offered me. No, I was tempted…'

'Cal…' She exhales the admonishment.

'Only it isn't what I want,' he says quickly.

'It isn't?'

He shakes his head. 'It's not justice. It's not what Margot would have wanted. He shouldn't be my focus or the reason for doing this podcast.'

'Then what is your reason?'

'Bella. Bella wants the truth. And I know a little of how she feels and I have the tools to help her.'

'And what do *you* want?'

'I want the truth too. But not just about Merrick and Barr. If that comes, it comes. What I really want to know is who is arrogant enough to think they can just knock off an imprisoned man and get away with it. It's so brazen – taking me and telling me what they're planning.'

'But who on earth would do that?'

'Someone with access and power. Which makes them dangerous. I don't know what to do, Shona. I can go to the police, but police and prison guards must be involved if they think they can get away with this.'

She grips his hand and the touch of her is reassurance.

'Shona,' his voice sinks to a horrified whisper. 'I think I was going to do it. To drop the case in return for them killing him – what kind of monster does that make me?'

She shakes her head.

'You didn't do it. And you were never going to let that happen. I know you, Cal. I love you.' She pauses. 'You need to tell someone.'

'I know. But what if it puts you and Chrissie at risk? I'd rather see Barr taken out than that.'

Shona stands and comes to his side of the table. She wraps her arms around him and he feels her strength flowing into his bones. Whatever the answer, he has made the right decision in telling her. He doesn't have to do this by himself.

After speaking to local police, they do a joint video call with Sarah and Bella to fill them in on what's happening.

'What did the police say?' Sarah's face is grave.

Cal shrugs. 'There's not a lot they can do. I didn't see the men, don't know where they took me. They've flagged our number so we'll be prioritised if we call 999 and they're sending someone out to take a statement and fingerprint the car. I don't think they'll find anything. These guys were professionals; they were wearing gloves.'

'Could you stay somewhere else for a while?' Sarah asks. 'They likely know where you live.'

Shona shakes her head.

'I'm not being scared out of my house. No way. And you're not stopping investigating. We'll be fine.'

Cal bites his lip. He knows these people don't mess around.

'I thought you were giving up on me,' Bella says, her face pale on the screen. 'I knew something was wrong.'

'I'm not giving up,' he tells her. 'But we need to work out what's going on and who we can trust.'

'Any theories?' Sarah's face is more serious than he's seen it for a while.

'It could be someone involved in investigating or prosecuting the case,' Cal says. 'Whoever it is, there must be something they don't want getting out and they're prepared to go to great lengths to keep it secret. Plus they have the connections to try and kill Barr.'

'This must mean we're getting somewhere with the investigation,' Bella says. 'You've been making progress, I know you have.'

'She's right,' Shona says. 'You must be getting close to something, Cal.'

'They have rather shown their hand,' he agrees. 'If the Merrick case was as rock solid as everyone said it was, there wouldn't be anything to hide. Of course, the other option is that Merrick knows something about someone else and this is a bid to stop whatever that is coming out.'

'Is it worth another try with him?' Sarah asks. 'Maybe through the daughter?'

He thinks of Melissa, the way she's crafted her life out of a loveless start.

'I can ask.'

'And maybe go back to the original trial lawyers,' Shona suggests.

'True. But if I do that, then it's going to get out that I'm investigating. I don't want to do anything to put you at risk.'

Sarah sighs.

'Then let's put out an announcement that we're pausing this series, make it look like you're complying.'

Cal looks at her pained face – knowing how much this will cost her, that she'll have to explain to her bosses, to advertisers, to the media. With everything going on at the production company this could be the podcast's death knell.

'Are you sure? The latest episodes are almost ready to go. Won't it damage you?'

'I don't know. But I don't see another way. This will give you cover for a short time. I'll sweet talk the advertisers and hopefully they'll stick with us.'

'It would buy us time to work out who's behind this.'

'You just have to make sure it works,' Sarah says, her voice hardening. 'And fast.'

-

With all that's been going on, Cal had almost forgotten about the photograph he sent to Detective Inspector Foulds.

'I've got your woman,' she says by way of greeting when he answers the phone the next morning, still bleary from catching up on his sleep.

'You have? Who is she?'

'This didn't come from me.'

'Of course not.' He holds his breath.

'Name of Daisy Williams. She and Barr were together for a short time in the 1980s. She was just a teenager.'

Cal remembers the cowed look on the young woman's face in the picture. What would it be like to fall in love with Jason Barr, to be in his thrall at such a young age? Surely she'll have insight no one else will into what makes this man tick.

'Where is she now? Can I talk to her?'

'I'm sorry. That's the bad news. She died in 1991. Drug overdose.'

His hope deflates.

'Our friend Jason was the one that got her hooked apparently. After they split she spiralled, getting into more and more trouble stealing to feed her habit. She was found unresponsive in a squat in the city. She'd been a good student in school as well. Only went off the rails when she met him.'

Cal feels despair. Is there no end to the damage one man can inflict?

'Have you had any hits on a yellow car? Can we talk to her family?'

'You can try. There's a brother left alive. Her parents are both dead now. You should be able to find him easily enough. We're still searching on the vehicle but I haven't had any luck, which likely means it was never pulled over or used in the commission of a crime. The brother might know, I suppose.'

'Can you send me his address?' Cal asks. 'I need to pay him a visit.'

CHAPTER THIRTY-NINE

CAL

The man behind the counter in the tightly packed shop at the fishing lakes is about the right age for Owen – grey haired with an angular face and red cheeks, he's wearing a checked shirt, sleeves rolled to his elbows. He greets Cal with a nod as he arranges a display of fishing flies in lurid colours, but his blue eyes are dulled, devoid of any sparkle.

While the man finishes tucking the fishing flies into place, Cal turns on the spot, taking in the displays of rods and lines, waders and clothing. Everything a dedicated angler could desire. For him, it's like being in a foreign country.

'They're quite something,' Cal tells him, pointing at the display.

'Put your money where your mouth is. Try one.' The man holds out one of the flies and Cal takes it, transfixed by its intricacy and luminous brilliance.

'I'm not a fisherman, I'm afraid,' he says, handing it back.

A brief memory of his father taking him as a child slips into Cal's head. After Margot died, those trips ended.

'It's one of the few times I find peace,' the man says. 'Get away from people.'

'Calm in a busy world?'

'Something like that.' His words sound heavy. 'What can I help you with then, if not fishing?'

'I'm looking for Owen Williams.'

'That's me.'

The man peers at him. Cal hates this part. Opening old wounds feels awful and he knows all too well how close to the surface these hurts lie. Gently, he explains who he is and that he's working on a podcast about a historic crime. As he talks, he sees suspicion in Owen's eyes.

'So this podcast's not about Daisy?'

'No, I'm afraid not.'

The man grunts.

'Then, what's it got to do with me?'

'I was approached recently by a woman who thinks an ex-boyfriend of Daisy's had something to do with the death of her family back in the 1980s. I think that's around the time he was with your sister so I wondered if I could talk to you about it.'

Owen's jaw is set hard. He shudders at the mention of his sister.

'Not sure there's anything to be gained from reliving the past. Daisy's been gone more than thirty years.'

Cal finds it strange how clammed up he seems to be.

'All the same, it would help the family, if you wouldn't mind?'

It's unusual, this level of recalcitrance. The air is thick with animosity.

The man sighs. 'If you wait half an hour, I'll see what I can do.'

-

When Owen closes up the shop, he hands Cal a box of fishing tackle to carry.

'Your shoes are going to get muddy,' he says, setting off into a wooded area. His tone makes it clear he doesn't care. Through the trees, Cal glimpses tranquil waters glinting in the sun. He follows Owen along a winding path that trails the shore until they are so far away from the shop and the car park he can barely hear the road. They set their load down on a wooden fishing platform that juts into the lake.

'The fish don't much like hearing voices,' Owen says accusingly.

Cal doesn't know enough about fishing to know if it's true. He touches the swallow tattoo on his wrist, wondering how he would feel if someone came knocking on his door asking to talk about Margot. In truth, he grabs any opportunity to remember his sister, but not everyone is the same.

Owen produces a folding stool and Cal stands uncomfortably behind him as Daisy's brother pours a milky coffee into a proper cup before screwing the lid back on his thermos. Then he opens a fat foil package and bites into a hunk of lemon cake. He doesn't offer to share.

A fish jumps in front of them and Cal can see the attraction of this peaceful spot – if there wasn't the atmosphere there is today. It should be relaxing talking with someone who can truly understand how he feels, but Owen clearly doesn't want him here.

The man throws the last bits of his cake into the lake and the surface is peppered with mouths and thrashing. A moment later it all dies down and the water goes still.

'Right then.' Owen glances over at Cal. 'What is it you want to know?'

'Do you remember a man called Jason Barr?'

Owen stills, stays silent for a long moment.

'Not really.'

'I think he dated your sister.'

The man's shoulders relax a little.

'Oh, yes. That's right. How did you know that?'

'I came into possession of some of Jason Barr's personal effects. There was a picture of Daisy in there.'

Cal pulls the photograph from his pocket and moves closer to Owen, holding it out. He's relieved to see the man's face soften ever so slightly at the sight of his sister.

'Daisy was obsessed with black-and-white film. She said it made her look classic.' He stares at the picture. 'So young. I'd forgotten.' Then his voice hardens again. 'She wasted her life.'

'We think it was taken in the mid-eighties,' Cal tells him.

Owen shrugs. 'Sounds about right.'

'Did you know Jason Barr?'

'No. A little, from school. He dropped out at fourteen though.'

'How did Daisy meet him?'

Owen doesn't look up, carefully folding the foil wrapping from his cake. He doesn't answer the question.

'My dad wouldn't have him in the house. Said he was bad news and banned Daisy from seeing him. Not that it made any difference. She didn't listen. Got herself hooked on crack, all sorts.'

'Did he give her the drugs?'

'Maybe. But she had all the chances. Dad used to go and get her and bring her home, but she'd just climb out the bathroom window and go looking for him. What was he supposed to do, lock her up? Lost cause.'

Cal swallows at the bitterness he hears.

'What happened to Daisy?'

'They split up eventually but she was wasted by then. Started stealing. She stole from us, friends, shops. She was forever getting lifted by police but it did no good. By the end she was living in this squalid flat with boarded-up windows and rats in the walls. There's no helping some people…' Owen looks up at Cal, fierce. 'They'll drag you down with them.'

'I understand,' Cal says, though he can't warm to the man at all. He makes a mental note to check into his history. 'Once an addiction like that grips someone, it's almost impossible to get them free of it. They have to hit rock bottom first.'

'There was no coming back from her rock bottom. She was found dead,' Owen says, his eyes on the dark shadows in the still water in front of them. 'Had been lying there a while.'

'I'm sorry.'

Owen shrugs. Silence falls.

'What do you want?'

'I'm interested in the car they're standing next to. I've been trying to find out whose it was and if Jason might have been driving it.'

Owen shades his eyes against the burst of bright sunlight that has broken through the clouds and illuminated the platform. He doesn't speak.

'Owen,' Cal says, struck by knowing. 'Was it *yours*?'

The man clears his throat.

'I lent it to Daisy when I went away for the summer. She'd just passed her test. I don't know what she did with it or who she let drive it.'

'What year would that be?'

Owen is sullen and silent so long he wants to scream.

'Eighty-six,' he says eventually.

The world is bleached in sunlight and Cal can't think properly. 1986. It fits.

'There was a big scratch on the wing when I got back and I was furious.'

'What did she say?'

Owen shifts in his chair uncomfortably.

'She said it wasn't her. Bloody good car. I miss it. Don't make them like they used to. All electric nonsense now.'

Cal looks down at the picture, almost afraid to ask.

'I don't suppose you can tell me what colour it was?'

'Why does it matter?'

Cal's conscious of his heart beating in his chest, the light refracting from the water.

'Just curious.'

'It was yellow,' he says, shortly. 'A yellow Datsun Sunny.'

CHAPTER FORTY

BELLA

She goes to meet Cal for lunch. The rain is relentless and her clothes are almost steaming as she sits in the pleasant chain restaurant in town, early and waiting for him. Bella's drunk two cups of coffee before their allotted meeting time and feels jangly and wired. She should have told him about the approach she's made to Merrick, but the words tangled inside her.

He's perfectly on time. From her table, she can see him shaking the drips from his coat when he comes in the door and tousling the water from his grey-brown hair, which he is wearing short but not short enough that you can't see the curl in it. Bella wonders at the faith she's placed in him. Where she would be now if she hadn't turned up on his doorstep that day.

He smiles as he slides into the booth.

'Sorry – hope I'm not late. Going to need a canoe to get home.'

There have been flash floods in parts of the city this week. It feels to Bella like the world knows her torment. They order food and talk about her family, the boys, his daughter in Edinburgh. Eventually, she can't contain her anxiety.

'Have you heard anything more? From the people who want you to stop investigating?'

Cal looks around to see if anyone is listening and shakes his head slowly.

'No,' he says, reaching into his leather bag that has been drying on the seat but is still blotchy from the rain. 'But we did find a yellow car.'

He slides the picture across to her and Bella feels the jolt of nausea at the sight of a young Jason Barr. It takes a moment for her to notice the young woman next to him, wearing an expression of adoration that makes her almost as sick.

'But this is black and white.'

'I found the owner. The woman is Daisy – her brother owned it and lent it to her. In 1986.' Bella looks up at him. 'It's possible she let Jason use it.'

'Where is she now?'

Bella stares into the young eyes, cannot fathom why someone with so much hope and potential is smiling at that brute.

'Dead,' he says softly. 'Not that long after this.'

She looks up sharply.

'It wasn't… him?'

Cal waggles his head, and she frowns, unable to decide from his movements if the answer is yes or no.

'Not directly. It was drugs.'

'I didn't think drugs were his thing?'

'They weren't later and he didn't take them, but we do think maybe he was involved in moving them around the place when he worked at the nightclub. That's never been confirmed but my police contact thinks it's likely to be the case.'

'So the car – he could have been driving it that day?'

'He certainly had access, so we know it's possible. If he was making drops or picking up supplies for his employer then he could have been anywhere. But' – he sighs – 'until I can track down colleagues from the club and persuade them to talk then that's all we have, and it's far from evidence.'

'It helps me though,' she says. 'To know it's not impossible. That maybe I'm not going mad after all.'

Bella's eyes smart and she tries to smile through the choked feeling, the memory of them in the field that day in the bright sunshine, the sky Mediterranean blue above and the land a riot of sunshine yellow, so few cares in their hearts, though they didn't know it then.

A jolt and a flash in her mind. An arm raised. A fist slick with blood. In the here and now she gasps and in the past she can hear a scream then a silence.

Bella's mouth fills with saliva. She closes her eyes, swaying and throwing out a hand for support, so that it hits the faux leather seat with a thick thump.

'Bella? Bella are you okay?'

He is beside her. His arms holding her up, such a gentle contrast to the violence of the memory, calling for water, and she wants to sink into him, this man who has so many answers. That strange combination of strength and tenderness. She feels herself flushing even as these thoughts compete with the horrible images. His hands on hers, guiding them to a cool glass, condensation dripping down the outside, like the rain on the windows.

Gradually, she's coming back to the room. She feels damp and cold, her jeans are still wet from running through puddles and she is tearful in a childlike way. She wants her dad.

'Is she okay?'

The concerned voice of the manager penetrates the fug.

Cal speaking. 'I think she's just had a funny turn. Give us a moment. Maybe a sweet tea if you could?'

The man bustles away, and the air clears, the sounds of other diners eating, cutlery clinking, coming back into being as the spectacle ends. Bella is drenched in embarrassment. She puts her hands to her face, trying to cool the burning.

'It's okay,' he says beside her, his hand on her back like a weighted blanket. 'Just breathe. Take your time. It's a panic attack. I've had them. It will pass.'

And he's right – as her breathing steadies, Bella feels the tightness in her neck loosening, her chest relaxing, the world coming back into shaky focus. The manager is suddenly there again, proffering the tea and fussing over them, asking if they need a doctor, can he bring them anything else, was it the food, an allergy?

'No, no,' she hears Cal say. 'Just give us some space. I'll let you know if we need anything. Just a funny turn. It's warm in here.'

She lets those words float in her mind as she sips the scalding tea and feels the sugar enter her bloodstream, coating her teeth and taking her sharply back to her teenage years when she started drinking tea to belong and had to drown it in sugar to stomach it.

'I'm sorry,' she whispers when she can speak.

'It was a shock,' he says, 'that's all.' But he's looking at her curiously, as if he knows it's more than that.

'I saw something.'

She swallows.

'Do you want to tell me?'

She does the same head waggle he did earlier and he laughs, taking his hand from her back. Bella looks away, embarrassed by her attraction to him. He makes her feel safe, that's all. So silly. She's a married woman who loves her husband, not a giggly teenager anymore. The thought makes her glance at the picture of the girl, Daisy.

'I was thinking about that day and I *saw* a few snippets, a hand with blood coming down and I heard a scream. I think it was Mum.'

A tear makes a voyage to her chin. He passes her a napkin and she dabs at her face.

'I'm sorry,' he says.

'Isn't it good? If I can remember? That things are coming back to me?'

'Define good,' is all he says, with a wry smile.

Bella exhales.

'I have a confession to make.'

She wasn't going to tell him, but she can't keep the secret when he is taking so many risks.

'Yes?'

'I went to see someone, about reconciliation and mediation.'

'Oh,' he says, waiting. 'How did that go?'

'It's not relevant in this case apparently. They do things like that with young offenders these days. And Lachlan Merrick is so close to the end of his sentence. There was a pilot project offered to my dad back when it happened,' she tells him. 'He told them to get stuffed.'

'I can understand that.'

'But the man I talked to. He said if I wanted to, I could approach Lachlan Merrick and ask to be put on his visitor list.'

She chances a look at him, still sitting beside her in the booth. His face is neutral. She feels it is deliberately so.

'He helped me make the request.'

'I see.'

She waits for a reaction. He doesn't seem angry. Which makes her feel worse for keeping him in the dark.

'I feel bad for not telling you.'

He looks away. 'You shouldn't. This is your story. Your family.'

'You're not going to talk me out of speaking to Merrick then?'

'No. But think very carefully about it,' he says. 'It can't be undone. And you may not get what you need from it.'

'I think my husband is going to be totally against the idea.'

'I would be too in his shoes. But sometimes you have to listen to yourself.'

CHAPTER FORTY-ONE

CAL

He draws up at the house, relieved to be home. A moment of silence before the front door is thrown back and Chrissie emerges, grinning, Rocket dancing around her in his ancient lumbering Labrador way: it's not elegant but it does telegraph the dog's happiness at having Chrissie home for the weekend. He hugs his daughter tight. She's thin but strong beneath baggy dungarees and her red curls tickle his face.

'How are the exams going?'

She pulls a face.

'Don't ask. Nearly over at least.'

Inside, he finds Shona taking a slow-baked pork dish from the oven, the smell of garlic bread filling the room. He kisses her, the dog under his feet, Chrissie pressing a glass of wine into his hand and turning the music up so they can hear the latest track from a band she follows. For a moment, he feels truly happy – the house is so much busier and alive with Chrissie here. He catches Shona's eye and sees the emotion mirrored in her expression, experiencing another beat of awe for how perfectly they connect. She can't know how much she means to him, it's almost impossible to express the depth of it.

When dinner is over they load the dishwasher and open another bottle of wine. They've already filled Chrissie in on the situation with the case and the threats made, including his abduction. He hates worrying her after all they went through last year when he was attacked by Jason Barr, but he isn't willing to take any chances. Cal goes through the production company's informal security plan with her and she agrees to be vigilant until they resolve the mystery of who's behind the threats.

'I want to help with the case, Dad. It would be good experience.'

'What about the exams?'

'Under control, I promise.' She grins.

A journalism student, Chrissie is learning investigative journalism, helped by her instinctive way with people and talent for patiently gathering information.

'I could do with an extra pair of hands – there's so much to research and track down. Can't promise that it's going to be interesting.'

'I don't mind!' Chrissie's eyes gleam.

It's a relief to think he'll have someone to share the burden.

Shona clears her throat. 'Let's hope it's deadly dull. We've had enough excitement already. But I'm game if Chrissie is.'

'There are several strands we need to pursue,' Cal says, opening up his laptop to show them both his plan. 'The first is having another go at tracking down more people from FIRE, the club Barr worked at in the 1980s.'

'What about Diane?' Chrissie suggests.

Margot's best friend was by her side when they went to the club and has lived in the area all her life.

'I asked and she didn't know anyone else but maybe she could do a social media post about it and see if anyone wants to reminisce about the old days. We also need to get a sense of where work might have taken Barr when he was there. I'm interested in Daisy's brother Owen, too.'

Cal isn't sure how likely it is that they'll be successful poking around in the club's past again. Photographs from FIRE were used in the trial of Jason Barr for Margot's murder. The doormen used to demand suggestive pictures – and worse – from the girls queuing. Barr's team argued that the images showed Barr and Margot knew each other and she'd consented to sexual activity with him. The jury bought it.

It still makes Cal itch with anger, but the truth is that anyone who worked there might be wary of him and the podcast. Maybe Chrissie stands a better chance than he does of getting people to talk.

'We need to have a try at digging out some contacts without attracting too much attention,' he tells her. 'Why don't you start with Diane and see what you can find.'

She already has her notebook open and is jotting down ideas. It's strange, relinquishing control of strands of the investigation like this.

'I've also been thinking that we should try and work out where I was held,' Cal says, as Shona sets down cups of tea in front of them.

As much as he doesn't want to think about it, this should be a major line of enquiry.

'How would we do that?' she asks. 'You were blindfolded. Even the police have said they can't help.'

'Well, the building I was in is unusual for this area. You'd expect to be in a farm building, or stone barn. It was more like a Portakabin.'

Shona settles in the chair beside him.

'There aren't that many of them around, I guess.'

'We could try figuring out exactly where I was dropped off afterwards, and then work outwards in a circle from there using satellite view. If we can find the location then we stand a chance of linking it to the people behind this.'

They run through the other open threads of the investigation and Cal feels himself relaxing – buoyed by their support. It reminds him of last summer when Chrissie came to Loch Tay and helped out on the case of an unidentified walker who'd died in the hills. It blows his mind how fast time has gone and how capable his daughter is. It's not that long since she was obsessed with horses and Pokémon.

It's late by the time they stop talking through the angles and agree the next steps. After taking Rocket for a walk around the field, Cal snuggles in next to Shona. Falling into sleep is like turning off the world.

CHAPTER FORTY-TWO

CAL

Through painstaking poring over Google Maps, they manage to find the layby where Cal was dumped after the abduction. After that, he and Shona get to work, studying satellite images in ever increasing circles from there. At first Cal is sceptical this will work, but when he sees how Shona's approaching the problem and her scientific dedication to the task, he starts to believe they stand a chance.

'There really aren't that many places that could fit the bill,' she tells him. 'I'll flag any that look likely and we can go through them together.'

He glances up from his laptop. 'How far out are you looking?'

'You said you think it wasn't more than ten minutes' drive from where they left you?'

'I can't be sure, but it felt about that.'

'I'm starting with a five-mile radius, then ten and fifteen to be sure. It's not foolproof but it's a start.'

Cal smiles, watching Shona switch into scientific mode, lost in the data.

They break for a tray of bacon sandwiches and mugs of coffee. The smell rouses Rocket, who has been lying asleep on Chrissie's feet but rapidly starts drooling, white laces of dribble dripping from his chops.

'So disgusting,' Chrissie says affectionately.

She has spent the morning on the phone to Diane going through the lists of people Margot's friend can remember from her days at the club and is now trawling social media trying to locate them in their current lives.

Cal makes them all down tools and they take the sandwiches out into the garden. The sky above is a field of clouds. It's a moment of calm and he has a horrible premonition that it won't last. He hates this creeping sense that something dark is on the horizon. The feeling of dread is a bad habit of his, so he presses down on it and hopes he's mistaken.

-

A few hours later, Shona has the search narrowed to eleven different buildings.

'I've made a few assumptions,' she says. 'You couldn't hear any roads or other people so I've guessed that there aren't many buildings nearby, ruling out villages and groups of houses. These...' she clicks through them, 'seem to fit the bill. They're modern or pre-fab in construction, isolated and either rural or industrial locations.'

'This is incredible,' Cal says.

'So now what do we do?' Chrissie peers at the screen over Shona's shoulder.

'I guess we let the police know.'

-

He makes the call to the number they were given and is amazed to reach the officer right away. But the response is less than enthusiastic.

'What did they say?' Chrissie and Shona have been watching him.

He shakes his head.

'He sounded sceptical. Said they can't go on a wild goose chase when we have so many possibilities.'

Shona makes a noise of frustration. 'We need to narrow it down, then.'

'I don't see how we can do that,' Cal says.

She stares at the map in front of them, little arrows marking the possible locations.

'Maybe we just go and take a look.'

'I want to come,' Chrissie says quickly.

Cal holds up a hand. 'Hang on, I'm not sure this is a good idea.'

'We could plan the approach to each location, go for walks next to them – we've got the perfect alibi with the dog,' Shona says.

As one they turn and look at Rocket, who is snoring on the sofa, his paws twitching.

'Come on, Dad.'

'I don't love this idea,' he tells them. 'But if we're really careful and all we're trying to do is establish which is the right one and then retreat… maybe it's okay.'

'We'll be careful,' Shona says. 'You can share the co-ordinates with Sarah and she can track our progress as an extra security.'

Cal is conscious that Sarah's job and the future of the podcast is on the line. Not to mention the torment Bella is going through. Maybe they have to take risks to get answers.

'Fine. Let's give it a try.'

Shone smiles and takes his hand.

'Just a group of innocent people out for a walk.'

CHAPTER FORTY-THREE

CAL

The next day is overcast and heavy, the clouds seeming to press down on them. Cal feels oddly jittery about their scouting mission but he buries the misgivings. Shona has worked out a route and they start with the closest options, the first a sawmill that Cal quickly discounts. The air is ripe with the scent of freshly cut timber.

'It didn't smell like this. I'd remember.'

The next two sets of buildings are less clear cut, but they persuade the dog out of the boot and set off on a walk that skirts each of the properties. He's able to eliminate them fairly rapidly.

'The windows are too big,' he says when they approach the first. 'That's not it.'

The second of the two is a set of derelict Portakabins on the edge of a farm and, at first, Cal is hopeful, but then dogs start barking and a man immediately emerges from a barn and eyeballs them. He shakes his head at the others and they retreat to the car.

After a stop for coffee and cake they set off again.

Cal notices Chrissie is quiet.

'Loads of the avenues I go down for the podcasts end up coming to nothing,' he tells her. 'If it doesn't that's fine. It's a nice day out and we've eliminated some possibilities.'

'It's not that,' she says. 'I just can't believe they took you.'

Back in the car, they drive through a brief rainstorm and emerge on the other side in blazing sunshine. Cal loves the moods of the Aberdeenshire weather, and the fact that the only thing you can rely on is it changing.

This location is proving difficult to pinpoint on the ground, so Shona pulls up the satellite view on the maps app and they find the single-track road to what looks like a disused quarry.

As soon as they bump onto the track, Cal experiences a lurching sense of déjà vu. He glances in the mirror and sees the focus on his daughter's face, deciding not to mention anything yet in case his instincts are wrong.

His nerves increase the further they drive down the track, which is banked on either side by big mounds of earth and sand. The mounds close down the view, making him feel claustrophobic. This is not at all the sort of place anyone would go for a walk, so their cover story will be useless if they're caught. Signs announce industrial works and danger ahead. His sense of foreboding ratchets when Shona tries to message his producer an update.

'No reception here,' she says quietly.

The road is so narrow that there is no place to turn around. Reluctantly, Cal keeps going, turning off the radio so they can concentrate properly. The tension in the car has risen and no one speaks. Just as he thinks the road is going to go on forever, it opens out and there is industrial machinery and a series of squat buildings ahead of them. Rocket whines, sitting up in the boot and clearly picking up on the atmosphere.

'What do you think?' Chrissie leans forward between the seats.

'There's no one here,' Shona says, quietly. 'We could take a look.'

Cal turns the car so it's facing the exit, then unclips his seat belt and opens the door.

'Stay here,' he says. 'Shona and I will scout around, first.'

Feeling watched, despite the eerie desolation of the site, Cal and Shona head towards the buildings. There is a chill running through him and he resists the urge to hold her hand. It feels like it felt back then, like he was at the end of the world. The main door to the building is locked with a hefty padlock and chain. When he rattles it, the sound seems to reverberate.

'This is it,' he tells Shona. 'I'm sure it is.'

'How do you know?'

'It's a feeling, maybe the smell…'

He can't articulate it, but the fear he's experiencing reminds him of Bella's visceral reaction to Barr's voice, the event that kicked all of this off. Sometimes you need to trust your instincts.

They look back at the car. Cal can see Chrissie emerging and he waves to her.

'Stay there. We'll be back in a minute.'

He and Shona skirt the building, thrashing through foliage that has grown up against the sides of it. At the far end there's another door. Here, the windows aren't boarded up and he peers in through the dust and grime. There's a table, the familiar carpet tiles, walls he recognises.

'This is it,' he tells Shona, not sure why he's whispering. 'Definitely.'

She takes out her phone and starts snapping pictures.

Cal tries the door and it pops open. He wants to turn and run.

Instead, he steps carefully over the threshold, nostrils filling with the mustiness that his body finds indistinguishable from threat. Shona presses against him.

'We should be quick.'

He strides forward and through a doorway, finding himself in a corridor he recognises, that shabby bathroom at the end. He gestures to the room he was kept in.

'There. That was it.'

Shona's filming him, keeping a record of it all. He's ashamed to realise that his hand is shaking as he points at the pile of furniture. The water bottle they gave him is still on the floor. All the emotions come rushing back. He startles when Shona touches his shoulder.

'You okay?'

He shakes his head.

'I thought… for a while I thought I might not see you again.'

She presses him into a tight hug. He feels her strength flow into him.

'Come on, we don't need to stay – we've got what we came for.'

They're just out of the door and pulling it back into place when he hears the noise. It sends an alarm racing through his entire body like a cold sweat. It's Chrissie.

He can't decipher the words, but he hears the urgency in her voice. Panic paralyses him for a split second and then he grabs Shona by the hand and they blunder round the side of the cabins, tearing through the bushes and nettles to reach the car. They make it in time to see Chrissie scrambling down the side of one of the vast slag heaps, slipping in the sand and rocks.

She tumbles to the bottom, her ankle buckling as she lands. As they run towards her, Chrissie pulls herself up, hobbling to the car while Rocket barks from the boot.

'Dad,' she shouts when she sees them. 'There are cars coming. Two Land Rovers. I was watching from the top and saw them turn in from the main road.'

They bundle Chrissie into the back, Cal frantically trying to calculate what options they have. Slamming the door, his heart pounds a dreadful beat.

With only one route in and out, there is nowhere to hide.

CHAPTER FORTY-FOUR

CAL

They have a few minutes' grace until the approaching vehicles find them as the track twists and turns from the road, but there's little he can do. Except one thing. Without speaking, he guns the engine and accelerates out of the car park, past the rusting machinery.

'What are you doing?' Shona sounds breathless.

Cal presses his foot to the floor, the tyres sending gravel flying.

'There was a tiny dead-end turning on one side of the main track. I saw it on the way. If we can get there first, then just maybe we can hide until they go past. That's all I can think of.'

'But if it doesn't work then we'll meet them head-to-head.'

'I know. But I think it's our only hope.'

Cal's never felt less certain but if he doesn't commit to the idea they're lost. He hunches forward over the wheel, taking the turns as fast as he dares, the high walls of the banking either side closing in on them.

'Go Dad, go go go.'

Chrissie puts a hand on his shoulder for a moment and her trust galvanises him.

'Make sure you're belted in,' Shona tells her.

The anxiety in her voice chills him.

Every second Cal expects to see the cars approaching. It's excruciating driving blind, slowing for the corners and then racing along the straight stretches.

'There!' Chrissie points to a cutting in the bank.

'Hold on.' He brakes at the last moment then turns the wheel hard into the cutting. It's only twenty metres deep and so he takes them as far in as he can, the nose of the Volvo almost touching the wall at the end. It's like being in a tunnel. He winds down the window a fraction, listening for the hum of the other vehicles, holding up a hand for silence. He can see Chrissie in the mirror, her face taut. Shona puts a hand on his knee, her fingers gripping tight.

A moment later two cars shoot past the mouth of the cutting so fast they send clouds of dust billowing. Cal's chest tightens. He can barely breathe.

'Do you think they saw us?' Shona breathes.

'I don't know. Let's hope not.'

If they're found in here there will be no escape. Cal has a horrible feeling the men in those cars won't mess around.

'I'm trying to remember how far it is to the next turning for them,' he says, starting to reverse to the exit. 'We need as much time as possible to get out before they turn around but I don't want them to see us in their rear-view mirrors.'

'Wait.'

His daughter unclips her belt and opens the door before he can protest.

'Chrissie!'

Breathless, he reverses after her as she limps to the opening of the cutting, staying close to the wall and peering around it. She holds up a hand to him to stop and he waits, eyes fixed on her.

A second later she changes it to a thumbs-up and he reverses fast out onto the track, wheels spinning as he turns. Chrissie grabs for the door and dives into the back seat.

'Go, quick,' she shouts.

He hits the accelerator, concentrating hard on the bend ahead. Shona is twisted in her seat, staring back at the horizon.

'There's something coming.'

'Dammit. They must have seen us.'

Cal grips the steering wheel hard, taking the road as fast as he dares. Bits of gravel are thrown up by the wheels to ping against the car. It seems like the main road will never come. On the next straight section Shona turns to peer behind them again. He chances a glance in the mirror and can see the first car turn the corner behind.

'I think we're almost there,' he says. 'Hold tight.'

He pushes his foot to the floor and prays. Behind them, the dot in the distance seems to be getting closer.

At last, the tarmac of the country road is visible ahead of them. They shoot out onto it and Cal doesn't wait, forcing the car to accelerate quickly. It's not far to the A96 but there's a sharp corner followed by a set of crossroads ahead and he thinks they can lose their pursuers in the village the other side. He knows there's a small car park behind the bakery. Beside him, Shona grips the door handle, bracing against the fast turns.

Cal makes it into the narrow car park, sliding nose first into a space and cutting the engine. His back is sticking to the seat, his T-shirt damp and sweaty.

'We need to get out,' he urges. 'Let's go into the bakery.'

Rocket whines from the boot.

'What about the dog?' Chrissie asks.

'I'll take him,' Shona says. 'You two go in and I'll walk him round on my own. It's less conspicuous.'

There's no time to argue with her. Shona tugs Rocket towards the street while Cal locks the car and helps Chrissie hobble to the bakery's coffee shop. A table at the back is free and they skirt the room to reach it.

They both turn their seats away from the window and door. They're hidden but Cal feels a desperate urge to look and see what's going on. It's excruciating, waiting. He thinks of Shona, worrying that she'll be spotted. He's about to go out and find her when his phone buzzes with an alert.

I'm in a pub with the dog. Stay put.

He breathes out again and fires off a message.

I'll text when it's clear.

'The cars have come into the square,' Chrissie says, glancing over her shoulder. 'They're parking. Two men getting out – one from each.'

The room seems hot all of a sudden.

'Where are they going?'

'They're just looking around.'

Frantic, he turns to look for an escape exit Chrissie could take to get to Shona if she had to, but he's not sure she'll manage alone with her ankle.

'They're heading this way,' Chrissie says, her voice high, panic rising.

'Look at me,' Cal tells her, holding her gaze. 'We're having a normal chat. Stay calm.'

Inside, his heart is galloping.

A moment later, the waitress appears beside them with a tray of coffees.

'Are these for youse?'

'No, we haven't ordered yet,' he tells her, taking the opportunity to peer out to where the men are striding towards the shops, splitting to take separate buildings in their search.

The waitress follows his gaze.

'Ach, they canny park there, like. They'll be in rare trouble with Alan.'

As she speaks, a man dressed in a high-vis tabard strides across the square.

'Ooh,' a woman at the next table chuckles. 'Here we go.'

Everyone in the bakery is watching now, many with delight, as Alan hails the drivers of the cars, which are parked partly in the road, blocking traffic. They can't hear what he's saying, but the gist of it is clear from Alan's purple face and gesticulation. The men who were searching the square have returned to the vehicles and an argument has clearly kicked off. Cal watches, intent, as Chrissie takes the menus and the waitress departs.

'What's happening?'

'Looks like they're in trouble with local parking enforcement.'

He holds up his phone, zooming in tight to get a photo of the men. It's distant and grainy but better than nothing.

One of the men is on his phone, another gesticulating angrily, but Alan clearly isn't giving up. Cal holds his breath as the thug steps closer and closer to the parking attendant, menacing him with his height and bulk. Long moments pass as they eyeball each other. Then the thug's head jerks to one side, called back by another of the men. With a last glare, he backs away, each step torturously slow, a threat in itself.

A moment later, the sun flashes on the blacked-out windows of the vehicles as they slowly cruise the line of shops in the square. When they reach the end, tyres squeal as the first vehicle accelerates hard, leading the other away. Cal sinks back in his chair, sticky with sweat and fear.

'That was too close,' he says, shakily.

He grabs his phone and texts Shona the all-clear, but as he does, another message pops onto the screen. It's Bella.

I heard from the prison.

Cal watches the dots that indicate she is still typing.

Merrick got my message. He says he'll see me.

CHAPTER FORTY-FIVE

CAL

Bella barely speaks as Cal drives her to the prison. He lets the silence settle around them, glancing across at her occasionally to find her biting at her fingers without seeming to realise what she's doing or where she is, her eyes sightless and her mind in the past. As well as shaken by his trip to the quarry, he is full of misgivings about this visit, worried that an encounter with Merrick will tip Bella over the edge. When he parks the car, he waits a moment for her to register that they've stopped.

'Oh. We're here.'

The rain rattles on the windscreen and Cal swivels in his seat.

'We don't have to be. You don't have to do this, Bella. Your mother and sisters wouldn't want you to go through more pain. It isn't going to bring them back.'

'You sound like my dad, and Noah.'

'Sorry. But say the word and I'll drive away from here.' He tries for levity. 'There's a great breakfast place just down the road.'

She sighs, half smiling at him, though the effort is too great for her to sustain it. 'It's something I need to do. It's hard to explain, but I can't keep going as I am.'

And he, more than anyone, understands that.

'Right then.' He opens his door and pushes himself out into the car park, grabbing a large golf umbrella from the back seat. 'Let's go.'

This time, Cal and Bella are met by Tariq at the door of the prison and taken through security and to a private room instead of the visiting hall. Their shoes make wet marks on the linoleum and it squeaks beneath their feet, loudly announcing their presence. Bella's face is pale but her lips are set into what Cal has come to recognise as a line of determination. She is strong, he reminds himself – what she has had to overcome is something from the depths of nightmare, but it has hardened her like tempered metal.

The room is simple – a table screwed to the floor, with a chair for Lachlan Merrick on one side and two for Cal and Bella on the other. Tariq sits back against the wall, an observer and supporter. For both sides, he realises.

'Any time you want to, we can just stop,' Tariq tells Bella. 'You can get up and leave the room whenever you want.'

Bella nods and her eyes meet Cal's. There are butterflies of nerves in his own throat so he can only imagine how she must feel. They perch on their chairs and wait, nervously, for Merrick to be brought through. It crosses Cal's mind that the convicted killer might refuse to come from his cell at the last minute like Barr did in court – he thinks the disappointment will break Bella if that happens.

But, what feels like hours later, the door opens and Merrick is led in by two prison officers, his gaze flickering anxiously across the waiting group before lighting briefly on Bella and darting away as if he's been scalded. As he pulls up the chair opposite, Cal can see Lachlan Merrick's hands are trembling. Why has he agreed to this?

It's horribly fascinating seeing this man again, trying to understand what led them here. Cal barely listens to the introductions Tariq is giving, instead conscious of Bella beside him, the way her hands are tucked between her legs, the muscles in her arms taut.

How are they even supposed to begin?

Tariq looks at Bella and nods encouragingly.

'Thank you for meeting me,' she says softly.

Her words seem to surprise the man in front of them, and he lifts his bowed head for a moment. Panicked eyes seek the counsellor for reassurance.

'I'm sorry. About what happened to your family.' Merrick sounds cracked and desiccated, the words wrought from his throat. It has the feel of a rehearsed opening.

'It wasn't you, though, was it?' Bella peers at him and everyone in the room is silent and still. 'It was Jason Barr.'

'I pled guilty in court,' Merrick says. 'I'm responsible. I don't know Jason Barr. I'm sorry.'

The man stares at the table as he speaks and Cal finds himself wishing he could see his eyes, try and divine the truth or lies.

'I just...' Bella pauses. 'I need to know what happened to them. To me, too. I need you to tell me what happened that day.' A single tear makes its way down her face. 'If it *was* you, then I need you to tell me why.'

Cal is surprised to see Merrick's eyes are now swollen with tears. The man's face is red as he shakes his head from side to side, looking more and more uncomfortable by the minute.

'I can't,' he says. 'I wish I could, but I can't.'

Cal feels Bella deflate next to him – she slumps from her upright posture to one of defeat. This was a mistake.

'Please,' she whispers.

'You don't understand,' Merrick says. 'I wish I could. I want to help you. You're the same age as my daughter. I used to see your mum out with you all the time. She was always playing with you and smiling.'

'You watched her.'

He nods, dipping his head in shame, though Cal catches a glimpse of his contorted features.

'I'm sorry,' he says. 'I shouldn't have done that. I was out of my head on all sorts back then. It's no excuse, but your family just seemed so…'

'So… what?' Bella appears fascinated and repulsed by him, leaning towards Merrick in her desperation for scraps of information.

Merrick takes a deep breath and when he looks up at Bella his eyes are filled with regret. 'So perfect,' he says.

'It was,' Bella says, choking a little on her tears. Cal feels a lump in his throat, and a glance at Tariq shows he's not the only one feeling emotional. 'Why did you have to take it away?'

Merrick drops his head to his hands.

'I'm so sorry,' he says. 'I wish I could explain to you how sorry I am.'

'That doesn't help me,' Bella says, and Cal can hear the frustration in her voice. 'Just tell me what happened that day. I can't remember it all and it's driving me mad. I need to know.'

Merrick shakes his head again, back and forth.

'You don't understand,' he says. 'I *can't* tell you.'

'Why?'

The word fills the room, expelled with force from Bella's lips.

The rest of them freeze, listening to the air ringing with the sound of her desperation.

The shutters go down on Merrick's expression.

'Because I don't remember,' he says, his voice a monotone. 'I wish I could, but I just don't remember what happened that day.'

Bella stares at him. Then she pushes back her chair and walks from the room.

Cal is moments behind Bella, following her down the corridor. She's moving so fast he has to jog to keep up with her pace. Her face is scarlet and her breath shallow.

'I can't breathe,' she says. 'I need some air.'

His mind whirrs with confusion. Bella is the one who doesn't remember. *She's* the victim, the person who needs answers to move on with her life. What damage can the truth do now? Seeing his reaction, Cal's sure Merrick knows more than he's saying.

Together they wait to be buzzed out of the secure area. Cal watches Bella jangling beside him and he wants to put a hand out to steady her but he's afraid he will make it worse than it is already. Tears course down her cheeks. When they are released, Bella rushes out of the door without waiting to pick up their belongings. Cal mutters an apology to the officer at the desk and bolts after her, hit by needles of cold rain the moment he is out of the door.

'I don't believe him,' she shouts over the weather, her hair plastered to her face, mascara trailing down her cheeks, making her unrecognisable. 'Why isn't he telling me the truth?'

Cal shakes his head. He doesn't know what to do to help her. Witnessing Bella's pain is cutting something open inside himself. In the end he simply opens his arms and she steps into them. The rain melts his shirt to his back and water trickles down his neck but he stands there as she sobs, drenched in the kind of despair he knows can devour you.

CHAPTER FORTY-SIX

CAL

Cal drives slowly north. The rain has stopped now but the clouds are still ponderous, Bella silent beside him. Exhaustion tugs at his eyes, forcing Cal to open the window so the blast of cold air slaps him awake. He thinks back to Tariq's serious face when he went into the prison to gather their belongings, Bella waiting in the car.

'I'll talk to him,' Tariq had said. 'I hope she's okay.'

And Cal had just nodded, because they both knew she wasn't.

'We try to prepare people,' Tariq said, apologetically, 'but sometimes there just aren't the answers they're looking for.'

As they drive up the coast and into Aberdeenshire, the North Sea thrashing the shore out of sight to his right, Bella falls asleep against the window. Cal can't get his mind off her younger self, Izzy, along with Gail, Philippa and Allegra, left behind in that heat-baked slice of woodland by the side of a field, their blood soaking into the ground.

When he drops her off, Cal is glad to see her husband Noah opening the door, light spilling out into the darkness as he wraps Bella in a hug. It's a relief to see her cared for. He watches as she goes into the house, not looking back.

Twenty minutes later, he feels the tension in his shoulders loosen as he turns into his own driveway and sees the wood-clad building with its long glass windows, light glowing from them. When he parks, he sits and watches it for a moment, too tired to get out of the car and into reality, content just to observe. But then the door opens.

Cal reaches for his rucksack and steps from the car, smiling at Shona in anticipation, his day immediately brightened. This relief is interrupted when he sees her face is grave.

'Hello love.' Cal stops in front of her. 'What is it? What's wrong?'

Shona's eyes are soft, her hands clasped tightly.

'They've been trying to reach you.'

He thinks of his phone, turned off for the prison visit and then discarded in his bag, too much on his mind, too many things happening. The world seems hyper-real; the drip drip of the eaves and the bright green of the trees behind the house. In the distance, the sky is rearranging itself to reveal slivers of blue.

'Who has?'

'It's your mum,' Shona says, folding him into her arms like he did Bella only this afternoon. 'She died a few hours ago. I'm sorry.'

–

He feels only numbness and nothing. The thing that has anchored him to earth has suddenly been cut and he is truly alone. The last one of his family of origin. Even though he expected this, the news is impossible to take in. Cal's immediate reaction is that he has to jump in the car and drive south… but then he realises. It makes no difference. No one is waiting for him.

Shona takes him inside, her touch gentle, settling him on the sofa and making tea that will cool before them because he cannot imagine drinking it.

'I'm not upset,' he tells her, stupidly. 'Well, I am. I must be. But I'm just trying to understand it.'

My mother is dead, he tells himself. *My mother is dead.* He repeats the words in his head until they lose all meaning. It's a curious and terrible thing. He knew this was coming and yet he never expected it to be real. All of a sudden, there are things he realises he forgot to tell her. Things he should have asked, should have said, and the opportunity is lost forever.

Rocket clambers onto the sofa and rests his head in Cal's lap and it is now, one hand in the dog's fur and the fingers of his other hand tightly wound in Shona's, that he can cry. Hot, fat, childish tears of regret and anger. They aren't tears just for his mother, but for Margot and his father. The fractured family that has been taken away from him piece by piece. It's clear to him in this moment that there really isn't a way to make things right and there never will be, no matter how many years Jason Barr rots in jail.

CHAPTER FORTY-SEVEN

BELLA

The visit to Merrick has triggered something inside her. Bella feels unstable, like she's rocking on the edge of a drop and can't catch her balance. She's desperately afraid that the floodgates are about to open. When she closes her eyes, she sees moments from that day, flashbacks of Philly's small legs, her face upturned, starfish hands grasping. Or Gail, so much bigger and faster than Izzy… she wants to catch up to her sister even now. She needs to know.

But, now the knowledge feels close, she almost doesn't want it. It feels like it might engulf her.

'Come on, love,' Noah says. 'Time for bed.'

She feels like saying no, she doesn't want to sleep, but that's childish and she has to rest eventually. Even if, when she does, the dreams will come.

She nods but doesn't move. He reaches for her hand and holds it gently, planting a kiss on her cheek. He knows. Bella pulls back and studies his tired face. He can't have aged in a few weeks, it must have been happening stealthily, but she notices it now in a rush – how their children are almost grown and starting independent lives, how they have reached a point her mother never did. Her upbringing was so different to the one her sons have experienced. This normality stolen from her, denied her.

Why does the loss have to strike anew? Again and again. Waves battering the coast. Hurting those around her, the ones for whom she should be safe harbour.

But she cannot express this to Noah. It's too much. So she smiles and lets him pull her up from the sofa and hold her hand as they take the stairs, one step at a time, like she is a child.

The dream comes in the early hours.

The same: the field, the waving heads of corn in the endless reaches, the bright blue sky. It feels different this time, though. Less a technicolour memory and more a reality. She can actually taste the day – the heat and the summer, the hot earthiness of it. Everything is so green, the bright yellow flowers aglow. In the dream, she spins on the spot and marvels at the lushness of the trees and the pureness of the day. She knows there has never been one more beautiful.

But as they walk, it gets darker. Black clouds start to encroach on the perfect blue. Bella frowns. This isn't how it's supposed to be. The scent of the oilseed rape is noxious. Beside her, Philly starts to cry. She reaches for her little sister's hand but can't touch her, fingers stretching into nothingness as Philly's cries escalate and exert an inexorable pull on her heart. The cries get louder. Panicked, she spins, scanning the path for her mother and Gail.

She thinks they are off in the distance, but she can't quite see them, or hear them. Where is Jet? Bella is frozen. Beside her, the crop rustles, sending sharp prickles into her. Someone is there. Someone is waiting for them. She starts to run.

The dream shifts. All she can see is sky. It's blue again but there is a smell she cannot bear, even worse than the pungent flowers. A sharp tangy wrongness. Old coins and metal. There are flies buzzing around her, lifting and landing. She wants to scream because they will not leave her, there are just more and more. She tries to move but it hurts and she is paralysed. Her fingers twitch and meet fur. Jet's tongue on her face, the dog's whimper. No one will ever understand the way she and Jet understand.

Then, above her. A face looming into view. Urine trickles from her, soaking her shorts. The fear is so pure and animal, it takes over every muscle in her body, every part of her is imbued with it. She wants to run but she is frozen. The man comes closer. It is *him*. There is blood on his hands and there is a streak of red on his face. Bella knows. She knew, even then, what he had done. Finally.

He gets closer and she wants to shut her eyes, hide away from him, but she cannot. She needs to see his face clearly. This is the moment she has been waiting for, the knowledge she needed.

She stares up. His face is a cloud above her, obscuring everything. Taking up her whole world.

Even in sleep, her heart stutters.

It is not Jason Barr.

CHAPTER FORTY-EIGHT

CAL

The evening passes in a blur. Cal calls Chrissie, feeling awful about telling her as she is days away from the end of her exams, and then he speaks to Allie, his ex-wife, to let her know. Shona cooks and he manages to eat, though it seems that the food tastes different in some indefinable way and he could not afterwards say what it was. Together they walk Rocket around the field, arms linked, not speaking. Tomorrow, there will be more calls to make and arrangements to put in place, but there is no urgency any more. It means the world that Shona is beside him and that she knows he just needs to inhabit his own thoughts for a while. She is his family now, she and Chrissie, and he never ever wants to let go.

It's hard to admit that he has been impatient for this moment. Watching his mother decline has made him feel so helpless. But, now that she's gone, he needs more time to get his head around it.

'It never could have been made right, though, could it?' he says aloud.

'No,' Shona murmurs, beside him. 'I'm not sure it could.'

'I don't even know what she wanted for her funeral,' he says. 'She refused to discuss it.'

'It's more what *you* want that matters now,' she says softly.

Cal realises he hasn't checked in with Bella. He opens his phone and stares at the screen, trying to find the words, remembering the way her body shook when she cried in the rain. In the end, he decides it's too late and he doesn't want to disrupt her evening.

At bedtime, he expects to lie awake with thoughts of both his mother and Lachlan Merrick's strange denial of memory in his mind, but sleep comes hard, plunging him into dreamless darkness. When he wakes, the sun is sending beams of light through the gap in the curtains. He can hear Shona making coffee and chatting to the dog in the kitchen. The world feels a bit more manageable again.

When he's had his morning coffee and walked Rocket, Cal speaks to Spencer and they discuss the arrangements for his mother to be moved to the funeral home today – he will travel down and see her in her casket and choose the service and details of her burial next to his father. He already knows the funeral will be small. There aren't really any friends left alive and so many of them fell away after Margot died as his parents became hollow shells of their former selves, but Spencer says he will be there and as well as Chrissie and Shona, Allie will come and his sister's old friend Diane. Whatever, it is enough. He doesn't want the song and dance, the heartfelt eulogy. It is too hard to know what to say.

After a morning of admin, Cal is desperate to throw himself back into work so he can feel normal again. He sends Bella a message asking if they can talk and while he waits to hear from her, he settles at his computer to research the old quarry site he, Chrissie and Shona found.

It seems so long since they escaped from it, though it has only been a few days.

As he dives into work, his body starts to release some of the unbearable tension and, the more he focuses, the more like himself he starts to feel. Dwelling on his mother's death is only going to send him into dark places. Instead, Land Register of Scotland searches take him down a rabbit hole of shell corporations and into lists of limited companies with impenetrable names. They all seem to run in a circle, no end in sight. Frustrated, he finds a pad of paper and starts sketching out the way the companies seem to slot together.

'What are you trying to hide?' he mutters to himself.

Eventually, he has to give up. It all seems to come back to a name. Comet Holdings. Cal frowns. The name is oddly familiar but he can't place it. He leaves the table and paces the room, taking his mind through the details of the case. Where has he seen this name before? And then something nudges at him. Cal grabs his main file of documents for the podcast – woefully far from paper free – and scrabbles through it, not sure if he's correct, but nerves tingling all the same. When he reaches the page, he stares in disbelief.

'What the hell?'

Rocket jerks his head up at Cal's tone and gives one deep throaty bark.

Agitated, Cal pushes away his chair and paces the room, hand over his mouth as he assimilates and the pieces slot neatly together.

Finally it makes sense.

The company that owns the quarry – Comet Green – is similar to the name of the company that owned the club where Jason Barr worked in Birmingham – Comet

Holdings. That is the place where his sister met her killer, where Owen's sister Daisy fell in with the same man. Cal returns to the laptop, cross-checking to be sure he's seeing what he thinks he's seeing from one to the other: they have the same registered address, an accountancy firm in the Isle of Man, and they appear to be UK subsidiaries of another firm registered there.

Who are these Comet people and why do they have links to both the quarry and the club? Does Jason Barr know something they don't want to get out? Maybe the abduction was wholly due to his links to Barr and nothing to do with Bella's case at all. In many ways that would make more sense. But, then, they knew about Merrick. They asked him to stop investigating. They're linked to Allegra. They have to be.

CHAPTER FORTY-NINE

CAL

A call coming in from Bella distracts Cal from his puzzling. He snatches up his phone, eager to check how she is after the events of the day before. Hopefully being back with her family and a good night's sleep will have helped her. But when he hears her voice, Cal knows that isn't the case. If anything, she sounds worse than she was when he dropped her home.

'I've decided,' she says, before he can even ask how she is. 'We need to stop.'

Cal swallows.

'What do you mean?'

'The podcast. We need to stop it. It's not doing any good.'

'I know yesterday was hard,' he begins, feeling on shaky ground, surprised at her vehemence. 'But we are making progress…'

'No!' She's almost shouting now, her voice filled with tears. 'You don't understand.'

'Okay, okay…' Cal tries to soothe her, worried about how distressed she sounds. 'Let's talk about it. Tell me what you're thinking.'

Can she really have believed Merrick yesterday when he said he was responsible for the deaths? As far as he's concerned, they both came out of the interview room knowing there is more to the story than the convicted killer is telling them.

'Seeing him dislodged something,' Bella's breath hitches. 'Because, last night, I had a dream, only it wasn't a dream, it was a memory. It was that day. I know it was.'

'Stay calm Bella, you're safe now. Just take your time.'

He waits as she sucks in raggedy breaths.

'In the dream I was in the ditch. I woke up. There was the most horrible smell and all of these flies were buzzing around me. The sky was so blue above and I could feel Jet's fur – she was sort of lying on top of me – but I was so frightened. So afraid to look. It was all quiet and I felt sticky and my head hurt and then... I saw him.'

'Who? What do you mean?'

'He came to look for me. He was covered in blood and Jet started growling. His hands were sticky red and he saw that I was awake and his face was right over me. I was so scared because I knew I was going to die. Jet was crying. I'd forgotten it, I'd forgotten it all but it was there inside me.' Bella sobs for a moment.

'And then what happened,' Cal asks, gently.

'Then he turned and he ran. He left me there. He left me alive. Why did he let me live and not them? I always assumed it was a mistake and he thought I was dead but it wasn't like that. He knew I was alive.'

Cal can hear the guilt that has filled her, taking up every available space.

'Who was he?' he asks. 'The man you saw, was it Jason Barr?'

Bella's voice rises again.

'No, that's just it. It was Merrick. I've been wrong all this time.'

CHAPTER FIFTY

CAL

The drive to the funeral home passes in a moment. Cal feels none of the wretched splitting he did when his mother was alive. Instead, a sort of emptiness has opened inside him. The funeral director is elegant in his compassion, performing a choreographed dance of guiding Cal through the various options for the service and the burial. He chooses the things she would have chosen, or he thinks she would have.

Afterwards, the man leaves him with his mother's coffin. It's closed and he doesn't want it opened. He finds he doesn't need to see her. She's gone and he hopes she's finding a peace that was lacking in the turbulence of her life.

As he sits vigil, waves of grief pass over him, but they aren't only for his mother. Cal shouldn't be here alone. Margot should be by his side. He knew her for such a short time, really. Just nine small years. And yet she left an indelible impression on her younger brother – he adored her and he's carried her with him ever since then. When he closes his eyes he can almost feel her beside him.

Back at his mother's house, there is only a quiet sadness. As if even the building knows she is gone. But then he steps inside and Cal is surprised to realise he feels different.

He walks slowly through his childhood home, thinking of all the items he agonised over in clearing it out, and the guilt he felt starts to dissipate. Cal stands in the hallway and shafts of light stream in, dust dancing in the glow. He closes his eyes and he breathes in the last of this place.

Even the boxes of Barr's belongings in the living room don't hold the same fear and sway for him. They're just mementoes. Scraps of cloth and photographs can't hurt him. He will bin the rubbish and turn the letters and pictures over to Foulds, he decides. He's due to meet her shortly and he'll take them now, get them out of his life. They can sit in a police archive in case they are ever needed. He'll never be finished pursuing Jason Barr – he knows that now. But he doesn't want them here.

Decisive, he crosses the room and closes the flaps of the boxes of paperwork, leaving the one filled with scraps of cloth to take to the tip later. One by one, he hefts them into the boot of his car, dusting off his hands when he is finished and looking around the empty living room in satisfaction. The estate agent has viewings lined up for this weekend. It is time for someone else to claim this house, maybe a family who will tear down walls, redecorate and make it their own. They can fill it with laughter and happiness and that might start to paper over the cracks of the past. He's ready to let it go.

-

Cal crosses the nature reserve to where Detective Inspector Foulds is waiting for him on Margot's memorial bench. A brisk breeze has risen, stirring up memories and playing with the detective's loose brown hair. It flies out behind her as he approaches and she looks wilder and freer than her usual buttoned-up professional demeanour. He has never seen her in jeans before. She holds up two cans of gin and tonic.

'Thought you might need this.'

He smiles. 'Shona sends a hug.'

Foulds grins. 'She's a good one.'

'I know.'

'Don't do anything to mess that up, eh?'

'Not in a million years.'

He laughs and sits down beside her, a wave of emotion cresting at how close he feels to Foulds, how much they've been through together. They've had their differences but they have the same battle scars. In front of them, ducks are dipping below the surface of the water, popping up in random locations. Chrissie used to love watching them when she was small, toddling in front of the bench, her wild red ringlets like a halo, the spitting image of the aunt she never met.

'I'm sorry about your mother.'

'Thank you. In some ways it's a relief. She was wasting away, no quality of life.'

It strikes him that it's a very long time since she had any of that anyway.

'Must still be hard though.'

'It is. Thanks.'

They crack their cans and chink them gently together in a toast. Cal touches the plaque on the bench softly, like a talisman. His sister would have been almost sixty if she'd lived. He might have been an uncle to her children; Chrissie might have had cousins. So much was taken with her, all that potential and possibility. Just how Bella feels.

He takes a breath and fills Foulds in on the events of the past weeks.

'And Bella now says she was wrong and it was Merrick all along?' The detective stares at him.

'That's what she told me.'

'And you? What do you think?'

Cal sighs. 'I'm just not buying it. Merrick was weird in prison. It seemed that he genuinely wanted to help but then he said he couldn't remember that day.'

Foulds raises an eyebrow.

'If he can't remember how does he know he did it?'

'Exactly. And why did he drag her over there to see him? Something's wrong with it all.'

'So what are you going to do?' She slugs at her can as a group of runners pass them and flustered geese stalk angrily from their path.

'I don't know. It doesn't really feel like I have permission to continue. But there are maybe other strands of the investigation I could look into in the meantime.'

'Yes, back up a little. We need to talk more about the fact you were *abducted*. That's a new low, even for you.'

'Yes, fair enough. Thanks for the security advice.'

'What are Police Scotland doing about it?'

'Still waiting to see... I don't think it's a priority for them, but we found the place I was taken and I've passed the information on.'

Cal fishes in his pocket for a piece of paper on which he has written the diagram of ownership he has tracked through Companies House and other public records.

'This is the organisation that owns the quarry where they took me. The same people seem to own the club where Jason Barr worked. There must be a way we can find out who's behind it all. I've reached a dead end – it's a network of corporations and holding companies ending in the Isle of Man.'

Foulds takes the paper from him and studies it.

'Leave it with me. I'll see what I can dig out.'

'Oh, and I also have some boxes for you.'

'Boxes?'

'Of Jason Barr's personal letters and things.'

Foulds looks at him in astonishment, then shakes her head.

'Do I even want to know where you got those?'

'Maybe not.'

They stand and he touches the plaque in farewell to his sister. Remembered, always. They walk back along the boardwalk, taking the looping route to the gate, bulrushes tall and proud beside them, grasses swaying and encroaching onto the walkway. Cal sees fish darting beneath them in the swampy environment, a V of geese in the sky above. When they've transferred the boxes of paperwork to Foulds' car, he watches as she drives along the street and out of sight. He's still determined to get justice for Margot, for Allegra and her family. But, without those boxes, he feels lighter.

CHAPTER FIFTY-ONE

CAL

Foulds calls him sooner than he expected. She sounds uncharacteristically excited – almost giddy.

'I've managed to get someone in forensic accounting who owes me a favour to take a look at that corporation.'

'They found something, I take it?'

She wouldn't be calling if not. He feels the welcome thrill of a connection sparking. With the withdrawal of Bella's support, it has been feeling like this case is over before it's begun. He's dreading breaking the news to Sarah that their broadcast suspension might need to be permanent – after everything she's done for him, this is not the way he wants the podcast to end.

'Well, it's all run through offshore accounts and various shell corporations that make actual ownership a bit impenetrable, but the reason he was able to come back to me so fast is it pinged for a connection to a known person of interest.'

'Who?'

'The land for the club and the quarry both trace back to a man called Wayne Gandy.'

'I know that name.'

'He's a self-proclaimed property tycoon. Hails from Manchester originally, but more often found in the Med on the back of a yacht with toned beauties half his age, these days.'

'Someone called Wayne used to run the clubs back in the day. Are you saying he still owns the land?'

Cal draws to mind an image of a thickset, bald man pictured occasionally in the press. A character cut from the same cloth as Jason Barr in physical terms, only dripping in expensive gold accessories and normally seen grasping a glass of champagne, his hand on the leg of a much younger woman. Something about Gandy has always made his skin crawl.

'Yes. He styled himself as a bit of a gangster back in the day, working his way up from one small club to a chain of them, but has appeared to go legit in the last twenty years. He sold off the bars and clubs business and went into aggregates and rubbish disposal. Apparently there's serious money in it. Then he moved into developing luxury high-rise buildings in northern and Scottish cities – all penthouse flats, rooftop bars and glossy gyms at the top of glass towers.'

'Wonder what he's compensating for?'

'Right. But he still owns the quarries and slag heaps – and the older properties, even though he doesn't manage the clubs and pubs anymore. Those are all leased out to independent and, as far as we know, legitimate businesses. Proving it is another thing, but we believe Gandy's empire is built on criminal foundations with the proceeds laundered to within an inch of their lives.'

'When Barr worked for him back then, he could have been up to his eyes in whatever dodgy dealings Gandy had going. If he was involved in the behind-the-scenes business, the boss man could have an interest in helping cover up his other crimes and keeping him out of jail.'

'It's more than plausible,' Foulds says, sounding impatient.

'It's always felt to me that Barr has a guardian angel protecting him. Yes, he went down for assaulting the women he followed from the clubs, but it took a long time to identify him and he's slid out of so many other sticky situations.'

'Gandy is extremely well connected, but…'

'But if it is him behind the offer they made me, why does he want Barr dead now?'

'Maybe Barr knows something Wayne Gandy doesn't want you to find out. Or maybe he's finally become too much of a liability. He's back in prison yet again. That's not going to fit Gandy's modern image.'

Cal's scribbling thoughts on his notepad, lines and arrows linking the different parts of the investigation, giving credence to suspicion.

'This is really helpful. Thank you.'

'Wait. I haven't told you the best part.'

He can hear a fizzing energy in her voice.

'More? Is it my birthday?'

'Guess what else this network of corporations owns?'

The prickly sense that comes when a case is really starting to split open runs down Cal's arms. He has a sudden inkling.

'What?'

'The farm and industrial buildings next to the Carlo murder site.'

Cal stills, pressing the phone harder to his ear. Synapses crackle in disbelief.

'Say that again.'

'Gandy owns the buildings where Lachlan Merrick used to work. All three of these sites are ultimately under the same ownership.'

'But… how is it possible we didn't know this?'

'He's a wealthy man. Fingers in lots of pies. Good accountants on his payroll. He holidays with his top money man in Monaco. There was no reason to link these places before – they're so far from each other and owned by different shell corporations. You have to be really looking hard. When Merrick confessed, no one bothered to follow up on the land ownership.'

'My God.'

The quarry, the club and the farm buildings, all in different parts of the country, linked. That gives Barr a reason to be in the area. Cal's mind races ahead of itself.

'Maybe Allegra saw something. If they were using the farm for drugs – storing them there,' Foulds says.

But Cal thinks about what they know of Jason Barr – the predatory urges he submits to time and time again.

'Or maybe she was just in the wrong place at the wrong time. If Barr was moving drugs through there, all it would take is for her to catch his eye.'

His heart constricts as he thinks of Bella and her family innocently crossing the field towards the woods that beautiful June day – the sun bathing them in heat and light. Did they capture the attention of a monster?

'What about the forensics? How can Barr have left nothing behind?'

It's good to talk this through with Foulds. She's seen so much over the years and he values her opinion.

'They weren't difficult targets were they?' she says. 'We know Allegra was quickly immobilised and the girls were too young to fight back. Whoever it was took the knife they used away from the scene.'

'But they would have been covered in blood, surely?'

'You've been there. It's an isolated spot. With a river. Maybe whoever it was got into the water and washed it all away. Forensics weren't what they are now back then. Now we might be able to find traces of him, but Police Scotland aren't going to order retesting while a man is in jail for their murders. I wouldn't if I were them, even if they have any items left to test.'

He thinks back to the file. His heart is galloping.

'Do you think they have anything?'

'Hang on – I've got a list here,' Foulds says. He waits for her to check. 'They have the girls and Allegra's clothes that were at the scene. Shoes, bags, buggy and three towels.'

'Four,' Cal says, automatically. 'There were four of them.' He remembers Bella's account of them packing that day.

'Three,' Foulds corrects. 'They didn't have one each.'

'Oh. Okay.'

'Lunchboxes, picnic blanket. That's about it. But these are things that could be retested.'

When he gets off the call, Cal thinks back to the reports of the yellow car parked in that other piece of woodland. Another piece of the puzzle linking Barr to this case. Individually, these things are circumstantial, but together they add up to more, surely?

He pulls up a map on his phone and studies the area – dropping a pin in the place he thinks the yellow car must have been. The police always operated on the assumption that the killer came in from the road Allegra walked along. But, if the yellow car was connected to the crime, that makes the escape route the opposite direction to the country road, further away from the scene.

Cal stares at the screen, thoughts triggered by Foulds' words clicking together. He expands the size of the map, realising that the pin he has dropped is on the edge of the river. Maybe the water wasn't so much barrier as opportunity. A roadway. He walked close to this spot when he left Bella on the rocks to remember her family. If someone parked there, they might have walked along and seen the Carlos swimming. If they followed them and lay in wait, all they would have to do is retrace their steps to the water. It isn't deep. Yes, the banks are steep and covered in undergrowth, but what if you simply waded upstream? There was no blood spatter that way, no drops of telltale red, he knows this from the police report. But maybe this man was clever. Maybe he mopped it all up before he set off. It's not impossible. It certainly fits Jason Barr's level of calculation and sadism.

Then Cal remembers the shirt found in Merrick's possession. Tucked away at the back of his wardrobe like a guilty secret. Soaked with Allegra's blood. The two men must be connected. Are they joint killers? That doesn't fit Barr's MO at all. Frustrated, he shoves the mouse away from him and rakes his fingers through his hair. There's got to be a way to uncover the truth. He just can't see it yet.

CHAPTER FIFTY-TWO

CAL

Cal crosses Piccadilly Gardens and weaves through Manchester's thronged streets, which are teeming with life and sound. Waiting for a tram to pass, he crosses the tracks and turns the corner to see the gleaming glass front of Gandy's latest commercial property development – sixty-six storeys of retail and apartments in a phallic glass tower, a hotel on seven of the floors and a rooftop pool and gardens high in the sky. It is rumoured to have cost more than £200 million and it's undeniable that over the years Gandy has brought the city prosperity and attention – opening doors to the social scene of the Manchester elite. He has dined with the mayor, council members and local MPs as well as the city's footballers and celebrities. He's powerful – thick, beringed fingers in so many pies.

Cal keeps tight hold of his folder of documents – he's spent the last few days researching Gandy and preparing to interview him for a fake profile piece. Sarah arranged the chat through Gandy's PR and gave his name as Christopher Longacre. It's the name he was born with but it's oil in his mouth to use it. The plans could be in vain. It's possible Gandy will recognise him anyway. He swallows, looking up at the glassy façade and the roof high above. It may feel that nothing could happen to you in the midst of this thriving metropolis, but he knows this plan isn't without its risks.

Hesitating, he wonders if it's worth it, but then he thinks of the miserable room he was locked in, he thinks of Bella and her nightmares and of Barr in his prison cell. Steeling himself, he sends Sarah a text message to tell her that he's arrived. She immediately responds with a thumbs-up emoji. If he doesn't message her in the next hour she's going to raise the alarm and that knowledge gives him the confidence to carry on.

Through the revolving doors and into a sleek lobby, Cal is signed in by a bored receptionist before taking a lift that is so fast and smooth he barely feels it moving. When the doors slide back, he sees he has indeed been magicked to the sixty-sixth floor, where he follows a high-ceilinged, marble-clad hallway to a door at the end. It's deathly silent up here, far from the rest of the world below. Before he can ring the bell, the door swings back to reveal a young, blonde woman with a perfect tan, short skirt and high heels.

She thrusts a hand towards him. 'I'm Ellie,' she says. 'We spoke on the phone about the profile. Come in. Wayne's just getting out of the hot tub.'

Cal steps into the brightest, most ostentatious apartment he has ever seen. The floors are the same rolling marble as the hallway and he can barely make out the joins where the slabs meet. Floor-to-ceiling windows greet him, with a vertiginous view of the city and a panorama of sky. The apartment is immaculate – garish artwork on the walls in great slashes of loud colour and a masculine scent that makes him want to gag. Sandalwood and ash, perhaps.

Ellie leads him further into the open-plan living space, which has a gleaming kitchen at one end and a sea of soft furnishings at the other. He agrees to a coffee and strolls to look out at the view. On a side table is a collection of ornate frames. Cal peers at them. Gandy with the leader of Manchester City Council, with a succession of celebrities, and, with pride of place in the centre, the president of the United States. He squints at a picture at the back, his heart lurching as he sees one of a man he knows with Gandy. Quickly, he slides his phone from his pocket and snaps a shot of it.

Before he can hide the phone, Ellie is back with his coffee, announcing the man himself.

Cal holds the device up.

'Just taking a picture of this incredible view,' he bluffs.

'You have to fly high to get that view,' a voice says.

Gandy is flushed with heat, wearing a white fluffy robe monogrammed with his initials. Now in his seventies, he is still an imposing physical presence. He frowns when Cal turns towards him, as if trying to place him, then pumps his hand with a meaty fist and indicates that he should sit on one of the designer chairs arranged around a floating fireplace. Electric flames flicker hypnotically in front of them. Cal's arms prickle.

'I'll have a Coke, Ellie,' the beefy developer demands, seeing her setting the coffee on the low table between them.

'Intimidated?'

Cal's mouth fills with saliva. He looks blankly at Gandy for a moment until he realises the tycoon is gesticulating at the apartment and the tower, expecting adulation. 'Impressive, isn't it. For a boy from nowhere?'

'It's quite something,' he says, recovering his calm. 'How does it feel to finally be in here after all the years of development?'

The soft open question works perfectly. Cal hits record on his phone as Gandy starts to boast and doesn't stop for ten minutes – all Cal has to do is prompt him with the occasional interested noise. Ellie brings Gandy his drink and he waves at her to set it down, then the PR retreats to the edge of the room. Cal is conscious of her opening her mouth to interject a couple of times, but Gandy allows no entry to the conversation.

Ten minutes later, Cal decides he's had enough of the PR spin.

'I did want to ask you,' he starts, cutting Gandy off full flow, 'about allegations that your early businesses were linked to less than legitimate enterprises?'

Gandy stops talking, his mouth fish-gaping at Cal's sudden transformation.

'Come again?'

'We have evidence that your nightclubs were hubs for importing and dealing cocaine as far back as the 1980s. I've spoken to several people willing to go on the record.'

It's chilling seeing how quickly Gandy's face changes – his eyes become dark, the bonhomie vanishes.

'Hang on. I recognise you. Who are you?'

'I work for a true crime podcast, Mr Gandy.'

The man jabs a fat finger in the air.

'Lovett. Cal Lovett.'

Warning creeps along Cal's spine. That this man knows his name is no small detail.

The developer spins angrily towards Ellie. 'This is your fault. Why didn't you check him out properly?'

'She's got nothing to do with this.' Cal rises from his chair, faced off against the larger man, only a flimsy coffee table between them.

'I think you should leave.'

Cal feels the physical threat but he thinks of Margot, of Bella, and he presses on.

'Does that mean you aren't going to answer the question, Mr Gandy?'

'I don't know where you get your information, but I haven't been involved with the nightclubs in decades.'

'But you do still own aggregates business Comet Green, including an Aberdeenshire quarry. And that business is linked to Comet Holdings and a string of other incorporations registered on the Isle of Man?'

'Those are perfectly legitimate companies. Your insinuations are slanderous.'

His voice is quiet, more dangerous for the coiled threat within it.

'I was abducted and held on your property, by men with keys and access to it, two weeks ago. Those men warned me off the case I have been investigating, Mr Gandy, and I'd like to know what interest you have in it.' Cal decides to take a flying leap into the unknown. 'Why do you want Lachlan Merrick to stay in prison for a crime he didn't commit?'

'This is fucking ridiculous.'

Gandy rises to his feet, purple-skinned against the bright white robe. Cal sees Ellie swallow and step forward, wringing her hands. She can't be that much older than Chrissie. He hates that she's involved and yet it feels like a witness is the only thing stopping Gandy from punching him in the face or throwing him off the sixty-sixth floor.

'Why would men linked to your property want to threaten me, Mr Gandy?'

'Get the fuck out of here. Now.'

Cal wants nothing more than to turn and run from this place, but he holds his ground.

'It would be an awful shame if someone were to investigate your business dealings, Mr Gandy. After all these years and the legacy you've built. Wouldn't it be a pity if it came crashing down?'

'You've got nothing. You'll be hearing from my lawyers. Ellie, get Jeremy on the phone right now.'

'And yet I've managed to establish that you also own the land next to where Allegra Carlo and her children were murdered. With your men warning me off the case, I'd say that provides ground for some questions, wouldn't you?'

Cal isn't prepared for the strength of Gandy's reaction. At the mention of Allegra's name, he freezes, his face draining of colour and his fists clenching. But then he seems to get himself under control and a calculation comes into his eyes.

'That is nothing to do with me.'

'But you know about it?'

'I'm saying nothing with that on.'

Gandy points to the phone recording on the tabletop.

Cal reaches down and stops the recording. He holds the phone out to show he's not faking it.

'Off the record.'

Gandy shakes his head.

'Not so fast. This has nothing to do with me and my business, and I want your word that you'll leave me out of it.'

Cal holds his hands up, nauseous at having to deal with this man for information. He's met Wayne Gandy's type before. He's a bully and Cal would bet a sexual predator too. But he swallows down his misgivings, feeling closer to an answer for Bella than he has been so far.

'Fine. If that's the case then I won't go after you.'

Cal has never lied to an interviewee, but he's lying now.

'Wait, I'm not sure...' Ellie's voice is a thin reed in the testosterone.

Gandy doesn't look at her, just waves his hand like she's an irritation.

'You can go now,' he says, not taking his eyes from Cal. 'That's all I need today.'

Ellie stutters and then seems to think better of intervening. A moment later, they hear the door to the apartment shutting behind her. Cal is glad she's out of there.

Gandy sits down, one arm along the couch back, crossing his legs in a way that almost gives Cal a view he really doesn't want.

'I should have dealt with that lunatic back then. That man's been nothing but trouble.'

'What do you mean?'

Cal's senses are tingling.

Gandy sighs. 'He was a bouncer at FIVE in the 1980s, that's on the record. He also did some... deliveries for me from time to time. But I stopped using him for those other jobs in 1986. He was promoted to head of security at the club so he didn't have time.'

The hulk-like figure stares his meaning into Cal. They both know what that date means.

'But before then he did deliveries to the farm warehouses near Coupar Angus?'

Gandy rubs his nose with the back of his hand.

'I believe so.'

Cal's vision starts to cloud at the edges, starbursts of colour in his sight.

'So you *knew* it was him? Back in eighty-six?'

Another shrug.

'And you didn't think to tell the police?'

Gandy laughs, as if Cal's an idiot.

'It wouldn't have been good for my business to draw any heat or attention. There were bigger fish to fry, Mr Lovett. In my trade sometimes there has to be collateral damage.'

Cal swallows. 'Collateral damage?'

He thinks of Bella shivering in a ditch, blood-soaked and motherless.

'Look, Jason Barr was a naughty boy. I considered dealing with him because he was a problem for me, shitting on my doorstep. But he promised to keep a low profile – and his mouth shut about various things – so he got to live.'

'And you promoted him.'

Cal feels hatred for the man in front of him boiling up inside.

'He was useful to me.'

'So Lachlan Merrick wasn't involved?'

'I've no idea, Mr Lovett. Maybe the two of them planned it together. I don't know the details and I don't care.'

'So why did you come after me two weeks ago if you don't care? They were your men.'

'There are people who will be compromised if you don't stop poking around. I was doing someone a favour. No good deed goes unpunished Mr Lovett.'

'Who were you doing the favour for?'

Gandy laughs. 'Time for you to leave.'

Cal forces himself to stand, shaky and ill.

Before he takes a step, Gandy adds: 'I would keep your word. We know where to find you, and the people you care about.'

Rattled, Cal strides from the apartment, letting the heavy door slam shut behind him. He jabs at the button on the elevator, waiting impatiently for the lightning-fast journey to the ground, back to reality. He can still taste Gandy's aftershave in the back of his throat as he heads for the outside. Once he's free of the building, Cal keeps walking, faster and faster, weaving his way through groups of students and business people out buying lunch.

Only when he is two streets away and realises his phone is buzzing against his chest, does Cal stop and lean against a wall, sweating and clammy.

'You alright, mate?'

He nods at the passerby.

But it isn't true. He isn't alright. Wayne Gandy knew Jason Barr was a killer in June 1986. He played God and he let him run free.

Cal's sister Margot was killed in September.

If Gandy had done something, anything, she would still be alive.

CHAPTER FIFTY-THREE

CAL

Cal walks the streets of Manchester aimlessly, his equilibrium completely scrambled and his mind going in circles after his conversation with Gandy in his sky-high paradise. He feels greasy from having sat in the same room as the man, for even having breathed the same air. It's long been a cornerstone belief for Cal, a notion that has driven *Finding Justice* forward, that someone always knows something. And someone did. Someone knew everything and did absolutely nothing.

Fury gives way to grief and confusion. By the time he finally stops pounding the pavements, Cal is footsore and his mouth is dry. The clouds above have turned black and he is lost, far from Piccadilly station, his train long gone. Disorientated, he takes a deep breath and pulls his phone from his pocket. Sarah has called him twice. In his hand, he's still holding the phone he showed Gandy. The dummy. Using the other handset, he fumbles a quick message to Sarah. *I'm out.* Then he falls back against the cool brick of the alley. A moment later, the reply comes in. *Got it. Every word.*

There, in his inbox, is the audio file of his conversation with Wayne Gandy. He thinks about calling his producer back, but she isn't the person he needs to speak to right now.

Another cornerstone belief of his has always been that he needs to protect his sources. All journalists know this. It's something he's taken as seriously as doctor patient confidentiality – he has to be trusted or people won't talk to him, he has to be a man of his word. But he cannot honour that standard with Wayne Gandy. How can he let this pass? He can't act like it never happened and go back to his normal life. He just can't.

It may have taken him two hours of walking to reach this conclusion, but in the end Cal knows he is not going to stay silent and let a man like Gandy get away without consequences. Margot is dead because he said nothing and Cal is going to burn the whole world down if that's what it takes to make him pay. He'll take that goddamn tower apart brick by brick.

Until now, the recording was an insurance policy. Now it's a smoking gun. Decision made, he opens his phone and presses call. If Detective Inspector Foulds is surprised to hear from him, she doesn't let on. Instead, she listens while the words pour from him: the confirmation that Barr worked for Gandy delivering drugs around the UK, that he was there in that location when Allegra and the girls were attacked, that Gandy knew he was the killer and said nothing.

'And you've got evidence of this?'

'I'm sending you an audio file now. It has the whole conversation. I'm also going to put it on the podcast.'

'Hang on, are you sure about that?'

'One hundred per cent.'

'He'll come after you, hard. Men like him don't piss about.'

'I know. I don't care.'

'Cal. You don't mean that. You're angry and upset. We need to think this through. We can use this information to get him in a way that doesn't come back on you.'

There's a long pause. Cal listens to the soothing static of the office behind Foulds. He thinks of Shona and Chrissie and his heart rate steadies.

'You're right,' he says. 'I know.'

CHAPTER FIFTY-FOUR

CAL

Cal walks to Manchester Piccadilly Station and buys a scalding cup of tea for the train, sitting in a daze all the way to Birmingham New Street. By the time he makes it to Tamworth, he is exhausted, barely able to walk the streets to his mother's house. He picks up a fish and chip supper to eat and all he can think of is calling Shona to say goodnight then crawling into bed to sleep.

The house is chilled and silent. He closes the door and makes his way to the sad, battered kitchen table. The place looks scruffy and worn with almost everything gone. He eats without pleasure, feeling bloated by the greasy meal and wishing he'd picked up a beer to go with it. Then his gaze flickers to the old bottles of alcohol left on top of one of the kitchen cupboards, still out of Margot's reach decades after she died. He hasn't got round to clearing them out yet – was just going to bin them.

Cal strides across the room and reaches for a half-empty bottle of Jack Daniels, hidden behind a bottle of sherry his mother used for cooking. It must be ancient but he doesn't care. He unscrews the cap of the bottle and pours four fat fingers into a mug, relishing the way the alcohol hits the back of his throat when he slugs the first mouthful. He drinks it fast and pours another, relieved to feel it numbing his senses and blunting the sharp edges of today's pain. He's trying not to think about what Foulds is doing with the information he shared. She'll try her best, but the political will to act may not be there and it could just be hushed up or buried. If it doesn't work, he will set the truth free himself. He has the recording.

Mug in hand, he wanders through the house, pausing in the doorway to the living room, taking in the dust and emptiness. Only old furniture remains – the estate agent said to leave it in place to assist the imaginations of prospective buyers and then he will have to hire a van and junk it all. In his memory, a smaller version of himself toddles across the room and into his sister's arms. He can hear laughter in the background. Coming back to himself and wiping blurry eyes with the back of his hand, Cal shakes his head at how maudlin the combination of today and the neat Jack Daniels is making him.

When he composes himself, he realises that the room isn't quite empty – there's the one remaining box of Jason Barr's scraps, taunting him from the corner. All of a sudden, he can't bear to be in the room with the box any longer. It shouldn't be in the house. He looks at his watch. It's still early – he can't drive after swigging the scotch, but he can take the box down the road to the communal bins and be rid of it once and for all. Ideally, Cal would watch it go up in flames but there is little space in the cramped back garden and he can't imagine the neighbours would be thrilled with him pouring petrol on the lot.

Setting the empty mug down on the floor, he crosses the room and hefts the box into his arms. It smells old and dust billows up from it, along with a moth-eaten, mouldy smell.

'Time for you to go.'

Just as he turns for the door, the old cardboard disintegrates and the bottom of the box collapses, dumping its cargo at his feet.

'Shit.'

Of course. It's like a curse, sometimes it feels he will never be free of this man.

Cal grabs a bin bag from the kitchen and returns to the living room, stuffing the items into it one by one – old doilies and the sampler he saw before. As his hand reaches for a faded length of material, he comes to an abrupt stop. Cal stares at the fabric, blinking to be sure he's seeing what he thinks he is. It's an old towel. And though the patterns on it initially look abstract, from this angle they resolve themselves into countless tiny fish.

His fingers hover above the fabric. It's a coincidence, isn't it?

But now he can't bring himself to touch it.

Cal sets the bin bag to one side and steps back from the pile. Foulds' words resound in his head. Only three towels. Not four, like he thought. It seemed such a tiny detail, one easily put down to someone being mistaken. But what if there wasn't a mistake?

Cal leaves the living room, going to the kitchen for the tongs. Back beside the towel, he lifts the fabric and spreads it out.

Is that a stain on the material? Brownish and faded almost into imagination.

Bile rises in his throat.

He is such an idiot. He's had this here all along. He's touched the contents of the box, upended them on the floor and he was about to throw them away.

Setting down the tongs, he drops his head to his hands. He clearly isn't thinking straight and he doesn't know for sure what this means, but as he kneels there, he can't shake the suspicion that he's looking at traces of Allegra's blood.

CHAPTER FIFTY-FIVE

CAL

When he finally gets back to Aberdeenshire after co-ordinating with Foulds and police officers from the Manchester and Scottish forces to tell them what he knows, exhaustion descends on Cal. It's a welcome surprise to find Chrissie waiting for him and he wraps his daughter in his arms when she appears on the doorstep.

'Surprise!'

When Chrissie lets go of him, Shona leans in for a kiss.

'We thought you needed some family time,' she whispers.

With Rocket snuffling at his legs and the two people he loves the most here with him, Cal is the closest to peace he's been in a long time. He follows them into the house and they cluster round the table, catching up on the events of the last few days – the plans for the funeral in a couple of weeks and the progress on the Carlo case.

'Bella hasn't come back to you?'

Cal shakes his head at Shona. 'She wants to be left alone for now. I'm not going to push it.'

Chrissie's face is pale.

'So this man knew? He knew what Jason Barr did?'

Her voice wobbles as she joins the dots. Cal reaches for her hand to steady her.

'Yes. He knew.'

'If he'd said something, done something, then…'

She looks at him, eyes shining with tears.

'We can't go down that rabbit hole, love,' he says, wishing he could take his own advice. 'What's done is done.'

After cups of tea and slabs of dark chocolate, Chrissie opts for an early night. Cal and Shona clear the dishes and curl on the sofa, tired but desperate to spend time together, a mindless TV drama playing in front of them. Cal doesn't see more than a minute of it. He jerks awake to find the programme has finished and Shona is asleep too, her head on his shoulder. His watch tells him it's gone midnight.

Gently, he shakes her awake.

'You should go to bed. I'll take Rocket out and lock up.'

She groans. 'What time is it?'

'Late. Go to bed, I won't be long. Love you.'

Shona kisses him sleepily. He turns off the kitchen lights and calls the dog to him. Rocket lumbers from his bed reluctantly, old bones cracking as he struggles to stand, his eyes as bleary as Cal feels. It is mean to rouse him but better now than at three in the morning when the dog decides he can't wait for the toilet. His bladder isn't what it was when he was younger.

When Cal closes the back door quietly behind him, the cold air is a shock. Nights in May can still be brutal here, making him wish he'd grabbed a jacket. Briefly, he debates returning for one, but the harsh and instant alertness is a refreshing slap to the face and there's a perverse relish to it. Rocket seems perkier now too – trotting off to the field edge when Cal had assumed he would simply want a quick plod around the garden. Reluctantly, he follows, driving his hands into his pockets and shivering at the way the chill cuts into him. The night is blustery, trees in the distance rustling their agreement that it's far too late to be out here.

Now that he is awake, his mind starts to agitate the calm waters. Instead of feeling satisfied with the investigative success, the more time has passed since he talked to Gandy, the more Cal feels sick at the conspiracy of silence that has kept Jason Barr out in the world hurting women. Only when it was convenient to him and his associates did the developer try to do anything and that was only to threaten and intimidate Cal. He does wonder who it was that Gandy was doing the favour for and if he's ever going to be able to find out.

Yawning so widely his jaw cracks, Cal decides to call an end to Rocket's nighttime snuffling, letting out a low whistle that brings the Labrador ambling to his side and a wet nose to his hand, looking for a treat.

'I didn't bring one, boy. Sorry. Bedtime.'

As they turn, he experiences a slash of foreboding, almost déjà vu. He is filled with sudden certainty that there will be retaliation for talking to the police about Gandy, that these men operate by their own rules and reasons, that they have informants everywhere. Perhaps his mind has noticed a flicker of movement or heard a sound from across the field because, a second later, there is a bright flare of light from the house.

Cal freezes in confusion, every nerve on end. It is Rocket who erupts first, raising his hackles and letting off a volley of barks. A moment later, there is a whomp and whoosh of flame. Now, Cal starts to run, the earth slipping beneath his feet, his legs seeming so slow and powerless no matter how much effort he puts into the sprint. The house is bobbing on the horizon, the light uncanny and wrong. Chrissie. Shona. He tries to shout, but his throat is closed and all that comes out is a gasping croak.

Adrenaline pumps through him, his breath ragged and his eyes blurred by tears.

They're in there, in his house, sleeping unaware.

And someone is trying to kill them.

CHAPTER FIFTY-SIX

BELLA

Bella wakes, drenched in sweat and confusion, her legs tangled in the sheets. She fights to get free, sitting up and pressing her feet to the floor, breathing heavily. Noah is asleep behind her, the house is quiet and the room lit only by the light of the alarm clock. Only one in the morning; there is still so much of the night to go. The thought of it fills her with dread. She strips off her sodden T-shirt and pulls another from the drawer, tip-toeing along the landing to the family bathroom instead of using the ensuite.

Bella stares at herself in the mirror: sees a woman drained and horrified, her skin yellow in the false light, her arms goose-pimpled, shivery now the hot sweat has gone. She lifts her damp hair off her neck and breathes steadily. She doesn't want to think about Lachlan Merrick and Jason Barr, but she cannot help it.

All the certainty she thought she had has been turned on its head in an instant, because of a dream. It sounds nonsensical. And yet, she would swear her sleeping vision was a memory of that day. How can she have been so wrong about it all? Now she feels sure that Lachlan Merrick was there.

It's so confusing. Has this whole endeavour been a perimenopausal fever dream? When she thinks of Cal and the faith he placed in her, she feels so guilty. He's called again today and she hasn't even listened to the message. Shame seeps from her pores with the sweat. She wants to know why Merrick let her live. If he'd killed her too then she'd be with her mother and sisters. Immediately, Bella feels more guilt – then her father would have been left alone.

Emotions have wired her awake. Sleep is now going to be impossible. Instead, Bella walks through the house, making her checks on the boys, trying to be comforted by the silence and calm that only comes at night. Dawn feels too far away to be real.

Finding herself in the living room, turning in circles, she picks up the remote and clicks on the screen, flopping down onto the sofa. Maybe if she watches some television for a moment she will drop off and even if Noah finds her here in the morning with a cricked neck and stiff limbs it's better than keeping him awake with her tossing and turning.

She flicks through the channels, flitting moth-like from one to the next, unable to settle on anything. The news channel pops into view and she lets it sit there, ticker tape running across the bottom, presenters in their smart brightly coloured jackets with perfect smiles.

That's something to come out of this, at least. Bella no longer fears the news in the way she used to. If anything, she's bingeing on current affairs, giddy at the fact that it no longer clamps her heart. As she sits, her eyes glaze. She turns the volume down low, a murmur in the background as she feels her eyelids getting heavy. And then they snap open. She must be hallucinating, on the verge of sleep.

Bella sits forward and stares at the ticker tape, waiting for the spool of stories to scroll round to the start. How is this possible? She sat in front of him only days ago.

The story slides into view once more.

Convicted killer Lachlan Merrick rushed to hospital: condition critical.

Is he dying? Is it finally over?

Why does she feel like she's going to cry?

CHAPTER FIFTY-SEVEN

CAL

Cal has never sprinted as fast as he does now. They reach the edge of the garden and he vaults the fence while Rocket tears around to the open gate, barking ferociously. The sound of smoke alarms pierces the air. His voice is back and he's screaming their names.

A silhouette against the red light reveals a dark mass by the house. As he runs towards it, the figure lights a match and Cal sees the glass of a bottle with a rag stuffed into the top jumping into flame. Alive with horror, he accelerates towards the figure, letting out a howl that's somewhere between war cry and pain. Launching himself at the man, he throws all of his weight into the bulk, knocking them both to the floor. The bottle flies off into the lawn and the grass bursts into flame as it smashes, the heat searing Cal's skin. Rocket's barks fill the air around him, as he tries to scramble to his feet, only to be socked by a punch to the guts from the figure.

Cal grunts in pain, collapsing, winded.

He has to get to Chrissie and Shona.

But before he can recover, a boot meets his ribs and he curls up involuntarily as pain fireworks through him and the kicks keep coming. There is nowhere to hide.

'If you won't fucking listen, we'll have to make you.'

The voice is gravel and pain in his ears.

The house is burning. He has to get up. *Get up. Get up.*

'Shona! Chrissie!' Cal shouts as loud as he can, not knowing if they're awake, if they're trapped, if they've been overcome with smoke... Their bedrooms are on this side, *oh God.*

The man places another kick in Cal's gut. Rocket is in a deep bark frenzy and then, out of the corner of his eye, Cal sees a blur of yellow fur as the old Lab launches himself at Cal's attacker, snarling, all teeth instead of softness.

There's a screech of pain from the man and a whimper as he punches Rocket away from him. The dog goes flying to the ground, letting out a yelp that strips Cal's soul from him. Summoning every last ounce of energy he has, he shoves up from the ground, tasting the blood in his mouth, the anger and fury and fear all distilled into one. He shoves the man back, hard so he goes stumbling and almost drops but manages to scramble up. The assailant starts to run away, fleeing the scene.

Cal dives to the Lab's side, hand meeting soft fur, but then there's the shatter of glass and a burst of flames behind him and he feels the tears pouring down his face as he turns to run in the other direction, leaving his beautiful, brave dog lying in the flowerbed.

-

As he makes it round the house, Cal hears the sound of his daughter calling his name.

'Chrissie!'

He barrels into her, finding her barefoot on the gravel, her face illuminated by the flames of the burning building so he can see the dark pooled fear of her eyes. He takes her arm and tugs her away from the house.

'Are you okay? Chrissie – talk to me.'

Her mouth opens and closes, no words come out but she nods. He can see the shock in her eyes.

'Chrissie? Where's Shona?'

'Isn't she with you? She went back!' Chrissie finds her voice, shouting over the roar of the fire. 'She went to look for you.'

Panic rising in his chest, Cal plunges his fingers into the pocket of his jeans, scrabbling for his phone. He passes it to Chrissie.

'Call 999. If you need to, run. There was a man here, Chrissie, I don't know where he went.'

'Go, Dad, go to Shona.'

Cal races to the back door and shoves it open. Smoke billows in great clouds, choking him, forcing him back for a moment.

'Shona!'

He screams her name, dropping to his knees and pulling his T-shirt over his face. He can see flames through the kitchen, in the lounge. Where is she? Propelled by fear, Cal crawls into the kitchen, unable to see much in the dark, trying to stay beneath the thick blanket of smoke and remember any fire safety he's ever been taught. He crawls around the room, one arm outstretched, trying to feel for her.

If she was in a bedroom she could have come out of a window so she must be here somewhere. Cal crawls fast into the living room, where the flames are undulating on the far wall, oddly beautiful. Illuminated by the fierce light, he gasps as he sees her, a shape on the floor, overcome by smoke. He knows how fast this can happen, that he needs to get her out.

Rising to a stooped position, he makes it to Shona's head and grabs her under the arms, turning to drag her towards the back of the house, not daring to look at her face, not daring to think. Something beside him crackles and falls. He doubles his efforts and pulls her along the floor, coughing, trying to stay low.

The kitchen, which previously felt so dense in smoke, is a relief. He can see the doorway ahead, sense the dark night and the fresh air, the movement of a hovering shadow. Chrissie? All he needs to do is get there. It's a few metres. He's done it. But Shona is heavy in his arms, he can't breathe. His ribs are on fire with the pain from his beating. Cal feels himself slowing, crumpling. Without knowing how, he's on the floor, head ringing and face pressed to the wooden boards, sucking in desperate breath and choking.

Keep going. He has to keep going.

Crawling now, getting closer.

'Dad?! Dad?!'

All he has to do is crawl towards Chrissie's voice. But all the power seems to have left his arms, like he's in a horrible dream where he's helpless, watching them suffocate.

And then there are hands on him, tugging. No! She shouldn't be in here. He wants to protest. *Stay outside.* Chrissie.

'Dad! Dad! You have to move.'

She slaps his cheek and he jerks back to himself, forcing his arms and legs into action, though it's treacly and slow. Where is Chrissie? He can no longer hear her. All he can do is try to drag himself free.

Just as he thinks it is hopeless there is air. Fresh clean, beautiful air. Rolling onto his side and coughing, coughing, the taste of burnt ash filling his mouth. Cal's eyes open and his mind starts to clear as he drinks in oxygen and looks up to see a sky full of stars, twinkling relentlessly through the acrid smoke.

He lifts his head, senses whirling. Chrissie is kneeling next to Shona, calling to her, shaking her. Cal crawls to them.

'Chrissie? Is she okay?'

His voice is hoarse, painful.

'I think she's breathing, but she isn't waking up. Help me, please, someone help us.'

Rising to his knees, Cal shakes Shona, calling to her to come back to them, remembering how he shook her awake only a little while ago on the sofa. She needs to wake up. He has to wake her.

'Come on, love, come on.'

The sound of sirens pierces the background. In the far distance, Cal can see the lights of the fire engines thundering along the A96 then vanishing from view on the corner. Above them, the barn is a vision of hell.

CHAPTER FIFTY-EIGHT

BELLA

Bella jumps up from the sofa and rushes to the kitchen, where her laptop is plugged in and charging, the dishwasher singing the end of its cycle. Standing at the kitchen island, she types in the address of a news website, frantic for more information about Merrick. But, when she finds it, there is no satisfaction. The brief story contains barely any information at all – marked as breaking news, details to follow.

Pacing the room, she chews at her fingernails and waits for the journalists to update the story, stopping to refresh the page every minute or two.

'Come on, come on,' she mutters under her breath, nerves singing with tension.

Should she wake Noah? No, what could he possibly do to help? After a few minutes of agonising and refreshing, Bella forces herself to stop and make a cup of tea. She studiously ignores the laptop, making the drink weak and milky and wiping up the drips she's made on the surface slowly, eking out the moments.

Eventually, she draws up a stool at the island and settles herself with the laptop in front of her, hands clasped around the mug. She'll wait until dawn if she has to. But it doesn't take that long. After twenty minutes, the story refreshes into a fuller version and she leans into the screen, hungry for the details.

> Lachlan Merrick, the man convicted of the 1986 murders of Allegra Carlo and her young daughters Gail and Philippa, has been taken to hospital after an incident in his jail cell. The BBC understands that Merrick was found unconscious following a possible suicide attempt. Prison officers are believed to have revived him at the scene and he was transferred by ambulance an hour ago. There has been no update on his condition.
>
> Merrick admitted killing Allegra and her daughters in the late eighties. The crime shocked the nation for its brutality and he was sentenced to life imprisonment. Merrick has been the subject of a recent true crime podcast, with some speculation that he may not have been solely responsible for the deaths…

Bella doesn't need to read any more, doesn't need to think about the fact that this development will splash her family's trauma on the front of the tabloids again. Her breathing is shallow and her hands are trembling. She doesn't know what to think. Did he try and kill himself? Was that because of something she said to him? She presses on the thought to see if it makes her feel guilty. It doesn't – the sensation is something more akin to discomfort, coarse fabric rubbing on her conscience.

The house is grave-like, still. She doesn't want to have to break this news to Noah and the boys. Somehow in the last few months, she has become a fragile object to be tiptoed around and Bella doesn't want them looking at her like that anymore – she wants to be the strong, engaged parent she thinks her mother would have been. She was that person before she heard his voice, standing in this room. It broke her apart and she wants to be put back together.

In fact, there is only one person she wants to talk to right now, and the realisation that this is the case shocks her. She thought she was done with him, that she had firmly closed that door, but standing in the quiet of the night, Bella finds she really wants to speak to Cal.

CHAPTER FIFTY-NINE

CAL

Cal leans forward and takes the biggest breath his scorched lungs can manage. Tilting Shona's head back and pinching her nostrils together to make a seal, he breathes into her mouth, terrified that he will only be making things worse. The breeze is carrying the smoke from their blazing home away from them, but the air tastes of ash and heat.

Again and again, he breathes for her as the sirens travel closer, each moment taking forever as he contemplates losing her. All his fault. She went back to look for him.

Just as a fire engine thunders down their driveway, Shona starts coughing and convulsing. Chrissie calls her name and he grips her hand, unable to draw enough breath to speak. She's drifting in and out of consciousness but alive, definitely alive for now. They roll her onto her side and Chrissie runs to guide the first responders to them. Not that they could miss the scene – the burning house must be visible for miles.

Kneeling on the gravel, Cal feels the tears mingling with the soot on his face. As the ambulance pulls up to them, Chrissie sinks down next to him, both of them holding onto Shona as if they can keep her in this world by force of will. He wants to ask his daughter if she's okay, but he can't. He can't say anything. They're both crying.

Then there are people. So many people. Paramedics with oxygen and clear voices, moving them aside, asking them questions, taking control. The terror of responsibility subsides – but into its place slides the worse reality.

Another fire engine joins the first, men and women spilling efficiently from each, knowing what to do, moving fast. Shona is given oxygen, Chrissie wrapped in a foil blanket. Cal is helpless, watching.

A man grips his arm, gentle and commanding.

'Where is the mains water point?'

Cal staggers to his feet and guides the fire officers to the hatch, watching as they connect more hoses and train them on the roof of the house, a great blissful arc of water that it seems will never be enough, turning to steam where it hits the burning rafters.

Unable to confront it, he tugs the arm of one of the firefighters, signalling that he needs him to follow.

'We need to get you seen to,' the firefighter shouts.

But Cal shakes his head and pulls him round to the other side of the house. His heart breaks all over again when he sees the shape of the dog on the lawn.

'Please,' he croaks. 'Please help him.'

'What happened to him?'

'The man who did this hurt him. He tried to protect me.'

The enormity of it hits Cal as he sinks to his knees, sobbing, and buries his nose in Rocket's fur. His brave, brave dog. Only a few minutes ago he was snuffling in the darkness, nosing out night smells. He didn't deserve this. Cal has to leave him, he needs to go back to Shona. It feels like he's being torn apart.

'Hey, his tail is moving!'

'What?'

Cal lifts his face and stares, his hands still stroking the dog's soft nose.

'Rocket? Good boy. Good dog.'

Rocket's tail thumps the floor again. Twice. Then his nose twitches and he tries to move because he'd do anything for Cal, follow him anywhere.

'No, no, stay,' he says, lying down next to the dog. 'Good boy. Good dog… stay.'

'Hold on, be right back.'

The fireman runs around the side of the barn out of sight.

Cal puts his head close to Rocket's, planting kisses on his fur, trying to soothe him, hoping he's not in pain. A moment later, the fireman is back with a colleague and a stretcher.

'We'll get him to a vet,' the woman says, rubbing Cal's shoulder. 'Poor wee dug. You go, pal, go to your wife. We've got him.'

He can barely see for the tears in his eyes and the smoke in the air. He kisses Rocket's head one last time, then staggers back to the other side of the house, not caring about the screaming pain in his own ribs or the destruction of his home. Only caring that his family are alive. For now.

CHAPTER SIXTY

CAL

Cal travels in the ambulance with Shona, following Chrissie, who has been whisked away first, holding tight to his hand before she went, her eyes big and afraid. He felt like the worst parent ever for not going with her. The fact that the paramedic advised him to stay with Shona makes him cold inside.

'She's going to be okay,' were the last words he said to his daughter, but he has the most awful, wrenching feeling that may not be true.

He keeps having flashbacks to a time he almost lost her in the past when they were run off the road in the Highlands. Helpless, he holds Shona's hand as the paramedic monitors her and the blue lights take them flying along the roads to Aberdeen. Cal stares at her face, imprinting her features in his mind and begging whatever higher power might exist to make her well, terrified that she is about to be taken away from him forever. It's all his fault. His work has endangered her again and all for his stupid quest to find justice for people who don't even want it.

'Hold on,' he tells her, over and over. 'I'm here.'

Her face is streaked with soot and her fingers are loose in his. They both reek of smoke. He cannot begin to care what they have lost back at the barn right now. The blaze was under control by the time they left, but not before fire seemed to have ripped through everything. None of it matters.

'We'll be there really soon,' the paramedic reassures him as they watch Shona's eyes flutter open and closed. 'Keep talking to her, we need her to stay awake. Shona, quine, stay with us.'

Cal squeezes Shona's hand again, relieved to feel a small response in her fingers this time. He half registers that he feels shaky and awful, sore from the pummelling he took from the arsonist but he shoves that aside. His mind is fixed on Shona as well as teeming with guilt at Chrissie having to travel to the hospital without him. A police officer told him they are taking Rocket to a twenty-four-hour vet. Cal has utterly failed to protect those around him.

The drive to the hospital seems to take forever, but they finally reach accident and emergency and the paramedics swing back the doors to slide Shona's stretcher out of the vehicle, Cal following in their wake as they rush her to the waiting doctors. Cal leans over the trolley to kiss her and whisper goodbye before she is wheeled away from them. He cranes his neck to watch her go through a set of double doors and then they flap closed and she is gone.

Chrissie is there and he puts one arm around her as they watch the trolley disappear.

-

The next hour is filled with checks – both he and Chrissie's blood oxygen levels are supplemented with high-flow oxygen. Cal's ribs are prodded and wrapped in a bandage, painkillers are administered and a cut above his eye that he hadn't even noticed is glued together. Once he has been given the all-clear, Cal calls his ex-wife, Allie, and tells her about the attack. He's braced for anger but she immediately switches into crisis resolution and they make plans for her to travel to Aberdeen in the morning.

'Shona's strong,' she says softly. 'She'll fight. And I know you'll be blaming yourself, Cal, but you are not responsible for what a homicidal lunatic decides to do.'

'Thanks Al,' he says, his voice breaking. It's both painful and beautiful that they've reached this stage, he realises. They're not in touch day-to-day, but she knows him better than almost anyone.

'Stay in touch,' she says. 'I'll be there as soon as I can.'

He passes the phone to Chrissie then paces the hallway, his eyes on the doors Shona was taken through, willing them to open.

A couple of police officers have been and gone, taking a brief statement from him and Sarah's contact details for more information on Wayne Gandy and the podcast investigation. They rapidly realised Cal was in no position to go through it all carefully. Smoke-addled and crazed with worry, until he knows how Shona is doing, Cal can't concentrate at all. He alternates between checking on his daughter and returning to the corridor to wait for news until finally a woman with a stethoscope around her neck comes through the doors.

Cal feels dizzy as he watches her approach, desperately trying to read the neutral expression on her face to predict whether she's bringing good or bad news. His stomach drops away like he's freefalling.

'Are you Shona's partner, Cal?'

'Yes. I am. How is she doing?'

'She's doing okay. We intubated her to give her plenty of oxygen and she's brighter than she was. We're going to need to keep her in for observations until later today at least. I'm worried about the amount of smoke she's inhaled and she has some small burns. But I'm cautiously optimistic. She's asking for you if you'd like to see her?'

Relief makes him weak and Cal staggers a little as he follows the doctor to Shona's bedside. She looks small against the bright white sheets. They've cleaned the soot from her face and her blue eyes crease in a semblance of a smile when she sees him at the door. She lifts one hand and he rushes to her, taking it and pressing kisses into her palm.

'Oh love,' he says. 'I'm sorry.'

Shona can't speak with the tube in her mouth, but she fixes her gaze on him and shakes her head. Her eyes then widen as she looks behind him and she starts making noises that send a nurse nearby towards them in alarm. Cal realises what she's asking.

'Chrissie's fine. Don't worry. She's asleep down the hallway. Allie is on her way.'

Shona sinks back against her pillow, twin tears spilling down her cheeks. Her grip on his hand tightens as she relaxes and lets heavy eyes close. Cal sinks onto a chair next to her and holds tight, watching as she sinks into sleep.

Eventually he realises he needs to update Chrissie, so he slides his hand from beneath Shona's and stands, uncomfortable at the seized position he's been in. He reaches for his pocket and realises his phone is crammed in there, digging into him. Pulling it free, Cal glances at the screen. It seems strange that this ordinary object is still here when so much else around him has gone. It's a vestige of a previous existence. A line of missed calls appears on the home screen, like a dull thud of memory.

As he walks back into the hallway he thumbs open the screen to see it is Bella who has been trying to reach him. Has she heard about the fire? She can't have done, surely? It's three in the morning and no one knows. Filled with foreboding, Cal hesitates, then presses her number and waits in the sterile corridor, aware again how he stinks of smoke and his eyes are scratchy.

'Cal? I'm sorry it's so late… early, I mean. Did I wake you? Have you seen the news?'

'What?' Cal knows he sounds abrupt but he can't think properly. 'You didn't wake me. I'm at the hospital in Aberdeen.'

'Hospital? Why? Are you okay? What's happened?'

'Yes. We're okay. It's been a close shave. Someone set fire to our house.'

Bella's shocked gasp confirms that she had no idea.

'Who would do that?'

'I think it was someone connected to Wayne Gandy, Bella. He warned me off the case and instead I've taken my recordings to the police. He's the kind of person to go down fighting. I should have realised. I've been complacent, consumed by the need to know, no matter the cost.'

'Cal it's *my fault.*'

She sounds stricken and he shakes his head even though she can't see him.

'No, Bella,' he says firmly. 'It really isn't on you.'

The line muffles and he knows she's crying. He makes an effort to soften his tone.

'Why are you calling?'

She clears her throat. 'It doesn't matter – it's not the right time. It can wait.'

Cal is tempted to agree with her, glancing down the long corridor with its pale walls and stretch of dull linoleum to where a light is flickering like a paranormal phenomenon, but something in her voice makes him pause.

'Tell me.'

'It's been on the news. Lachlan Merrick is in hospital. They say he tried to kill himself.'

Her voice trembles as she speaks.

A cold feeling snakes down Cal's spine.

'Tonight?'

'Yes. Only a few hours ago. They don't know if he's going to pull through.'

The timing sends chills through him. All of a sudden he can't breathe. His mind racing, Cal sets off down the corridor, not sure where he's going, just needing to move, though he is too far away to help.

'Bella, wake Noah and the boys,' he tells her. 'Go somewhere else.'

'What? Do you mean…?'

'I don't know. I'm overreacting. But don't take the chance.'

'Okay,' Bella says. 'We'll do it.' Then she hesitates, tears coming more audibly now. 'I owe you an apology. I can't tell what's real anymore. I don't know what to do. What would my mother think of me and the mess I've made?'

'No,' he says, fierce in his sudden certainty. 'We're so close. We're not going to give up. This is the moment. The worst possible second. All it means is we've almost done it.'

'You really think so?'

'I do. Keep the faith.'

'Keep the faith,' she whispers back, and then she's gone.

Cal keeps walking along the hallway, agitation growing inside him. What are the odds? His house set alight, his family threatened and left for dead, then something happens to Merrick at the exact same moment? He wishes his senses weren't so dulled by exhaustion and the pain in his body.

Gandy. It has to be him, or the mysterious friend he was doing a favour for. Is the property developer cleaning house, trying to ensure there's no one left to testify against him? It's audacious, and yet what he knows of the man tells him it's possible. He thinks of the reptile eyes and the meanness of him, the threat he felt in his proximity. Another chill runs through him. What else might he be doing to ensure silence?

Cal finds himself walking faster, his ribs sending shooting pains as he moves. His mind scrambles over the thoughts, putting two and two together… only he's not sure he's adding the numbers correctly. One thought overwhelms all others. What if Merrick isn't the only prisoner in danger?

Abruptly, Cal comes to a halt, his body aching. The insidious, darkest notion fills him. He could do nothing. Does he care what happens to that man? No. He could simply stop here, turn around and walk back to the people he loves. Plausible deniability intact.

He closes his eyes. So much grief and loss caused by one individual. The thick beef of his jowls, his cruel eyes and his inflated muscles form a clear picture. Cal can see every detail. Why would he even think of saving that monster? But just as he has resolved to go back, another face replaces that hated one. A stronger image. Dancing eyes and a crimson-lipped smile, her red curls falling over her shoulders, the scent of her perfume mingling so strongly with the lingering ash of the fire that he immediately opens his eyes to be sure she's not there beside him.

Margot was better than the evil that took her from them. She was a light that still burns fiercely for him, a part of his identity. Her lively independence and strength have been the blueprint for every woman he has loved since. He finds and adores those qualities in his daughter every day. What would his sister say right now, if she were here?

Slowly and tentatively at first, Cal puts one foot in front of the next, creeping along the corridor. As he moves, his steps become more deliberate, chasing away the dark thoughts and temptation that have threatened to consume him. When he reaches the electric doors, he steps into the cold night knowing that while some would do nothing, he is not that person and he will never be.

Outside, his breath forms clouds and the chill pinches his skin with witches' fingertips, but finally he can breathe. Cal presses his phone to his car.

When she answers, Foulds is instantly awake, unquestioning in her trust that his call matters. There are always people, he thinks, brimming with emotion, who will fight for justice with you. Who will take the mantel when you can't manage another step.

'Listen,' he says. 'There's not much time to explain, but I think someone's going to try and kill Jason Barr. Now.'

'He's in prison.'

'I know. It might even be too late.'

'Why are you warning me?'

The wonder in her voice startles him. Maybe he's mad.

'I wish I knew.'

Cal hangs up the call, swaying with tiredness and emotion. The hospital entrance doors slide open and shut repeatedly. He stands, frozen, the world imploding around him. All he can see is a cell and a makeshift rope. A moment of reckoning.

CHAPTER SIXTY-ONE

CAL

When he wakes in the early dawn, Cal's face is pressed to Shona's bed and Chrissie is asleep in the chair opposite. She is wrapped in a blanket with her head tilted back, grubby and tired, her hair a stinking halo around her, but she is there and alive. His phone, which he has charged in the nurses' station, is vibrating beneath his chest.

Guiltily, he answers, whispering his greeting to Foulds.

He watches Shona's breath easing in and out, her face mercifully blank with sleep.

'You were right.'

'What?'

'All hell has broken losc. We're trying to get in front of it before it hits the media.'

Cal rubs his face, still lost in sleep and confused about where he is and what's happening.

'He's… is he…?'

'They were just in time. He's pretty beaten up, by all accounts.'

Cal feels blank horror. Barr didn't die. Is that good or bad?

'So someone targeted us all on the same night? Me, Merrick, Barr?'

'It seems that way. We've sent protection officers to Bella's house just in case.'

'She won't be there. I warned her.'

Foulds sighs. 'Well done. I don't know who we can trust. This is a mess big enough to make those at the top start asking questions. There will be interviews coming your way. The Scottish prisons service has a crisis meeting planned for nine a.m.'

'It's Gandy – they need to look at him.'

'Wayne Gandy is in Spain. He travelled there yesterday.'

'That's a bit too convenient if you ask me.'

'Well, people are going to ask you, so get anything you've got ready to turn over.'

They ring off and Cal sits staring into the grey sky outside the window, emotion roiling inside him. Ever since he found out Jason Barr was responsible for Margot's death, he has fantasised about him dying or suffering. Now that he's been attacked, it feels a hollow victory. Bringing him pain isn't going to help.

He sees Chrissie watching him, her eyes wide and fearful.

'It's okay, love,' he whispers. 'Go back to sleep. Mum will be here really soon.'

'Is it him? Jason Barr?'

He shakes his head. 'Someone hurt him in prison, that's all. I'm sorry I woke you.'

She yawns and he watches as her eyes close, sleep claiming her quickly after the trauma.

Cal, on the other hand, is now wide awake. Gandy's audacity in striking three times in one night astounds him. The chances the man is going to willingly come back from the Med to answer questions are slim to none. He's pretty sure Gandy's yacht is berthed near Barcelona.

He has money and connections in many non-extraditable locations. His heart clenches at the thought the unpleasant kingpin has got away.

Stretching his neck to release the kinks, Cal thinks back to their conversation in the glass penthouse. There were definitely clues that someone else behind the scenes was owed a favour or pulling the strings with this operation, but who? His mind snags on the man in the photograph – is he the missing link?

CHAPTER SIXTY-TWO

CAL

The taxi drops them at the end of the drive to their ravaged house, but neither he nor Shona can face it yet so they stop to see Mary first. She answers the door straight-backed and beady-eyed. Rocket waddles towards them, tail wagging and squeaking with excitement. Cal drops to the ground to ruffle the dog's fur and rub his ears, and in a few moments his face is wet with Rocket's delighted slobber. He feels tearful at remembering how the Lab defended him.

'Vet says he'll be sore for a wee while and he's to take it easy,' Mary says. 'He's on more drugs than I am.'

She holds out a brand-new leash she must have bought for him. So many people have rallied around the brave dog. The fire fighters have sent him a Fireman Sam toy and a box of meaty treats.

'Here, take him down with you, he needs a toddle. I'll put the kettle on for when you come back. I'm happy to have him longer if you need. Betty in the shop found a bone or two for him and we've been just fine. The police have been in to talk to me a couple of times but I didn't hear anything that night, I'm afraid.'

Surprising all of them, Shona steps forward and envelops Mary in a tight hug.

'Ach there's no need.' Mary brushes away the affection, but as they turn to make the trek along the track to their property, Cal catches the pleased look on her face.

At the head of the path, he reaches for Shona's hand and threads their fingers together.

'Ready?'

She nods.

'Let's get this over with.'

Rocket snuffles the verge as they approach, sneezing at scents he finds and then shaking his head so his ears flap. The sound is music to Cal. They follow the dog slowly, keeping the pace down for Shona, newly out of hospital.

'I can smell it,' she says, sadly.

Cal can too – the stale after-smoke of bonfire fills his nostrils. It takes him back to the fear and chaos of that night. He reminds himself that they all escaped relatively unscathed. It doesn't help to dwell on what might have happened. Shona is walking beside him, not lying insensible on the floor, overcome by heat and smoke. All the same, he thinks it's going to take some time before he can close his eyes at night and not remember the moment he saw her there.

Gradually, they get closer to the structure, which has police tape flapping from the door, though the fire investigators have now finished their appraisal. Nearer to, Cal can see that the stone walls still stand, but the roof has caved in at one end of the building, and the wood cladding has gone entirely, the glass shattered or melted, leaving blackened walls and a hollow look, the shuttered eyes of the building staring at them, like the set of a disaster film.

Cal glances at Shona and sees the tears in her eyes. He wraps his arms around her and she buries her head in his shoulder.

'It's just stuff,' he hears her say, the words muffled.

'We'll rebuild it. It's going to be just like it was before, I promise. Better, even.'

The woodshed and their cars have survived the blaze, apart from damage to the body work, which is peppered with burn marks where hot sparks landed. They stand beside them and look up at their home, silenced by the scale of the damage and their escape from it. The windows and front door have been boarded to stop looters, and investigators told them they managed to lock the back door at the intact end of the barn. Cal digs in his pocket for the key and holds it out on his palm.

'Shall we?'

'I didn't think we were supposed to go in, in case it isn't sound?'

'We can peer in. But I won't if you'd rather not.'

Shona swallows, her face paler than usual. Rocket is pressed against her legs, his nose twitching and his tail low.

'Maybe just a look.'

They round the end of the barn, and for a moment you wouldn't know there was anything out of the ordinary about it – if you couldn't smell the smoke. Cal slots the key into the lock and the door opens inwards to a gloomy scene. He turns on the torch on his phone and steps into the house.

'Cal…' Shona warns.

'I won't go far, love.' Rocket follows him to the threshold but he holds out a hand. 'Wait, boy, stay. Good dog.'

The animal whines his disapproval and thumps his tail twice, uncertain.

There is obvious smoke damage, but he opens a cupboard by the back door to see the dog's food and bowls next to lines of cleaning products. He closes it up again, unnerved at this evidence of their mundane normality, when so much of it has been shattered by the petrol bomb. Fire investigators have done their analysis and agreed the cause is arson. They've taken pictures and tested for accelerant. It all backed up Cal's memories of that night, though any footprints or car tracks of the perpetrator were mashed into the ground by the efforts to put out the fire. Now the police are pursuing their enquiries, but he can't imagine they're ever going to know who threw the bottle. In a way that doesn't matter – he's more interested in who ordered the hit.

'Are you coming back?' Shona's voice, soft and sad, brings him back to himself. He hates hearing her subdued – wants to restart the smile in her tones and bring her gorgeous sense of humour back. Even before the fire, he knew how deeply he felt about her. Nearly losing her has only crystallised that. A thought strikes him.

'One second...'

Cal tiptoes into the edge of the kitchen, winded by the sight of the blackened walls and rubble from the roof that he can see further in. Forcing his gaze back, he scans the surface in the corner and grins to see what he's looking for – Shona's phone plugged in where she always charges it at night and their car keys hanging on the little hooks. A picture of them with Chrissie is still on the wall. Feeling guilty for straying in so far, he scoops everything up and darts back to her.

'Look! We have transport. And... this.'

Shona looks like she's going to tell him off but then her face breaks into the smallest smile at the sight of the framed photograph and her phone.

'You shouldn't have done that, but thank you.'

'I think I left my laptop in the car, but I might be mistaken,' he says. 'Shall we go and check?'

Back round the house, Rocket still stuck to their heels, Cal clicks open the boot. There, discarded in a tired moment, is his laptop and the file he's been using for his notes on the podcast. He feels a mix of emotions looking at them, touching his bag. His hand lands on a hard lump in the side pocket. He digs his fingers in and they close around a small box.

Turning back, his heart thumping, he sees more tears running down Shona's face.

'I can't stop leaking,' she says, wiping her eyes.

'Oh, love.'

He hugs her tight.

'It doesn't matter,' she says, wiping her eyes. 'It's just *things* and we're all okay and that's what matters, but…' Her voice wobbles. 'It feels like everything is gone and we're going to have to start all over again.'

Cal wipes her cheeks dry and kisses them.

'I know,' he says, 'but look, starting again could be fun. You always regretted that kitchen worktop colour and now you'll have to choose a new one.' Her mouth twitches at his poor effort to cheer her up, though the tears continue. Cal takes a deep breath and his heart fills with clarity and certainty that takes him easily to his knees.

He holds out the small box in front of him, shaky with the asking but determined this is what he wants more than anything. Shona gasps and her hands fly to her mouth. Blue eyes peer over the top of her fingers, searching his face for meaning. He can't tell what she's thinking and suddenly his mouth is dry. But this is the truth and there's no going back.

'Shona,' he says. 'There is no one else I would rather start again with than you. Everything in my life is better because we are together. You are the smartest, funniest and kindest woman I know, and the most beautiful. I would rather be standing outside a burned building with you than anywhere else in the world.'

Shona's laugh bursts free and his chest fills with warmth.

'Will you do me the honour of marrying me? I want us to be together forever.'

She presses her hands to her mouth and looks at the gleaming ring, the diamond and sapphires sparkling even in this low light.

'Where did that come from?'

'This was my grandmother's ring. It's been on my mind for a while… I've just been waiting for the right moment.' She doubles over in laughter. 'This is not going quite how I imagined doing this, I'll admit.'

'You are such a romantic,' she laughs, wiping her face with the back of her hand and then pulling him to his feet. 'Expensive restaurant? Nope. Exotic holiday destination? Nope. Burned out shell of a building?'

'It's perfect,' Cal says. '*You're* here.'

Shona's expression softens into seriousness. Stepping closer, she takes his face in her hands and kisses him, slowly and deeply. Cal loses himself in the sensation, the taste of her. He can no longer smell the ash and soot. Everything else may be different, but *this*, this is the same.

When she lets go of him, he meets her gaze and sees a trace of the merriment he loves – it is still there beneath the surface and they will get through this like they get through everything else. He takes the ring out of the box.

'Is that a yes?'

CHAPTER SIXTY-THREE

EPISODE SEVEN: A POWERFUL MAN

Wayne Gandy is a man of means and a figure of influence. If you met him at the Liverpool races or a charity event, you might think the wealthy Manchester-based developer was a pillar of the community – as clean and shining as the towers he creates. You would be dead wrong. Finding Justice *has been working on an exposé of Gandy's supposedly legitimate business interests as part of our investigation into the deaths of Allegra Carlo and her daughters.*

We have discovered that Gandy was aware of Jason Barr's possible involvement in the crime just after it was committed. He said nothing. Not only has Gandy protected Barr from the consequences of that crime and allowed another man to take sole responsibility for the attacks, he ensured that Barr was free to continue hurting and killing other women. He has blood on his hands.

In today's episode, you will hear from the man himself that he knew about the crime and decided to do nothing. This undercover recording has been passed to police. We can also show that we have evidence Gandy's businesses imported vast quantities of drugs into the UK from the 1980s to 2000s, and that his now-legitimately run businesses are based on criminal enterprises and laundered money. Gandy has decorated the cities of northern England and

Scotland with glass towers while fuelling the grimy underworld of crime and poverty that comes with drug addiction.

Wayne Gandy hired sophisticated accountants to conceal his links to many of these businesses and police forensic accountancy specialists are combing through the details. Greater Manchester Police is leading that investigation. A spokesman said:

'Some of this could take months, but I can confirm that Wayne Gandy's bank accounts have now been frozen as part of a proceeds-of-crime investigation. We will be looking to seize assets in the near future.'

Gandy clearly thought he'd got away with everything. But now it's time to face the music.

CHAPTER SIXTY-FOUR

CAL

Lachlan Merrick is heavily guarded in the hospital – a level of security that seems unnecessary to Cal given the state of the convict at the heart of it. The man is obviously weakened by the attempt on his life, wasted and see-through, though he is tight lipped about who it was who targeted him, claiming he was asleep and didn't see their faces. It's an understandable reaction considering he is due to return to the prison to serve the rest of his sentence.

Cal and Bella pause in the corridor. Cal checks his recording equipment is working, then together they pass the two men on the door and enter the room, where a nurse is taking observations, a blood-pressure cuff round Merrick's arm. Melissa sits, anxious-faced, by the side of his bed and her father's head rests listlessly on the pillow, though Cal sees his eyes track their movements, flicking from one to the other. Bella stays slightly behind as they edge into the small private room, filling it with even more discomfort than there already is.

Merrick looks at Melissa, seemingly for reassurance or permission, and she nods at him. Her arms are folded, legs crossed away from her father, giving the impression that she would rather be anywhere but here. He clears his throat, and when he speaks it's like rusted iron and regret.

'I'm sorry about what I said before.' He looks at Bella as he says this, then his eyes fall and he addresses the sheets covering him on the bed. 'It's not true that I don't remember anything.'

Cal feels Bella's intake of breath. He waits for her to speak but she doesn't say a word so he fills the silence.

'So you do know exactly what happened?'

Merrick shakes his head from side to side. 'I wish I didn't. I've tried to forget but I can't. It comes to me at night, in dreams. I haven't slept well since that day. I don't remember all of it. I was out of my face on the smack, so there are some chunks of time that are missing, but… I remember enough.'

'Why did you keep it quiet?' Cal asks. He's appalled that it's taken until now and an attempt on Merrick's life before he's willing to break his silence. He will never understand people who conceal the truth while others are suffering.

'Because I was where I was supposed to be.' He looks at Bella again. 'I wasn't lying about all of it. What happened to them *was* my fault. I shouldn't be trusted out in the world. I've sabotaged every parole hearing I've ever had. Everyone is better with me locked away. I deserve it.'

A single tear runs down the man's cheek and Cal feels Bella recoil.

'You knew Jason Barr?' he prompts, taking an old photograph from his pocket and trying to get Merrick to regroup. It's the one of Barr and Daisy in front of the car, evidence of a piece of the past that has had ripples through time.

The look of utter dread and fear on Merrick's face says it all. He nods, transfixed by the image, his eyes glazed with memory.

'That's him. He used to come and pick things up at the warehouse. Sometimes with another man – Oscar, Owen? But usually on his own. He said his boss didn't trust anyone else. He was strong and confident – everything I wasn't. We got talking. He'd come and bum cigarettes off me, never seemed in a hurry to head back.'

Merrick turns his head away from them. The atmosphere in the room is tense and still, all eyes on him. 'I wish I'd never met him.'

'So how did he find out about Allegra and her family?' Cal asks softly.

'We were outside having a fag this one time and I could see her and her girls in the distance, crossing the field. I told him about her.' He closes his eyes. 'I was boasting to him, I said some stupid things about how pretty she was,' he swallows, 'about what I'd like to do to her. He was big and worked out and I was weedy and I wanted to impress him.' He looks fearfully at Cal. 'I was just talking shit. I used to watch her – I went too far with that, I know I did – but I would never have done anything. Not really. I didn't know what he was like. I didn't know what he'd do!'

'How long had you been watching her?'

Merrick closes his eyes as if he can't bear to look at them.

'Since they moved in. I saw the lorry on the day they arrived. She was gorgeous, but it was more than that. She had these beautiful little kiddies, and a dog and she was always out walking with them, smiling, having fun. My life… wasn't like that when I was a laddie. I just wanted it to be… you know…' He fixes his gaze on Cal with desperate eyes. 'I wanted to be part of it.'

Bella suppresses a sob. Cal wants to comfort her, but he knows the most important thing he can do for her right now is get to the truth.

'I don't understand,' she says. 'I still don't understand what happened that day. I remember you were there. But it's *his* voice I hear when I sleep. It's driving me mad.'

Cal watches Merrick's eyes watering. He looks at Melissa for help.

'Come on, Dad,' she says, the word sounding foreign on her lips. 'They need to know what happened.'

The room is silent and still, save for the machines monitoring Merrick.

'Please,' he says, 'can I have some water?'

A look of disgust on her face, Melissa picks up a cup and holds it so he can reach the straw. Some of the liquid trickles down the side of his chin. The convicted killer sinks back into his pillow, exhausted by the effort.

'Go on,' Cal says.

Merrick closes his eyes.

'I'm sorry,' he whispers. 'I'm so sorry. I want to die. They should have let me die.'

'After it happened, you could have told someone,' Cal says. 'He's been out there hurting other people. He killed my sister later that same year.'

Merrick's eyes jerk to Cal in panic and dread.

'He threatened me. Said he'd kill me if I told anyone.'

'I don't believe you,' Melissa shouts at him, emotion exploding from her. 'Why are you so weak? You cared more about what happened to you than saving other people! You're a coward.'

He shakes his head back and forth, emphatically.

'No, Melissa, no it wasn't like that, I promise. I *am* a coward, but…'

But his daughter stands, disgusted. 'I've heard enough. I never want to see you again, ever. You're nothing to me. Less than nothing.' She looks at Bella, tears running down both their faces, mirrors of grief and pain. 'I'm so sorry.'

'No, Melissa, wait, please,' Merrick pleads. The prone man lies bubbling and helpless as she walks away from him.

'He knew about *you*!'

She halts. All three of them do, shocked by his outburst.

Merrick's chest is heaving and he's clammy and pale. Cal can see the marks on his neck where he fought to be free of the ligature.

'What?' Melissa says, so quietly Cal can barely hear her.

'I'd told him your mum was pregnant. That I was going to be a dad. Afterwards, he said if I told anyone about him, ever, that he would find you and he'd do what he did to them.' Merrick is openly sobbing now. 'He said the most horrible things. I'd seen what he did. He killed those babies. He killed them all.'

This, finally, something that Cal believes.

Tears run down Melissa's cheeks.

'I wanted a family like that. I wanted my kids to have what they had. I haven't been a father to you. I know that,' he says. 'But this was the one thing I could do: keep you safe. That's all I had to offer you.'

It's hard watching Merrick cry so pathetically. The air around them is heavy.

Cal waits, torn between needing to listen and wanting to get Bella out of there.

'There's one more thing you can do,' Melissa says, her gaze darting to them, then back to her father.

'What? I'll do anything. I promise.'

Melissa takes a breath and it seems to lift her a little taller.

'You need to tell them,' she says. 'You need to tell them exactly what happened that day.'

CHAPTER SIXTY-FIVE

BELLA

She cannot stay in this hot, enclosed space with him a moment longer. Finding the strength in her legs, Bella spins and bolts from the room, past the guards on the door and down the corridor until she finds a line of empty seats and drops into them, spent. Even after all of this, she doesn't have the full picture. Snippets of memory and fractions of dreams haunt her. She knows it was awful, bloody, terrible. But not knowing has its own horror.

Her chest hitches and the tears keep coming. After a moment, Bella hears footsteps coming towards her along the hall and she thinks it's Cal, but when she looks up she sees Melissa, holding out a tissue to her and pressing another to her own face. After a beat, Bella takes it, and the other woman perches beside her on the bank of chairs, leaving a seat between them.

'He'll do it. He's going to go on the record.'

Bella wipes her eyes, unable to stem the flow of tears.

'I'll go, if you want me to. I understand you might not want to talk to me.'

It is tempting to lash out at Melissa, the child Merrick sinned so hard to protect. But the fight seems to have fled her body. Bella shakes her head.

'It's not your fault. You're not responsible.'

'I hate that I'm related to him.'

Bella thinks of her own dad, tireless and strong, remaking their lives after the worst possible thing that could happen to them. Then she thinks of the wreck of a man in the hospital room. The fact that he, too, loves his daughter. She reaches out and puts her hand on Melissa's. The two of them sit there in silence. She lets her thoughts drift to her mother and her sisters. That day is a distant nightmare. Finally, she has the chance to discover what really happened to her, to them.

A door closes further along the hallway and the two women turn to see the podcaster walking towards them, concern on his face. How does he keep doing this? So driven that he immerses himself in other people's pain over and over again. How does he kick to the surface? Bella cannot fathom it. She's grateful he does, but she doesn't want to drown in this pain forever. She needs to come up for air. In this moment, Bella decides. She knows what her mother would want. She's going to let Cal Lovett find the truth for her. But it will not define her. She's going to return to her family and *live*. The only act of defiance that matters.

CHAPTER SIXTY-SIX

EPISODE EIGHT: THE TRUTH WILL SET YOU FREE

This week, police divers searched the river close to where Allegra Carlo and her daughters were found on a hot June day in 1986. Working upstream from the beach where the girls played in the water in the hours before the attack, they searched the riverbed with their fingers, painstakingly looking for evidence. Buried in a cluster of rocks near the far shore, they found a rusted knife that has been there for almost forty years.

After being in the water for so long, it's unlikely much forensic evidence will remain, but, finally, police have the missing murder weapon. They know where the killer came from and escaped to. The picture is clearer now. This is because the man convicted of the murders, Lachlan Merrick, has finally broken his silence. This is Finding Justice *and I'm your host, Cal Lovett. Today we bring you an extended season finale. Listeners are warned that the contents of this episode are disturbing.*

'What happened that day, Lachlan? Start at the beginning.'

'It was hot. So hot. I was on shift and we had to keep taking breaks because of the weather. It wasn't like Scottish weather at all. Jason Barr came to pick up packages from the barn along from the unit where I worked and we got talking.'

'You and he had chatted sometimes before this? He knew you watched Allegra and her daughters when they were walking in the countryside. Tell us what you talked about that day.'

'I'd seen them, earlier, going to the river. I knew they were going swimming. I'd watched them do that once before. I told him… I told him I'd seen her get changed. That she was topless.'

'And what did Barr say?'

'He said we should go and take a look. So I got into his car with him… I showed him where to park in some woodland. From there you could walk along the river to where they swam. He'd given me some stuff.'

'You were high?'

'Yes. We were just watching them from the bushes and I was knackered and not seeing straight. I'd taken too much. It was so hot and I fell asleep for a moment. I don't think it was long but when I woke up he wasn't there and they were leaving the river.'

'What did you do?'

'I was on my own. I thought he'd got bored and left me. So I walked through the woods to go back the shorter way and when I got to the edge of the trees…'

'It's okay, Lachlan, take a moment.'

'He must have gone ahead to wait for them because he was lying in the field out of sight. I saw him jump up and… I heard her screaming. The two bigger girls ran and the dog was barking and barking at him. I went closer. I couldn't help it – he… hurt her. He used something to tie her hands and the baby was crying and crying so, he… stopped it.'

'Why didn't you help her?'

'I was so scared. I didn't know what to do and my head was all fuzzy and…' [Sobs] 'He looked at me when he did it. He kept looking at me. I thought he was my friend – I told him about them because they were special, they were perfect, a family. He watched me while he killed them, while he… hurt her. And it was like everything I loved, he hated. He saw how special they were too, but he wanted to destroy them. And he wanted me to

watch him do it. I hadn't seen who he was until that minute. I thought he was my friend but he was actually a monster.'

'Can you tell me what happened next?'

'I was a coward. I just stood there on the side of the wood and then the two girls... they ran back and I wanted to tell them not to, but... the bigger girl tried to help her mother and he pulled out a knife and he just stabbed her and he kept doing it. I didn't know he had a knife, I swear.

'Then the other girl... she tried to stop him and he hit her so hard that she went down and the dog bit his leg and he hit it too... It's the worst thing I've ever seen. He just kept doing it and then he looked at me and he smiled.' [Moans.]

'What did he do then?'

'He started walking back to me with the knife in his hand and I panicked. I thought I was next. I ran so fast, deeper and deeper into the woods. But he found me.'

'And he let you live?'

'He made me promise not to say a word. He told me what he would do to my girlfriend, to my baby... he said he knew people. I wish he'd killed me. I wish I'd died too. But I think he liked that I knew. He took something so special and he ruined it forever. And it's my fault. I told him about them. If it wasn't for me they'd still be alive.'

'Did you go back to the car together?'

'No. He left me there. When he was gone, I went back.'

'Okay Lachlan, deep breaths. Do you need to stop for a minute?'

'No. I need to say it. I've never told anyone. Not ever. I wanted to see if I could help her. I picked up her T-shirt and all the things that were scattered. I put the lunchbox in her bag and then I... I tried to stop the bleeding but it was so much, it was everywhere. He hurt her so badly. I used a towel to cover up the little one and then...'

'What happened?'

'The girl he hit. She moved.'

'Izzy Carlo wasn't dead.'

'The dog was lying on top of her in a little ditch. She must have been unconscious.'

'She remembers you. She saw your face.'

'I was going to pick her up, but she was so scared. I didn't know what to do and then a car came along the lane and the dog ran towards it and I knew they were going to see me, so I ran and hid behind the hedge. The man came over and I saw him be sick and I saw him find her and pick her up and run and so I knew…' [sobs]. 'I knew it was over.'

–

We can confirm that police are looking at Jason Barr as a second suspect after this podcast established he was in the area that day. We know he had access to the kind of yellow car that was spotted in the vicinity of the murder scene by independent witnesses, fitting Merrick's testimony.

In addition, further evidence has come to light. A stained child's swimming towel kept in Barr's possessions is now being tested by forensics labs for links to the crime. The case has been officially re-opened.

Given these developments, Lachlan Merrick's involvement and prison term will now be reviewed as he is prepared to testify that Jason Barr was the sole killer of Allegra, Gail and Philippa Carlo.

'This has changed everything we thought we knew about a notorious and bloody set of murders,' the Home Secretary told the Commons last week. 'The government is committed to reviewing all possible miscarriages of justice and to using modern scientific techniques to bring new prosecutions, where appropriate.'

When quizzed on Jason Barr, the minister refused to be drawn on speculation that the Carlos are the tip of the iceberg and that Jason Barr is responsible for a string of murders dating back to the late 1980s. We understand, however, that several police forces are reviewing cold cases with similarities.

Barr himself is currently unable to be interviewed. He has been placed in an induced coma after being attacked in his prison cell last week. It is not known if he will survive.

CHAPTER SIXTY-SEVEN

CAL

The final episode has gone out when Cal finds time and energy to put the last piece of the jigsaw in place. As predicted, Gandy has failed to return from Spain and has not been seen since the night of the arson attack, using his considerable resources and dubious connections to go to ground. He's been disavowed by reputable former colleagues and associates. Manchester City Council has taken back an award he was granted. They're renaming a hospital wing, former friends falling over each other to distance themselves from him.

Shona has gone back to work today, Chrissie is at university, and he has been reviewing his files in the static caravan they've placed on the land next to the barn, plans for the reconstruction of which are underway – on a grander scale than before, with an editing studio, library and upstairs bedrooms on the wish list when the insurance payout and the compensation from the production company come through.

He's decided to make his next series on Wayne Gandy, determined to ensure the connected criminal is brought to justice. An old BBC friend of his has an international private investigation company and they've discussed pooling resources and producing a TV documentary as well as a podcast. *Finding Justice* is expanding and Sarah is over the moon.

Focusing on Gandy seems a better idea than chasing Jason Barr's past. Barr lost a kidney in the beating he received in jail and the other was damaged. He'll be just well enough to sit in court for judgement, but he isn't going to be terrorising anyone else – there is lots of dialysis in his future.

The burning hatred he's felt for Barr for so long does seem to be fading, but Cal can't help but feel sad that he doesn't have direct justice for Margot. He will have to be content with watching the monster go down for other crimes. And that's definitely something. In time, he's hopeful it will be enough. At least Allegra, Gail, Philippa and Bella will be avenged. Foulds even thinks they'll be able to talk Barr into pleading guilty – and it's unlike her to be optimistic. Cal's heard that several journalists are sniffing around other unsolved cases. He'll let them take the baton.

In the meantime, he's been researching Gandy – looking through old newspaper articles and social media posts, talking to school friends and early colleagues, trying to build a picture of the web of people around the fallen-from-grace property developer. It's keeping him busy. It's also reminding him that there are other people out there who could have saved his sister and didn't.

Lifting the photograph from his desk, Cal feels that old firework of connection. He's known deep down, since he saw this picture in Gandy's Manchester penthouse, what it means, but the fire, the interview with Merrick and the ensuing furore has delayed him until now. He's been biding his time.

He sits back in his chair, lacing his fingers behind his head. It's a beautiful day outside. Summer is here. The sky is cloudless and insects are gorging on patches of clover. Workmen are replacing beams in the roof of the barn. It's time. Cal closes his laptop and reaches for his coat, smiling as Rocket lumbers to his feet.

'Want to come to Edinburgh, boy? Want to see Chrissie?'

At her name, the dog throws his head up and barks his agreement.

–

The drive south is easy enough. Cal parks at Edinburgh airport and he and Rocket take the last part of the journey on the tram, the dog a popular passenger, so happy to have his head rubbed by anyone and everyone. They disembark on Princes Street and he looks up at the majestic bulk of the castle, refreshed by the burst of sunlight that has broken through the claggy clouds. He's arranged to meet Chrissie in a couple of hours, but first he has one stop to make.

He and Rocket wait patiently on the street. He buys a cup of tea and watches the door of the courts. At five on the dot, the man he has been waiting for emerges, waving to a waiting bank of cameras and stopping to give a brief soundbite to a journalist. Jeremy Fishpool is expected to be confirmed as a judge next week. Well, he was.

Cal hangs back until he is done, then falls into step beside him.

'Now, look here, I've said all I'm able to today and…'

The words trail away as the advocate turns and sees who it is beside him. There's a momentary flicker before the bluster sweeps in – so easy to miss, but Cal sees it there and it further galvanises him. He waits a moment, letting Fishpool sweat as he matches his pace, stride for stride.

'It was you,' Cal says.

'I don't know what you're talking about.'

Fishpool glances around them, seemingly checking no one else is listening. Always mindful of image. His voice is thready and uncertain.

'You know, when I realised that you'd been acting for Gandy for years, I spent ages trying to work out what he had on you. It must have been something good for it to silence you over Merrick. But that's not it, is it? You've both got something on each other.'

'This means nothing to me, Mr Lovett.'

'Well, hear me out. I'm willing to believe you just did a really bad job with the Allegra Carlo case. After all, you were a junior advocate – you were working for a man later defrocked for drunkenness – and cutting corners probably felt justified given the public outcry. But you're not stupid, Jeremy. Somewhere along the way you must have realised that there were gaping holes in the case, that Merrick deserved someone to fight for him.'

Fishpool is staring ahead as if trying to pretend Cal isn't there. He knows he's getting to him.

'I suspect it's no coincidence that you started working for Gandy and his businesses around then. Maybe you knew he was protecting Jason Barr, or maybe you were just hooked by the money and the lavish lifestyle. It's a bit lost in the mists of time, but I know I'm close.'

'This is preposterous.'

'Fine, don't tell me. It makes no difference. Either way, the wrong man went down and you looked the other way. What's one drug addict locked up when he shouldn't be, eh? But then, Bella remembers something and I start investigating and you realise your earlier corruption or, let's give you the benefit of the doubt, incompetence, is about to be exposed just at the very moment you're being considered for a place in Scotland's judiciary. Not going to look good, is it?'

'This is a very pretty fairy tale, Mr Lovett,' the advocate says, his voice lofty, 'but that's all it is.'

'Maybe. But I do have some evidence that suggests otherwise. You've done legal work for almost all of Comet Holdings' businesses and we can connect all of that back to Wayne Gandy. You've been very careful not to be photographed publicly with him over the years, haven't you? Privately, you might have slipped a little.'

Cal holds out a copy of the picture he took of the one in Gandy's penthouse. In it, Fishpool and Gandy sit at what is obviously a lavish birthday party. The two men are deep in conversation, laughing. Gandy's hand on Fishpool's back. A cake sits on the table in front of them. Several very young women, girls even, are draped across the sofas around them.

Fishpool, brought to an abrupt halt, stares at him.

'I suggest you leave this well alone.'

'Or what? You'll huff and you'll puff and you'll blow my house down? You've already done that, Jeremy. I'm still here.'

'What you're suggesting is slanderous.'

'You both had a lot of dirt on each other, didn't you? So when you realised your past incompetence was about to be exposed, who else would you call on, but your old mate Wayne? He's the one with the connections to threaten me, to take out Merrick and Barr for you, to burn down my house. Never mind justice or decency as long as your way is clear to the bench? A shame that's not going to happen now.'

Fishpool's face is purple. He leans closer. The mask drops at last.

'We'll fucking destroy you,' he hisses.

'He's not here anymore, Jeremy. Gandy isn't going to fight your battles for you. You knew Lachlan Merrick was innocent and you bungled the case. Jason Barr should have been in jail but instead he murdered my sister. You are not going to destroy me. I'm in the process of taking you apart piece by piece. God knows what else you've been doing for Gandy over the years. What am I going to find when I dive into those dealings? How old are these girls in the picture, for a start?'

Cal rocks back on his heels, relaxed. Beside him, Rocket wags his tail.

The advocate reaches for his phone and brandishes it at Cal.

'I'm going to call the police. Now. This is harassment.'

'I don't think you will do that,' Cal says mildly. 'But I'm going now, anyway. I have more important things to do than speak to you. The *Edinburgh Evening News* has been gifted a very interesting set of documents to kick things off with. You might want to pick up a paper later. Goodbye, Jeremy.'

With that, he tugs on the dog's lead and takes advantage of the break in traffic to stride away from Fishpool, heading for his daughter and his life. Determined not to look back.

CHAPTER SIXTY-EIGHT

CAL

Bella seems tired. She's standing outside the Inversnecky cafe at Aberdeen beach when he parks and dashes across the road to meet her, making him worried that he's kept her waiting. He checks his watch, ready to apologise.

'Don't worry,' she says. 'I was up early. Can't sleep at the moment, so I walked down here and watched the sun rise.'

He gestures at the greasy spoon.

'Do you want to go in?'

Bella shakes her head.

'Do you mind if we walk instead?'

They cross the road to the broad promenade above the beach. The tide is going out, leaving the sand wet and gleaming, reflecting Aberdeen's acres of sky. Cal looks out at the North Sea, where container ships are dotted on the horizon. Maybe some of them are headed for east coast ports, with secret cargoes of drugs like the ones Gandy received and distributed for so long. Those networks will still be running. There's always someone willing to take the risk.

'How are you doing?' Cal asks. 'It turned out to be a lot in the end, didn't it?'

'Careful what you wish for,' Bella says eventually, stopping and turning to face him.

Her gaze pins him in place. He looks into her eyes and sees a version of himself from the past, one less accepting and more unsettled than he is now.

'I'm sorry,' Cal says.

'You don't have anything to be sorry for.'

A single tear slips down her cheek.

'You listened to the episode,' he says quietly.

Bella nods. 'I had to. I had to know. It triggered other memories from that day. They all fit what he told you.'

It's hard, looking the cost in the face and trying to weigh up whether or not it was worth it. He gets to leave the story behind, but Bella will be dealing with this for the rest of her life.

'I needed to know,' she says, as if able to read his mind. 'It's brought everything up but that was my only chance of getting justice for them. That's more important than my peace of mind.'

'Is it?'

Bella laughs. 'I think so. I'm seeing a therapist now. And talking to my dad more. That helps.'

A runner passes them and a dog barks from the shoreline.

'The parole hearing is tomorrow,' Cal says as they resume their stroll.

'I know. It looks like Merrick will be released. The sentence he's served is already so long and, now that they've tested all of the items from that day and found traces of Barr's DNA, the mood is bending in his favour, though you never know.'

'How do you feel about it?'

She shrugs. 'I don't know. He followed us and scared my mum with his obsessive behaviour. Then he led Barr to us. Without that, it would never have happened. I relive that over and over again. If only.'

Cal sighs, thinking of his own 'if onlys'.

Bella's phone rings in her pocket.

'Sorry… I…'

'No, it's fine; you should get that.' He leans on the railings while she takes the call, looking out at the grey-blue water.

A moment later, Bella joins him.

'That was Noah. He and the boys want to come and meet me to have brunch and go on the amusements.' She looks awkward. 'Do you mind…'

Cal smiles. 'Not at all.'

It's hard sometimes to accept that some of his subjects need to leave him behind. While he is in frequent touch with so many of the families whose stories he has covered, others want to walk away. Cal is a reminder to them of the worst times in their lives. He knows now which group Bella will fall into.

They walk back to the car, quiet and reflective, each lost in their own thoughts. There is a space between them.

He turns to say goodbye to her and feels a lump in his throat. This case has been different. Intertwined with Margot's in a way his other cases have not been.

Without warning, Bella throws her arms around him, squeezing him so tightly he's almost knocked off balance.

'Thank you,' she breathes.

Cal returns the hug, overwhelmed by a wave of grief for them both.

His own phone rings when he gets into the car. Cal feels wrung out and strangely lonely. He accepts the call absentmindedly, pulling his seat belt over his shoulder.

'Are you free to speak?'

It's Foulds. She sounds fevered, her voice higher and tensed. He lets the belt slide back.

'Yes. Is everything okay?'

'I've got some news for you.' Is she tearful? Is that what he can hear? 'That box of Barr's scraps and mementoes you gave me? I had it all tested. Not just the swimming towel.'

Cal stills. The sound of the waves and the seagulls retreats and all he can hear is the rushing of blood in his ears.

'And?'

'And we're getting hits. Testing is so good now. Tiny traces of DNA are still in there Cal. Along with a couple of other profiles, we found traces of Margot's blood.'

It feels like the world has stopped turning. His mind is slow, struggling to keep up.

'I… what does that mean?'

'The fact that it's blood means he can't just say it's because they were in a relationship or whatever line he pulled last time. But that's not all.'

'There's more?'

'We've got the yellow Datsun. We traced the ownership and it was sitting under some other vehicles in a scrapyard in Wales. We seized it and forensics sprayed the boot. Cal, it lit up like a Christmas tree. We're running more tests.'

Cal's vision is blurred. He cannot speak. As he sits, dumbfounded, trying to make himself understand, he has the strongest sensation that someone is sitting next to him. For a second he smells her perfume, and then it is gone.

EPILOGUE: NEXT SUMMER

CAL

The sand on the beach is perfectly white, scattered only with driftwood from last night's storm. The breeze occasionally rises up and whips their hair to the sky, but the water is so clear you can see the urchins clinging to rocks beneath it. When they discovered the Singing Sands together, Cal and Shona walked to it, but today they've brought their guests in offroad vehicles along the forestry track.

It's a ridiculous place to get married. But since the barn burned and their lives were upended, they've been throwing caution to the wind. They wanted to do it and they have. In front of him, Shona looks effortlessly cool in her ivory suit, her skin glowing. She squeezes his hand and Cal refocuses on the celebrant's words, holding his gaze on the beautiful blue of his wife's eyes. Absolutely his soul mate.

Released into a partnership he knows will last a lifetime, he leans in and kisses her deeply. Their guests applaud. Beside them, Chrissie whoops and Rocket lets off a volley of barks, hyped up by the electric atmosphere. Chrissie lets him off the lead and he darts to the water, plunging into the cold salt with his tail wagging.

Around them is a cluster of their closest friends and family: Margot's old friend Diane, DCI Lorna Foulds, Robbie whose mother's death he helped resolve, Shona's brother Graham and his wife, her colleague Cliff and a few others. They've kept it deliberately small. Up the beach, in the shelter of some rocks, a chef from the local hotel is grilling seafood delicacies and cases of champagne sit on ice. Waiting for this moment. Their guests stroll towards the bar, laughing, barefoot on the sand.

They hold back and watch them go.

'I love you,' he whispers in Shona's ear. 'Dr Williams-Lovett.'

She kisses him again, then they swivel to look for Chrissie, to bring her into a hug so she knows there will always be a place for her in the centre. But she's down by the water with Robbie, the pair of them deep in conversation, throwing a piece of driftwood for the dog.

'Interesting,' Shona says, eyeing Cal.

'Don't worry,' he says. 'I won't get carried away, I promise. They're probably just friends.'

But as they watch, Cal sees their fingers are touching ever so slightly, Robbie's dark head bent close to Chrissie's red curls. He smiles and turns away.

'Come on,' he says, tugging on Shona's hand. 'We need to get to the champagne before Diane and Cliff drink it all.'

As they follow the others to the area set out with chairs, tables and blankets, Cal feels a rising sense of euphoria. Not a loud, intrusive kind, but something integral and quiet. Surrounded by love. On cue, Rocket bounds past, spraying sand and seawater, making them laugh. Shona's hand is warm and soft, her face suffused with happiness.

It's like being in a dream. One he never ever wants to wake up from.

Yesterday, Jason Barr – already serving life in prison for the murders of Allegra, Gail and Philippa Carlo – had another life sentence added to his time. This one for the 1986 murder of Margot Lovett. Beloved sister, daughter and friend. Cal did not attend the trial. He made no personal statement. The man who killed her is no longer relevant to his existence.

Margot is gone, but she'll always be with him. Now, on this beach, he feels her in the air, in the sand between his toes, and in his daughter's distant laughter. With Shona pressed to his side, Cal takes a glass from the waiter's tray and holds it to the sky – smiling as he remembers her and finally lets her go.

Acknowledgements

It's strange coming to the end of Cal's story (for now). Thank you to all of the readers, reviewers and bookshops who have supported the series. You are all wonderful and it makes my day every time someone connects with one of my books. So many of you have taken Cal to your hearts and have been kind enough to message me about it.

Cal's fans were very much in mind as I wrote this novel. I hope you're happy with the parting shot of our true crime podcaster. He's infuriated me at times but the closer I came to the end of writing, the more I realised I am going to miss him! Please do stay in touch on Instagram at heather.critchlow or join my VIP Reader's Club at www.heathercritchlow.com for news of what's coming next and regular book giveaways.

A heartfelt thank you to my editor, Louise Cullen, who saw the potential for Cal and plucked him from her submission pile four years ago. She gave me the chance I'd been longing for and I am incredibly lucky to be working with her – her insightful feedback takes my books to the next level. Huge thanks also to the rest of the team at Canelo, including Alicia Pountney, Aidan Kavanagh and Kate Shepherd, who do so much to bring my books to readers.

Thank you to Siân Heap for a brilliant and thorough structural edit, Laurel Sills and Vicki Vrint for their copyediting and proofreading skills, and Andrew Smith for the gorgeous pink cover.

Cal never would have been on Louise's submission pile were it not for Charlotte Seymour, my tireless and tenacious agent. Having her in my corner to navigate the ins and outs of publishing is a true blessing. Thank you to the rest of the team at Johnson & Alcock – especially to Ed Wilson and Anna Dawson who have looked after me so well this year, and Hélène Butler and Magdalena Guzdziol for their foreign rights expertise.

Author extraordinaire Sam Holland was kind enough to read *UNSEEN* very early – sharing our latest works during the creation process was so helpful and she absolutely saved me from making some time-consuming mistakes. Thank you also to Niki Mackay, Jo Furniss, Rachael Blok, Kate Simants and Dom Nolan for their early reads and blurbs. I'm lucky to have such a talented and kind group of people around me. Pincers up to the Criminal Minds, sub support group and my other lovely writing friends as well – you are all brilliant.

My longstanding writing group of Tammye Huf, Gillian Anton and Chris May – thank you for reading and commenting on *UNSEEN* at our London lunches. You've been there since the start.

To the rest of my wonderful friends and family: I am lucky to have you all and so grateful to you for being fabulous cheerleaders for my books. Most of all, to Will, Rachel and Adam – I couldn't do any of this without you and I wouldn't want to. Thank you always.